MOTORCYCLE DADDY

LAYLAH ROBERTS

MOTORCYCLE DADDY

Laylah Roberts

Laylah Roberts

Motorcycle Daddy

Laylah.roberts@gmail.com

laylahroberts.com

Cover Design by: Allycat's Creations

Editing: Celeste Jones

Created with Vellum

LET'S KEEP IN TOUCH!

Don't miss a new release, sign up to my newsletter for sneak peeks, deleted scenes and giveaways: https://landing.mailerlite.com/webforms/landing/p7l6g0

You can also join my Facebook readers group here: https://www.facebook.com/groups/386830425069911/

BOOKS BY LAYLAH ROBERTS

Doms of Decadence

Just for You, Sir

Forever Yours, Sir

For the Love of Sir

Sinfully Yours, Sir

Make me, Sir

A Taste of Sir

To Save Sir

Sir's Redemption

Reveal Me, Sir

Montana Daddies

Daddy Bear

Daddy's Little Darling

Daddy's Naughty Darling Novella

Daddy's Sweet Girl

Daddy's Lost Love

A Montana Daddies Christmas

Daring Daddy

Warrior Daddy

Daddy's Angel (coming June, 2020)

Heal Me, Daddy (coming July 2020)

MC Daddy

Motorcycle Daddy

Haven, Texas Series

Lila's Loves

Laken's Surrender

Saving Savannah

Molly's Man

Saxon's Soul

Mastered by Malone

How West was Won

Cole's Mistake

Men of Orion

Worlds Apart

Cavan Gang

Rectify

Redemption

Redemption Valley

Audra's Awakening

Old-Fashioned Series

An Old-Fashioned Man

Two Old-Fashioned Men

Her Old-Fashioned Husband

Her Old-Fashioned Boss

His Old-Fashioned Love

An Old-Fashioned Christmas

Bad Boys of Wildeside

Wilde

Sinclair

Luke

1

Mowing the lawn was the last thing Sunny wanted to do.

Unfortunately, she wasn't the sort of person who could just ignore the fact that something needed doing. No matter that her feet were aching and she really just wanted to shower then collapse into bed.

She hauled herself out of her tiny car, and without bothering to even go inside the house, she tromped down to the small shed to drag her lawnmower out. She actually loved this shed. Everything was ordered just how she wanted it, and nearly all of her tools were pink. Even her lawnmower was pink with little rhinestones glued along the front of it.

Greg would have hated it. Greg had made her buy a plain black mower, even though she'd been the one to do all the outside maintenance. He'd claimed it was better to split the chores up according to their strengths.

Which might have made perfect sense, if Greg had any strengths. She snorted to herself as she started up the lawnmower. Something Greg would have told her off for.

Apparently, snorting was not ladylike.

Who knew?

Then again, who cared, right?

Only Greg. Maybe if she'd cared more, their marriage might have lasted. Then again, if it meant she got to push around a pink lawnmower with diamantes maybe she was better off without Greg.

She finished up her mowing, and wiped the sweat off her forehead. Her stomach growled, reminding her that she hadn't had time to eat the rice salad she'd packed for lunch today. Ronny, her boss, had over-scheduled her. Again. And again, she'd had to work through her breaks. Plus, she'd gotten home later than usual.

Today had been a gorgeous summer day. She was pushing her lawnmower back down to her tiny shed with its flower boxes planted in front of the small windows and its bright red, cheery roof when she looked across at her neighbor's backyard.

The houses on this street were all small but had big plots. Suited her. She liked working outside. Her neighbor obviously did not. His backyard was bereft of anything but a huge deck and grass. Lots of grass. Overgrown grass.

Shoot.

Drat.

You do not have to take care of that for him. He's not your friend.

Because she had so many of those.

They hardly ever crossed paths. He was usually gone by the time she got home and when she got up in the morning, the house was dark. Although she hadn't seen his truck in the driveway the last few mornings, so maybe he was away.

Which is probably why he hadn't noticed that his lawn mowing service hadn't been doing their job.

Just leave it, Sunny. Not your problem.

But if the grass wasn't cut soon, the homeowners association was likely to fine him. Paisley, the head of the association, seemed to have nothing more to do than go around handing out fines.

Sunny had once caught her measuring her front lawn with a ruler at seven in the morning, wearing yoga pants, and a work-out bra, with her enormous German Shepherd watching on menacingly. She'd received a fine later that day for her grass being a half inch too long.

She wondered how many fines her neighbor had already received for his long lawn, and the fact that his truck was often parked in the driveway instead of inside the garage.

Greg had loved all these rules. Had claimed it kept all the riff-raff out. Yes, he'd actually used that word.

Riff-raff.

Sometimes she thought he was an eighty-year-old trapped in a thirty-year-old's body. He'd been pissed when the neighbor moved in. With his motorcycle, and his penchant for Sunday afternoon barbecues with his rough-looking friends.

He'd gone on for weeks about a gang moving in, and property values going down.

Funny, how he'd claimed the opposite when she'd offered to buy out his half of the house in the divorce. Maybe she should have just sold this place. Moved on. But she loved this house.

Nope, she definitely didn't owe her handsome-looking neighbor who'd never once even said hello to her, anything.

So why was she pushing her lawnmower next door?

~

DUKE WAS IN A SHITTY MOOD.

He was tired. He was hungry. He was grouchy. He should have been headed to work, but he couldn't stomach being around people right now.

When he got in these moods, which didn't happen all that

often, he knew he needed to stay far away from other people. He couldn't trust himself not to say or do something he'd regret later.

He pulled his truck into his driveway, parking in front of the single car garage.

Stepping out, he strode over to the mailbox, frowning when he saw it was empty. Shrugging, he moved into the house. Shit. It was hot as hell in here. Turning on the air, he grabbed a beer out of the fridge. All he wanted to do was sit on his porch and have a quiet drink.

Alone.

He scowled at the sound of a lawn mower as he stepped outside. He'd heard it out front, but he'd hoped it was the neighbor across the road.

He froze on his porch, eyes narrowing in on the short figure pushing a bright pink mower down his thick lawn.

What the fuck? Who was that? And why the hell was his grass so long?

The service he used should have mowed them days ago. Holy shit. . .did that mower have jewels glued onto the front of it?

He stared at the woman who had her head down, her attention on what she was doing. As she grew closer, he realized it was his next-door neighbor. Fucking awesome. He'd seen her around a few times in passing. Mousy, quiet sort of woman. Her loud, obnoxious husband had moved out months ago.

Why was she mowing his lawn? Without his permission. Duke didn't mingle with people outside the Iron Shadows.

He didn't give a shit about his neighbor and what she did. Unless it impacted him. Which right now, it sure fucking did.

Calm. She's obviously just trying to do something nice.

He glanced down as his foot hit something, sending his mail flying.

Fuck. Fuck.

She'd touched his mail? He bent down and picked up the pile, spotting one that had been half-opened. Had she gone peeking? He took a look at what was inside that envelope, shock filling him as photos spilled out.

What the fuck was this? Why would someone send him photos? Unease stirred through his gut. Especially as he saw one of the photos was from last night.

When he'd been staking out the senator's family home. Senator Jonathan Robins. Assbag extraordinaire. Sex offender. Douchebag. A man that the Iron Shadows leader, Reyes, badly wanted to take down. Duke had been doing his stint on dickhead-watch. Not that he'd seen anything of interest.

Hence his current bad mood.

But now he was even angrier. Since it seemed like someone had been watching him. Taking photos of him.

And he'd never had an inkling.

Fuck. Fuck. Shit.

Someone knew. Who the fuck was it? What did they want? He turned the envelope over. There was nothing written on it. It hadn't been posted. He searched through the photos quickly, there weren't just photos of him in here, but also of Reyes, Ink, Razor, Spike and Jason. What the fuck?

The roar of the lawnmower brought him back to the present. She'd opened his mail? Had she looked inside?

He stormed towards the woman. He couldn't remember her name. Wasn't sure if he'd ever learned it, to be honest. The envelope filled with photos was clenched in his right fist.

Duke was a guy who was slow to anger. But once he let go it was hard to rein it back in.

The woman didn't even look up. She just plodded up and down in neat, even rows. Obviously, she couldn't hear him over the loud noise of the mower, but couldn't she sense him? Christ, anyone could sneak up on her.

For some reason, that made him even angrier.

He stepped in front of her, waiting for her to reach him. He knew the moment she saw him. Heard her let out a startled cry as the mower stopped a few inches from his black boots.

He glanced up from his boots to scowl at the woman. She was dressed in a long-sleeved, ugly-as-sin khaki shirt with something embroidered on the top right.

Clean Cut Gardening Services.

Hoping to get another client on her books, was she?

Not happening, sweetheart.

Her shirt swamped her, her green shorts came down to her calves, making her look like she was playing dress-ups in her dad's clothes. Her hair was hidden under an ugly straw hat that looked like a family of rats had taken refuge in it, nibbling away at parts of it. Her cheeks were flushed, sweat coated her skin. She looked worn out.

And his temper bubbled even further.

"Oh shoot, you scared me!"

She had a hand pressed against her chest. He moved to the side, turning off the mower. The silence was almost deafening.

"Funny that, considering this is my property and you're trespassing!"

The red faded from her cheeks and she took a step back. A smidge of regret filled him at scaring her but as he folded his arms across his chest, he remembered the crumpled-up envelope in his hand and that she was ruining the few hours of peace he had before having to go into the club.

"Tr-trespassing?" she stuttered; her voice so quiet he could scarcely hear her. "I'm not trespassing!"

"No? What do you call it when you're somewhere that you weren't given permission to be?"

"I-I'm mowing your grass." She pointed down at her mower.

He grunted. "Didn't ask you to."

She narrowed her gaze, a spark of heat entering her eyes. So she wasn't as meek and mild as she made out? Interesting...

Still, she really wasn't his type. He liked women who were submissive in the bedroom, but otherwise could take care of themselves. This woman would need constant care and assurances. He didn't have time for that.

"Are you that desperate for work you're over here mowing my lawn for free trying to drum up business?"

Her eyes widened, her mouth opening in shock. His eyes were drawn to those plump, pink lips. Hmm, for someone who was rather unremarkable looking, she had a very nice mouth.

It would look very pretty wrapped around a cock.

He nearly snorted. Like she'd ever give a blow-job. She had missionary-only written all over her. Probably closed her eyes and lay there until it was done.

Okay, enough.

She should not turn you on.

She's some nosy neighbor, probably in the homeowners association like Yoga Barbie who pretended to go running each morning just so she could spy on everyone.

Like she could run with those hugely-inflated fake boobs.

"No. Of course not. I was trying to be a good neighbor!"

"By opening my mail? You call that being a good neighbor? Because I call it a federal offense."

She went even more pale and he worried for a moment that she was going to faint.

Fuck. Shit.

He had to remind himself that she wasn't some prospect he was telling off for being a dipshit. She was a woman. She'd probably never been spoken to like this in her life. She couldn't even seem to swear for fucks sake.

Calm down, Duke.

All he'd wanted was a cold beer and an hour of peace. It would have reinstated his equilibrium. He knew that he was taking his bad mood out of her and it wasn't cool. . .

Unless she really had opened his mail.

She hadn't answered his accusation with a denial. He raised an eyebrow, holding out the envelope.

She swallowed. "I'm really sorry. I didn't mean for it to rip. There was so much mail in your box and the homeowners association gives out fines if you don't collect your mail daily. So I thought I'd get it out for you. I had to tug hard and that envelope ripped. I didn't see anything."

He sighed. Crap. He believed her. She wasn't some nosy cow out to poke around in his life. She was just a nice woman trying to be a good neighbor.

And you are a real prick.

He massaged his head. "Look, I—"

"I need to go."

She pushed the lawnmower around him and started up towards the side gate. He thought about going after her, apologizing. But the truth was he was probably better off letting her go. If this encounter stopped her from coming over here again, all the better.

He moved back up onto the porch. From his vantage point above her, he could just spot her in the waning light, pushing the lawnmower into that ridiculous garden shed of hers. Didn't she have any security lights? He scowled. What was that dick she'd been living with thinking?

And why the hell did he care? The guys had given him shit about buying a house in suburbia. This place was so normal and ordinary, it did seem like a strange choice.

But he liked that it was ordinary. That the worst he had to worry about was the neighborhood association fining him for breaking the rules. Although that fake woman who headed the association had made it clear that in exchange for sexual favors, she'd gladly turn the other cheek on any breaches.

He shuddered at the thought. He didn't have to worry about drive-by shootings or who was cooking up meth. This place reminded him of his childhood. Before he'd lost everything.

Darkness fell and the quiet soothed him. It also had him sighing with regret.

He'd been a real asshole.

Christ. He didn't even know her name. Knew nothing about her except that she was quiet, and she'd had an uptight suit living with her when he'd first arrived. He took another sip of beer, glancing down at the envelope in his hands. His outdoor lights were set to come on automatically and they'd switched on several minutes ago.

Unlike next door. Where there were no lights on at all.

He frowned. *The photos are what you should care about. Not your mousy neighbor.*

Except she hadn't seemed so mousy, standing there with her mouth open, her tanned skin flush with exertion. Those ugly, baggy clothes should have been a turn-off and yet he'd found himself wondering at the body underneath. Had he ever seen her in anything that wasn't baggy and several sizes too big? Not that he could recall.

Concentrate, Duke. Photos.

He picked up his phone as it buzzed. Reyes.

Meeting ten tonight.

All right. That gave him enough time to shower and eat. His stomach growled as he stood. He glanced over at the quiet house next door. Still no lights. Fuck. Had she eaten? Was she sitting there in the dark? Why?

Because she was scared of him?

He groaned and ran his hand over his face, exhaustion weighing him down. He didn't have time for this. She wasn't his responsibility. Just because she lived next door and she'd been trying to do something nice and he'd snapped at her, didn't mean he owed her something.

Yes, it does, asshole. Fuck. He wasn't used to anyone outside the club doing something for him without a motive. In fact, most of the time even those fuckers had a motive. She hadn't seemed to have any motive at all other than wanting to help him.

Wandering inside, he put the envelope down next to his keys and wallet so he didn't forget to take it with him. He picked up his phone to order a pizza. Without thinking about it too hard, he ordered a second pizza for next door.

The least he could do was make sure she ate.

Pushing her out of his mind, he headed to the shower.

~

"Shit. What fucker took these?" Ink demanded, glaring down at the photos as though they'd give him the answers he desired.

Duke leaned back in his seat, taking another drag of beer. He wished he could have something stronger, but he didn't want to stay the night in his room in the compound which was out the back of the main bar, behind a big concrete and wire fence.

So he nursed a single beer as he sat in Reyes's office and watched his closest friends study the photos he'd received.

"Nothing on the envelope, no note, damn fucking rude really," Razor drawled.

Duke looked over at Jason who was frowning but didn't offer anything then over to Spike who scowled, but kept his gaze on the door as though expecting it to open at any moment. Sometimes it was hard to figure out what was going on in Spike's mind. He didn't talk much.

"These are all photos of us doing surveillance on the senator," Ink said.

Yeah, that's what Duke had discovered after he'd had a chance to look them over. He snatched one out of Ink's hands. He turned it over and pointed to the image of a fox's head.

"Anyone know what this means?"

Spike grunted. "I might. Heard rumors of someone called the Fox. Assassin for hire."

An assassin? What the fuck?

"I'll ask around," Spike said.

"It's got to be a warning. To back off the senator," Reyes stated.

Duke nodded.

Ink rose and started to pace. "Why are we even bothering with watching the senator?"

"You want to let him continue what he's doing?" Reyes asked quietly. "I know it's fucking annoying but now is our chance to watch him, while he's here in Billings rather than spending most of his time in Washington where we don't have eyes on him."

"We never used to give a fuck what anyone else did so long as it didn't involve us," Ink spat.

"Ink," Duke said in a low, warning voice knowing Reyes wouldn't like any disrespect. He wasn't an asshole like their last leader, that prick didn't give a shit about anyone but himself, but Reyes still wasn't someone you wanted to cross.

Reyes stood silently and the tension in the room ratcheted higher.

"We got a problem, Ink?"

Duke tensed. Ink stared at Reyes then let out a deep breath and ran his hand through his blond hair. "No, fuck no. You know I don't have a problem with you. Christ, I just don't want us getting in a mess like we ended up in with Bartolli. If we're getting a warning from a fucking gun-for-hire then is it not a sign we should fucking stop?"

"Bartolli is dead," Reyes said in a deep voice. "I took care of that."

Fergus Bartolli, head of the Bartolli family, had been using the club to blackmail Senator Robins with photos of him having sex with a very young-looking girl. Photos where she looked drugged and out-of-it.

Duke had certain desires in the bedroom, but nothing like that fucking disgusting ass-wipe, Robins. He needed to be in control. These guys were the same. Most of them were Daddy Doms. It was how Razor met Reyes, at a BDSM club that catered for those who practiced age play. Razor had brought Reyes into the club. Eventually gotten rid of Smiley, their old President and started cleaning up the club.

Reyes liked his woman to be his Little girl. Didn't mean he was a pervert or anything. It was all consensual. Duke knew of a ranch a few hours away where most of the men there were Daddy Doms as well.

It had never appealed to Duke.

At least, he didn't think it did. A pair of lush pink lips and wide blue eyes flitted through his mind. What did his next-door neighbor have to do with anything? He shook his head.

"Duke?" He glanced up and realized everyone was staring at him.

"Yeah?"

"What you think?" Reyes asked, surprising him. He didn't always ask for others' opinions.

"I think it just makes me more curious as to what the fuck is going on," he drawled. "I ain't one to be scared off by some pussy who can't even show his face but instead has to send secret messages."

"What if those photos of him with the girl were taken in Washington?" Razor asked.

Reyes unlocked his drawer and pulled the photos out. Duke looked down at them. Mother-fucker, that girl looked young. "There's nothing distinctive in the photos to be able to tell when they were taken, but I'm thinking it was here since he'd have more eyes on him in Washington."

"But his wife lives here," Duke mused.

"Maybe he's got another property?" Razor guessed.

"I'll look into it," Jason told them.

Reyes nodded. "Then we continue. Spike, you have the next watch?"

The big man silently nodded.

Reyes glanced around at them all. "Anyone who doesn't want to continue doing surveillance doesn't have to."

Nobody spoke up. As he'd suspected they wouldn't.

"All right. Then everyone fucking be careful. Keep an eye out for anyone you think could be watching you and call for back-up if needed."

2

"You. . .you can't fire me!"

"Just did, sweetheart," Ronny told her callously. He leered at her. Her insides crawled. God, she hated him. He was a worm. No, that was mean to worms. He was a ferret. Or a rat. No, wait both of those animals could make nice pets.

He was a cockroach.

And the cockroach had just fired her.

"But. . .but. . .I work hard, I'm good at my job, I—"

He waved his hand. "Nothing to do with that. Although you did take too long on the Anderson job." He'd assigned three hours for a job that would usually take two days. She'd gotten it done in one day and worked extra hours without pay to do it.

Darn it. She clenched her hands into fists as anger pulsed through her. Was she really going to let everyone push her around for the rest of her life? Or was she going to stick up for herself?

The other night, when that asshole from next-door had basically accused her of trespassing and opening his mail, she'd ran home with her tail tucked between her legs. Not even the mysterious pizza that had turned up later, already paid for, made her feel better.

She'd thrown it in the bin without eating it, taking a quick shower before falling into bed. Not that she'd slept. No, she'd spent most of the night tossing and turning, thinking about that arrogant biker jerk.

"Then why?" she asked.

Ronny shrugged, looking bored. He sighed. They were standing in his trailer which he pretended to work from. The guys she worked with all joked that he spent the day watching porn and jacking off. She'd never taken much notice. It hadn't seemed right to gossip about the boss.

Even if he was a little cockroach.

Now, she looked around the messy place in disgust. The trash was overflowing, empty food containers lay everywhere and it stunk of sweat, garbage and old food. She wouldn't be surprised if there were actual cockroaches living in this dump.

Ronny hitched up his ugly shorts that were part of their uniform. His huge belly fell over the top of them, the buttons of his shirt straining over his stomach.

"Look, girly, I got places to go."

She narrowed her gaze at him. His father had been the one to hire her. And he'd always treated her with respect. She was the only woman who worked here and once he'd seen she knew what she was doing, he'd started giving her the more complicated jobs. The ones that required brains rather than just brawn. Which is all some of the guys had.

"You can't just fire me without telling me why."

He raised his arm. She grimaced at the pit-stains on his shirt, the smell wafting out. Her eyes watered. Jesus. Did he ever shower?

"It's the fucking economy. I'm losing money here."

Then why didn't he do some work instead of watching porn and masturbating?

She could feel her shoulders hunching over. She nearly left without another word, but then she remembered that she had a mortgage and bills to pay.

She needed this job.

She didn't want to lose it.

"So why me? Why not one of the other guys?" Most of whom took extra-long breaks and were always getting to work late and leaving early. Not one of them brought in as much revenue as she did. She was sure of it.

So why fire her?

Because you rejected him last week.

She swallowed the bile rising in her throat. She knew she shouldn't have gone to Friday night drinks. But Kev, one of the older guys she worked with who she actually liked, had asked her and she was tired of going home to a quiet, empty house.

It was so lonely.

But she should have listened to her instincts. The whole night had been uncomfortable and weird. She wasn't a drinker, and she'd felt a little silly ordering a sparkling water. Then when she'd gone to the bathroom before heading home, because she always seemed to need the toilet as soon as she got in the car, she'd encountered Ronny walking back into the bar.

He'd been stumbling, already drunk and when she'd reached out to help him as he'd tripped, he'd pushed her against the wall and kissed her. She'd tried to fight him off, but he had at least a hundred pounds on her.

He'd slobbered all over her, his breath reeking of garlic and bourbon, his over-powering body odor almost making her gag. She'd only managed to get away because another guy from the bar had come along and asked if she was okay.

She'd thought he hadn't remembered because he hadn't acted any differently towards her.

Until now.

Her body was trembling. This couldn't be happening. What would she do? Paying out Greg had left her with a hefty mortgage, she lived cheaply but she'd lose her home if she couldn't find another job quickly.

"I bring in more money than anyone else—"

"Now, that's just not true, sweetheart," Ronny drawled condescendingly. "Please don't beg me. It's a little pathetic and I really don't have time to listen to you. It's a simple matter of last on, first off."

Her mouth dropped open. That. . .that cockroach!

"I was not the last hire! You only hired Seb four weeks ago!" And he was completely useless. Spent more time taking photos of himself and posting them to Instagram than he did actually working.

"Yeah, but Seb is a friend. You're not. Now, don't cry, it makes you look pathetic. See, this is why my dad shouldn't have hired a woman to do a man's job."

That was it! No more! Even she had a snapping point. All her life she'd tried to follow the rules, to do the right thing. She never jay walked. She opened doors for people. She used her manners. She tried to spread a bit of kindness around. But this was too much. A red haze actually filled her vision.

"You sexist pig!" she shot out at him. "I ought to report you for sexual harassment!"

Ronny narrowed his eyes, his cheeks growing red. "I have no fucking idea what you're talking about. I've never sexually harassed you."

"You kissed me the other night in the bar."

He snorted. "As if I'd kiss you. Be like trying to kiss my great-aunt. No way I'd touch you with a barge pole. You try to tell anyone I did and I'll sue you for slander; we clear? My word against yours and ain't no one going to believe you, bitch."

He took a step towards her and her bravado faded. He was right. It would be a he-said, she-said situation. Unfortunately, she thought most people would believe him.

"All they'll see is some dried-up, plain woman trying to latch onto her boss because her homelife is sad and lonely. Now get out of my office and don't ever come back."

She turned around, knowing she'd lost. Now she just wanted out of here. She felt dirty. Ill.

Don't cry. Don't cry. Don't let him see he's hurt you.

She managed to hold it together enough to get out to her car. But it took her two tries to get it started. It wasn't until she turned into her driveway that she realized she was home and she had no memory of getting there.

Fuck. That wasn't good.

Panic had her gasping for breath. She parked in front of her garage. She didn't have the energy to get out and open the door. Greg had promised her a remote-controlled door opener. But as usual, he'd never come through.

And now she couldn't afford it.

She really, really couldn't afford it.

Ronny had sacked her. She had no job. No references. And around five hundred dollars in her savings account.

Fudge. Son-of-a-peach.

You're so pathetic, Sunny! You can't even swear properly.

If ever there was a time to swear it was now. What was she going to do? She couldn't lose the house. If she lost the house, she'd have to move in with her parents. She didn't even know where they were. Not to mention they lived in a tiny RV, travelling around, smoking pot and worshipping the moon.

She wasn't even joking.

She leaned her forehead against the steering wheel. She knew she should get out of the car. Without the air on, the car was becoming a heat-box. She'd worked a full day in the sun with no breaks. She was exhausted. She was dirty.

But she couldn't move.

Worry kept her paralyzed. Tears dripped down her heated cheeks. What to do? What to do? She wasn't sure how long she sat there, crying, but when a knock sounded on the car window, startling her out of her panic, it was dark and she desperately had to pee. She gasped for air, staring out the window in fear at the big figure looming next to her car. The doors were still locked.

She screeched as he knocked again. A headache thumped in the back of her skull and fear had her heart beating too fast.

Then a light went on and she found herself staring up into the frowning face of her next-door neighbor.

Awesome. Just what she needed. Another run-in with him.

Tears dripped down her face faster as she just sat there, exhausted, staring up at him.

~

What was he doing? Duke shook his head at himself as he gave in to the urge that had been tugging at him for the last hour.

He'd noticed her car pull up as he'd come in from his run. Half an hour later, as he'd left the shower and headed to the kitchen, he'd noticed her car still sat in the driveway. Which was unusual but she could have been heading back out.

He'd grabbed a steak to grill. But he'd found himself unable to eat in peace until he made sure that everything was all right.

The sun had set, but the nights in Montana could be cold despite it being summer. The street lights flickered on, illuminating his way. It really wasn't his problem to take care of her, but still, he found himself striding down her driveway. Christ, the car she drove was a piece of junk. He'd asked Yoga Barbie what her name was.

Sunny. It suited her. Even if it was a little unusual. Yoga Barbie thought she came from some sort of cult. Claimed she and her husband had broken up because she was a lesbian, because why else would she wear men's clothes?

As soon as the information had dried up and the sexual innuendos started, he'd walked off from her mid-word.

Yep, he could be a rude prick.

No, he didn't much care.

As he moved past her car, he glanced inside and stopped in shock. She was still in her car? He'd assumed she'd gone inside while he'd been in the shower.

Fuck. The car wasn't running. It had to be damn hot in there. Worry filled him, as he tugged at the door. Locked. Shit. He knocked on the window and she startled.

All right. At least she was alive.

He waited for her to open the car door or roll down the window but she just sat there, staring up at him. What was she doing?

Finally, he realized that she might not be able to see who he was and he pulled out his phone, turning on the flashlight app and shining it up into his face.

"Sunny! Open the door!" he barked at her. She didn't move. "Come on, it's got to be hot in there. Open the door."

Still nothing. Shit. Should he leave her alone? He was certain he was the last person she wanted around right now.

Yet his instincts screamed that she needed help. And he didn't have it in him to just leave her. There was something about the way she sat there, so still, it made him think that she was beyond making decisions herself.

So make them for her.

"I'm going to count to three and then I want you to unlock this door. One. Two." He paused. Fuck. Shit. *This is really working, asshole.* "Three."

No movement towards the door. In fact, she actually shied away from it.

He crouched down to make himself less intimidating. Not exactly easy, he'd been told many times how terrifying he could be. Worked well for him at the club, and his clients at the tattoo parlor he owned didn't give a shit.

But for quiet little subbies it could definitely be too much.

Was she a sub? She'd been unable to meet his eyes for long the other day, but that could be because she was shy. Or she'd been scared. The fact that she might fear him didn't sit right.

Time to find your softer side, man. Damn, if the guys could see him right now, they'd piss themselves laughing. While he wasn't as scary as Spike or cold as Reyes or volatile as Ink, he could rule with an iron fist. He hadn't reached the position of VP if he didn't have a steel backbone.

"Sunny, it's Duke," he said.

She likely already knew his name. Or maybe she didn't. He hadn't known hers. Then again, they'd already established that he wasn't a good neighbor.

"Listen to me, I need you to lower the window." He made an unwinding gesture with his hand, feeling like an idiot.

So he was surprised when a few seconds later the window actually lowered.

"Hey there, baby girl." The endearment surprised him. He'd never called anyone that before. But it suited her. She seemed so pure and innocent.

"What do you want?" Not the friendliest of greetings, but he knew he deserved that.

"I came over to check on you. Have you been sitting out here since you got home? Why the fuck didn't you have the air on? Or a window open?"

Soothing and sweet wasn't him. But he was irritated that she'd just been sitting here. Why wasn't she taking better care of herself?

He reached his hand through the open window, freezing as she shied back.

"Babe, not gonna fucking hurt you. Just checking your temp."

"You swear a lot."

"That so?" he murmured as he touched her forehead with the back of his hand. Fuck. She was way too hot and sweaty. Her dark-blonde hair was plastered to her forehead. He needed to get her inside and rehydrated.

"I'll try to watch that around you, okay?"

"Okay," she replied in a smaller, almost childlike voice.

A suspicion started to form in his mind. But right now, he didn't have time to think about that. He needed to get her inside and cooled down.

"When's the last time you had a drink, baby girl?"

"I don't know. Not thirsty."

Her head kind of lolled back, as though she didn't have the energy to hold it up right now.

He'd had enough. If he left this much longer, he'd be calling for an ambulance. Duke reached in and unlocked the door, opening it.

Then he unbuckled her seat belt. Her clothes were saturated with sweat. Fuck. Shit. Definitely had to be dehydrated. He'd get her inside then see about getting some water into her.

"What ya doin', motorcycle man?" she asked.

"Motorcycle man?" he repeated, hoping to distract her as he reached for her. Last thing he needed was for her to resist him. But right now, she seemed compliant and sweet. He lifted her into his arms. She was lighter than he'd expected. Those hideous clothes she wore did nothing for her.

"You don't like that one? How about biker babe?"

"Not very masculine," he muttered. "Where are your keys, baby girl?"

"Under the flower pot."

"What?" He froze, staring down at her. *Please tell me I didn't hear her just say that.*

"Oh, sorry, the flower pot with the purple gerberas with the white centers. Aren't they pretty?"

He had no fucking idea what the fuck gerberas were and since she had no security lights and he'd put his phone away to pick her up, he couldn't fucking see any purple flowers with white centers.

"Babe, what the hell? Why the fuck are your keys under a flower pot?" He carefully set her down on the small bench by her front door.

"You're swearing again," she pointed out.

He bit back an impatient retort as he grabbed his phone and turned to search for fucking purple and white gerberas among the freaking hundred flower pots she had. She leaned forward to undo her boots, nearly toppling over.

"What are you doing?" he barked, catching her.

"Oh. Sorry." She sniffled.

Nope. Christ. Last thing he needed was her crying. Seemed like she didn't have the liquid to spare, either.

"It's okay," he said gently. Look at him, being soothing. This shit was harder than it appeared. "Just stay sitting there. I'll help you with your boots, all right? Soon as I find the damn keys."

"That pot." She gestured over, pointing to a pot. When he turned his phone light that way, he saw that it held purple and white flowers that were apparently fucking gerberas.

Fuck him.

He lifted the pot, snatching up her keys. "No fucking safety lights. Keeps her fucking keys under a fucking flower pot and she drives a fucking car that should have headed for the junk pile a long time ago."

"There's nothing wrong with my car," she protested, her words almost slurring together.

Fuck. Shit.

"And apparently she sits in hot fucking cars and let's herself sweat out all the fucking liquid in her body," he muttered as he unlocked her door.

"Shouldn't leave it out, though. I'll get a fine. Screw it! I don't care. Don't. Care. Gonna be a rebel. I can do that. I can do what I want."

"Okay, little rebel. You stay there for me, all right?"

"Okie-dokie."

Duke didn't bother to look back at her, certain she would obey. He moved inside and switched on some lights and the air.

He turned back to go get her, only to find her standing behind him, swaying on her feet. Her boots were still on, and she'd left a trail of dirt through the house.

"Damn it, Sunny, I told you to stay put." He winced at the growl in his voice.

She stared up at him, blinking. "I made you mad again. Sorry, Daddy."

He froze. The fuck did she just say? Christ, was she delusional now?

"I'm not your daddy. I'm Duke. The next-door neighbor."

She just continued to stand there, staring at him. Fuck, how out of it was she? He grimaced, unable to believe he was about to say this. "Biker babe?"

"Biker babe," she muttered. "Bit girly."

She couldn't stay where he put her, but that she remembered? He rolled his eyes as he took hold of her hand and led her to a chair. She didn't sit, just continued to stand there.

"Sit, little rebel," he murmured. "Let's get you out of those boots and into the shower. You need to cool down."

She was shivering now with the cool air blasting through the room. She needed to get out of those sweaty clothes. He noted how red and flushed her cheeks were and her eyes were swollen.

Had she been crying?

Unease settled in his gut at the idea of her upset and alone as he unlaced her boots.

Well, she's not alone right now, is she?

"Can't remember last time I helped take someone's shoes off," he muttered.

"You'd make a good Daddy," she murmured. Her eyes were closed, her head slumped against the back of the chair.

"No plans on having children, baby girl," he told her.

"Me either." She snorted. "Gotta have a husband before you have kids, right?"

Well, not technically. But she seemed the type to map out her life perfectly. Definitely not his type. He didn't do forever after or happy little families.

"Don't have one of those. Used to. He was a. . .a jerk."

He pulled off her socks. Christ, why did she have such thick socks on? No wonder she was roasting.

He only ever helped someone undress when he was about to fuck them. And no woman he'd ever fucked would be seen dead in a pair of men's socks.

And yet, he wasn't concerned or grossed out in the slightest. Might have helped that she had the cutest feet, with cheery yellow nail polish on her manicured toe nails. Not at all what he'd been expecting.

But then, he was beginning to see that she was very different than he'd judged her to be.

"A fucking jerk." She looked ridiculously pleased at that.

"Don't swear," he scolded. Yes, he was a hypocrite. No, he had no right to tell her what to do. But right now, he didn't care.

"Swear if I want to swear," she said almost sulkily.

He raised an eyebrow. "Not while I'm in charge, you won't."

Maybe he had more of a Daddy Dom side than he'd realized. He shook his head. Or maybe it was her. She just seemed to bring out parts of him that he hadn't known existed. The urge to be indulgent was tempered by the need to ensure she did as she was told.

She was fucking with his head. The sooner he made sure she was okay and left, the better.

"You said you're not my daddy."

"And I'm not. But right now, I am looking after you. And you're going to be respectful and obedient, young lady."

Christ. Where was this shit even coming from?

"Greg wanted kids. I can't have them."

He winced. Fuck. She was going to be pissed once she realized how much personal information she'd given him. She couldn't have kids? Fuck. How old was she? Twenty-five at most, he was guessing.

"It's one of reasons he left me."

That fucking bastard.

"Then obviously you're better off without him, huh? Come on, you need a shower."

"There were other reasons. I'm too quiet and shy. I'm not corporate enough."

"The fuck that mean?" he snapped.

She started to giggle. "I have no idea. Duke?"

He froze. Was she growing more aware? That was the first time she'd used his name. He braced himself for her to get mad at him. If she told him to get lost, would he? Could he?

"Yeah, babe?"

"I like 'baby girl' better," she told him.

He waited for more. Nothing came. "That it?"

"Hmm, oh, and I don't really feel that good." She put her hand over her mouth and he quickly scooped her up, racing for the bathroom. Luckily, her place was an exact replica of his house.

Except her house looked like a home. It looked lived in. His house was a bachelor pad. Huge T.V., a pair of recliners in the living room. Only his bedroom had an actual bed although he had a few mattresses for when some of the guys crashed at his place.

He got her to the toilet just as she started vomiting. He crouched, holding her as she dry-heaved. Not much was coming up. When was the last time she'd eaten?

When the heaves stopped, he helped her lean back against the wall. He flushed the toilet and picked up her toothbrush, putting some toothpaste on it.

Her eyes were closed, her skin now pasty white.

"Baby girl, brush your teeth and I'll get your shower going." How the hell was he going to get her in the shower?

She opened her eyes. "Can't. Tired. Bed."

"Soon," he promised her. "Wouldn't you like to go to bed all clean? Brush your teeth, I'm going to get you some water."

Something with electrolytes in it would be better. He turned the shower on. Then moved into the kitchen. Her cabinets were neat. Glasses all in a tidy row. Yep, nothing like his place. He opened the fridge, frowning when he saw how little food was in there. A fucking head of lettuce and some tomatoes? And what was this shit? He pulled out a tub of gloopy-looking stuff.

Hummus? Seriously?

Shaking his head, guessing she hadn't been to the store this week, he grabbed a bottle of water.

When he returned, she was slowly scrubbing at her teeth, and there was a smudge of toothpaste on her chin.

It kind of looked cute. He shook his head. *Losing it here, Duke. You do not like cute. You do not like little rebels with wounded doe eyes who can barely meet your gaze.*

"Come on." He helped her stand up and turned her to the sink. "Spit," he commanded when she stood there.

Nope. Definitely not his type.

"Drink this, little rebel." He tried to hand her the bottle of water after she'd finished brushing her teeth.

She shook her head, wrinkling her nose.

"Sunny, drink." He held the bottle up to her mouth and she tiredly took a few sips. Not nearly enough, but he'd let it go for the moment. As soon as she was out of the shower, he'd ensure she drank some more.

Then he'd leave. His good Samaritan act done for the day.

Now, he just had to figure out how the hell to get her into the shower.

3

She was having the most delicious dream.

There was a really sexy man, gorgeous abs, wide shoulders, muscular arms and legs showering with her. His hands were calloused and they felt delicious on her skin. Although she wasn't sure why he was wearing his boxers.

"Take them off." She reached for the band of the shorts.

"Nope. They're staying on." He pulled his hips back while still holding her upright in the shower. She shivered. Too cold. She reached for the controls and he lightly smacked her hand.

"Owie." It hadn't hurt but she felt obliged to complain.

"Don't touch the shower controls," a stern voice said.

"Sorry, Daddy."

He had to be a Daddy, right? That was why he was bathing her. She turned and leaned her head against his chest.

Sexy Daddy.

"Fucking Christ, this has to be retribution for all the bad shit I've done."

Bad shit? What bad shit? And he really had to stop swearing.

"Baby girl, been swearing all my life. First word was probably fuck. Not going to stop now."

"Did I say that out loud?" she wondered.

"Yes, you did."

"Am I your baby girl?"

"For the moment," he muttered.

Tears filled her eyes again. He was going to leave her. Like Greg.

"Aw, shit, don't cry, sweetheart. You can't afford to lose any more fluids."

"Greg sometimes called me sweetheart, but never in that voice. I like your voice. It's rough and growly and deep. Greg had a girly voice. And it got really high-pitched when he was excited. Like when he was about to come."

He groaned. "That was too much information, babe."

"He has a really small dick too. Do you have a small dick?"

"Babe, please," he begged.

She risked a glance down. His boxers were plastered against his skin. "No, definitely not small. But then you're my fantasy, so of course you don't. I told him he was plenty big enough. That I wouldn't want anything bigger. 'Cause what does it really matter, right? Not like he did all that much with it. Few pumps and done."

"Jesus, I will do anything. . .anything for you to stop talking about dicks."

"Oh, I thought men liked to talk about their dicks. I don't know that much about men." She yawned. "I only ever slept with Greg. He seemed obsessed with his. But he was obsessed with most things. Hated almost everything I said and did. He really hated the next-door neighbor."

"Is that so?"

"Uh-huh, said he was bringing down house prices with his biker gang."

"Not a gang, babe."

She closed her eyes. "I think he was just jealous. Duke's way better looking than him. Definitely got more friends. Has a fucking sexy-as-sin bike."

"Don't swear."

"Why not?"

"Because it doesn't sound right coming from you."

That didn't seem to make much sense. "What'll you do if I keep swearing? Ooh, will you spank me? It's been so long since I was spanked."

She missed it. She tried to lean back to see him, nearly slipping over.

"Jesus, baby girl, will you stay still. You're like a slippery eel."

"Have you ever held an eel?" she asked suspiciously.

"I have," he confirmed.

"Bet Greg wished he had, his was more like a tadpole."

There was a moment of silence then her dream man burst into laughter. "Babe, you're fucking crazy, you know that?"

Her smile dropped and she hunched her shoulders. "Yeah. I know. Sorry."

"Hey." He tilted her chin so she was looking up into the prettiest pair of eyes she'd ever seen.

"Men don't have pretty eyes, little rebel."

"You do. Your eyelashes are all sooty and long. So pretty. You don't put mascara on them, do you?"

"Fuck, no." He looked horrified.

"That's good. Greg—"

"Babe, please, no more Greg stories."

She stiffened. What an idiot she was. No man wanted to hear about someone else's ex. Even a dream man. Although it was kind of cathartic to talk about him. Wasn't like she had anyone else to talk to.

"Sorry," she murmured.

"Come on, let's get you out of here. You need to drink some

fluids. You're cooler at least now. Damn foolish sitting in a hot car for over an hour."

"Who would do a silly thing like that?" she asked as he hustled her out of the shower.

"Who indeed?" he murmured.

She swayed as she stood, dripping on the mat. He swore and quickly put down the lid of the toilet, making her sit on it.

"The lid's down," she said confused.

"Did you need to go?"

She thought about that for a second, totally distracted by his fine ass as he turned around to get some towels. Ooh, look at his tattoo. Pretty. She was reaching out to touch him, when he swung around and caught her.

"Stop checking me out."

"But you're my dream man."

He crouched and wrapped the towel around her. "Believe me, I am in no way your dream man."

"Why would I dream you up if you weren't?"

"Because you're dehydrated and out of it," he told her, gently drying her off before briskly running another towel over himself then wrapping it around his middle.

That was a shame.

"You should take those wet boxers off," she suggested.

Huh, why had she showered in her underwear? She attempted to stand when he grabbed her shoulders.

"Whoa, stay where you are."

"Got wet panties."

He groaned. "I swear. . .I haven't been so bad to have to endure this kind of torture."

What was he even talking about?

"I'm going to turn around. Can you take your bra off yourself, while staying seated?"

"Of course, been doing it since I was fifteen. I was a late bloomer." She sighed. "There's still not much there."

He turned and she awkwardly undid her bra. Why wouldn't her hands work properly?

"I was thinking of getting boobs like Paisley's. Do you think I'd look good with her boobs?"

"Who the fuck is Paisley?"

"You swear a lot."

"So, I've been told," he said dryly.

"I didn't think my dream man would swear so much," she said as she stood and tried to pull her panties off. A dizzy spell hit her and she slumped forward, banging into his back. Her towel slipped down.

He swore as he turned and grabbed hold of her. He held her against him as he wrapped the towel back around her. Then he lifted her up and carried her into the bedroom.

Somehow, she'd lost her wet panties in the process. Ahh well. Wasn't like they were very useful anyway.

"Nobody likes wet panties."

"Depends on how they got wet in the first place," her dream man muttered. "Let's get you into bed and I'll go get some more water for you."

He set her down on the chair she had in the corner of the room then looked down at the pile of stuffies on her bed.

"I need Moody," she told him.

"Moody?" He turned back to her.

"Moody the monkey." She pointed at the worn, creamy-colored monkey. He picked it up, handing it to her. She seized hold and held him up.

"See, smiling." She turned him over and the smile on his face turned down. "Grumpy." She then hugged him tight and yawned. "Tired. Sleep."

"Not yet, baby girl," he rumbled. "You need to drink some more."

"No."

"Excuse me?"

She didn't know where her backbone came from. She was tired, though and she didn't feel like drinking. "No drinking. Sleep."

"That's not what's going to happen. Stay there." He lifted her up and she sighed.

"I like being carried. Greg. . ." she trailed off, remembering that he didn't like her talking about her ex.

"Didn't like carrying you?" he guessed as he tucked her into bed.

She sighed. "Don't think he could. He had puny muscles. Not like your big ones. I didn't know I liked big muscles until I dreamed up you."

Her eyes drifted closed and he shook her gently. "Stay awake, baby girl. You need to drink."

"Okie-dokie," she said as she drifted off.

CRAP.

That was hands down one of the weirdest experiences he'd ever had. And that was saying something, considering his life.

Hopefully, she wouldn't remember any of this when she woke up. He shook his head, recalling everything she'd said about her ex.

What a douche.

He stripped off his wet boxers then pulled on his clothes. Moving quickly, he walked next door and grabbed a couple of Gatorades from his beer fridge. He kept them here for the boys when they'd had a few too many.

He looked longingly over at his ruined steak before tossing it in the trash. He'd get something to eat later. He walked back into her house, noting where she needed some security lights. She could also use a deadbolt on her door. He strode into the bedroom to find her cuddling Moody. She was fast asleep.

He sat next to her on the bed. "Sunny, wake up."

She mumbled something then burrowed deeper under the covers.

"Sunny, wake up. Now." He injected a sterner note into his voice, expecting instant obedience.

"No." Her voice was childlike and he sighed.

Christ. Why him?

"Sunny, don't be naughty. I want you to wake up and drink your bottle," he quickly tacked on, "of Gatorade."

"Ew. Yuck. No."

Well, what the fuck did he do now?

You could leave.

Right. Like he could kick back and relax while worrying about her.

She's an adult she can take care of herself.

As though to disprove his thought, she rolled over with that damn monkey clutched against her chest. Then she stuffed her thumb into her mouth.

He nearly laughed. Right. Take care of herself, huh? If he hadn't come over to check on her, would she still be baking in her car? The thought made him feel ill.

She needed a damn keeper.

He took hold of her shoulder, shaking her lightly. "Wake up, Sunny. Now."

"Don't wanna go to school. Sick."

She'd feel even worse in the morning if she didn't rehydrate. He was uncertain what to do if she wouldn't listen to him, however.

What are you going to do, spank me?

He remembered that question all too clearly. He'd spanked his fair share of women, during sex. He enjoyed bondage and control in the bedroom.

But all of that was fully consensual. Sunny wasn't herself right now. Would she be mad that he'd stripped her off to her underwear to get her in the shower? And then she'd taken hers off and fallen against him. He'd tried not to look, he really had. But she had the prettiest breasts he'd ever seen.

She was right, they weren't big. But if she dared to even think about getting boobs like Yoga Barbie, he would...

What? What would you do?

Fucked if he knew right now.

Right, if she wouldn't drink then he'd just have to make her. He grabbed hold of her, dragging her up. Her eyes shot open and she stared up at him with a scream, flinging backwards. She kept a tight hold of her stuffed monkey.

"Don't hurt me!"

"I'm not going to hurt you. It's Duke. I have some Gatorade for you."

"Don't like it."

Her eyes were drifting shut once more.

"I don't care if you don't like it. You're damn well going to drink it." He pressed the bottle to her mouth and she pulled away.

"Eww, yuck."

"Stop being such a baby and drink it!"

She gaped at him, hugging that stupid toy tight as tears dripped down her face.

Fuck. What was he doing?

Acting like an ass, that's what you're doing.

"Sunny—"

"You should leave."

Tears tracked down her too-pale cheeks, making him feel like more of an asshole than ever.

"I can't leave until you drink something."

"Don't wanna. You're being mean."

More tears. Fuck. He couldn't take it. He felt something hard inside himself break a little. Fuck. Shit.

What the hell did he do now?

Christ. One thing he did know. He needed help.

4

"Duke, my man, what's up?" Razor asked.

"Got a situation."

"With what? Everything okay?"

"Yeah, kind of." He placed a hand on the nape of his neck. Christ, he couldn't believe he was doing this. But it was get some help or take her to the emergency room. And he'd rather not be tied up for hours, waiting at the hospital.

Duke sighed. "Look, I know you're into this Daddy Dom stuff."

"You want to ask me about that?"

He could understand Razor's confusion. He didn't think this was a conversation he'd ever have with the other man either.

"Yeah, well, I've got a situation."

"What sort of situation?"

"The sort where I need the advice of someone who is used to dealing with Littles," Duke said abruptly. He blew out a breath. "Look man, I've got someone here I'm fairly certain is a Little. I found her in her car, overheated and dehydrated and unless I can get some liquids into her, I'm going to be taking her to the emergency room."

"She won't drink? Is she responding to you?" Razor asked, finally getting the urgency of the situation. "What makes you think she's a Little?"

He looked through the bedroom door to check on her. She was lying on her side once more, but this time she wasn't asleep. She was just staring at the wall, looking so forlorn and lost he couldn't stand it.

Fuck, this is why he didn't do relationships. He didn't know how to look after someone's emotional health. He could barely deal with their physical health.

"She's given me a few hints," he said dryly, moving away so she couldn't hear him. Did calling him her dream Daddy count? "I managed to get her cooled down in the shower but now she's curled up in her bed, and she's refusing to drink."

"Look, obviously not all Littles are the same. It's not a one-size fits all scenario. Try speaking nicely to her. Coaxing her into drinking and praising her when she does."

"What makes you think I didn't do that already?" he snarled.

There was silence on the other end.

"Fine. I'll try, the thing is. . ."

"What?"

"I kind of snapped at her and upset her. She, ah, she. . ."

"She what?" Razor asked.

"She fucking cried all right?"

More silence.

"I'm not used to women crying."

"You aren't? There's a shocker," Razor said dryly. "Way to go, making a sick Little cry."

"Thanks, that's just what I needed right now. If that's all you've got to help me—"

"No, wait, listen, with Littles you have to sometimes be indulgent, treat them like the little princesses or princes they are. But you have to temper that with making certain they do as they're told.

Sure, they're spoiled, but they need to know the boundary. The lines that can't be crossed without punishment. One of those lines is putting themselves at risk. Obviously, not drinking when you've told her that she needs to is a risk to her health. Therefore, it's a line."

"But it's not like we have any rules," he argued. "She's not mine. We don't have any sort of relationship."

"Right, you're just doing this out of the goodness of your heart."

"Fucked if I know why I'm doing this. But it's either get this into her or call an ambulance."

"All right, so you might not have set rules for her, but you're all she's got right now and you're only looking out for her. Even if she wasn't a Little, you'd be trying to do this for her health, right?"

"Yeah, so what are you saying?"

"Littles might complain about rules, but they're there to make them safe. To make them feel secure. If you can't convince her to drink, you may have to be stern."

"I tried. She cried."

"Were you mean?"

"I don't fucking know!"

"You were probably mean," he muttered. "Strict doesn't require you to get all cold or yelling or swearing."

"I didn't fucking yell." But the other two. . .yeah, maybe.

"Give her a consequence if she doesn't do the behavior you require of her. Drink the Gatorade or I'm going to. . ."

"What?"

"Well, I don't know, that's up to you. What are you comfortable with?"

"She asked me if I was going to spank her earlier," he muttered.

"She did?" Razor sounded amused.

"Stop fucking laughing at me, you bastard."

"Sorry. . .sorry, it's just imagining you, the great, stoic, calm Duke Canton dealing with a Little with an attitude, yeah, it's fucking funny. You're never out of your depth yet here is this girl practically making you sweat buckets over getting her to drink."

"She doesn't have an attitude."

Probably not the thing he should have focused on right then. He shook his head. He'd quickly gotten dressed when he'd gone next door so at least he was no longer standing around in his boxers. Boxers that she had tried her best to pull off when they'd been in the shower.

She sure wasn't shy when she thought she was dreaming. He had to grin at that. She was going to be mortified if she remembered that part.

"Right," Razor said almost gently. "Sorry. She's sick and if you don't know each other well, then likely she's feeling vulnerable. You seen her Little side before?"

"No."

"Okay, then maybe her defenses are down. Best you get her to let you help her now before they come back up."

"So when you say I should get strict, I threaten to spank her?" Discomfort filled him. Not over spanking someone. But they didn't have a relationship. It felt wrong.

"Will you do it?"

"What?"

"Will you follow through?"

He sighed. "Fuck, no."

"Then I wouldn't threaten her with that. Follow through is important."

Holy shit. Was he really having this conversation?

"Are you sure I need to know all this? This is a one-time thing, never to be repeated. I just want to know how to get her to do what I want her to do without making her cry."

"Christ, man, if I knew that don't you think I'd be rich," Razor snapped back. "Just be firm. But don't be mean."

"Shall I threaten to take something away from her? Like the stuffed monkey she's holding onto for dear life?"

"Jesus, no!" he snapped. "For fuck's sake, man, don't mess with the stuffies. Bitch will cut you over that."

"Don't call her a bitch," he snapped.

"Hey, a generalized statement. Nothing against your girl. I mean not-your-girl."

He sighed. "I'll work something out. Thanks. I think."

"You're welcome, any more advice—"

He ended the call. Yeah, he didn't think he'd bother to go to Razor for any more advice. Right, what to use to get her to co-operate? Maybe he'd lucked out and adult Sunny was back. He peeked in on her. Still hugging that monkey. And her thumb was in her mouth.

He walked into the room and sat facing her on the bed. "Baby girl, it's time to drink now."

"No," she mumbled around her thumb.

How could someone who seemed so sweet and timid the rest of the time become so obstinate when they were sick?

"You're going to drink this whole bottle or there's going to be consequences," he warned.

She froze. "Consequences?"

"Uh huh."

She moved one hand behind her to cover her bottom. He wondered if her husband had been her Daddy. Duke guessed that if he had been, he'd fallen flat in that department like in every other one. He had to smile as he recalled her talking about his tadpole dick.

Although he wasn't sure he appreciated his cock being likened to a cold, slippery eel. He shook off that thought.

"You can't spank me!"

He raised an eyebrow. "No?"

"I's sick."

"You won't be sick all the time, though, will you?"

"That's not fair."

He nearly sighed with relief as rather than get teary, she was glaring up at him.

"I don't like that stuff." She pointed to the bottle he held.

He shrugged. "I don't much care since it's going to make you feel better."

"I don'ts need it since I feels fine," she tried to convince him.

"Is that so? Did I mention that naughty little girls say goodbye to their fun activities?"

"Like what?" she asked suspiciously.

"Like watching cartoons and coloring." It was a bit of a guess, but he'd spotted some coloring books tucked under a cushion in the living room. They looked like they had cartoon characters on the front.

She gasped; the noise comically loud.

"Now, are you going to drink the Gatorade like a good girl or do I need to go find a baby bottle to feed it to you?" Not that he fucking had one of those.

"I am not a baby." She snatched the Gatorade out of his hand and started to drink.

He let out a deep sigh. Thank fuck. He really had thought they were headed to the Emergency room. He ran his hand over his face.

"You look tired."

He glanced back at her. He glanced from the bottle to her mouth. Then raised an eyebrow pointedly. "Drink or do you need my help?"

She sighed but lifted it to her mouth once more.

"I'm fine. Just a few long days at work." He stood and stretched. Now that she was drinking, he felt better about leaving her.

Better, but still not great. Especially when she was in Little mode. How often did she go into Little mode? Did she normally have someone look after her?

"Was Greg, ah, your Daddy?"

"What?" She pulled the drink away. "No. That would be silly."

"Silly, how?"

"'Cause Greg never thought about anyone but himself."

Yeah, that sounded about right from what she'd told him about the man.

"I'm sleepy now." The bottle was only half-empty. But her eyelids were drooping, her words slurring. However, she still needed more.

He sat next to her on the bed. She scooted over and he pulled her against him, his arm over her shoulder, her head resting on his chest. He grabbed the bottle, holding it to her lips. He tried to ignore how good she felt in his arms. How nice it was to look after someone like this.

She reached for the bottle but he pulled it back. "Uh-uh, conserve your energy, baby girl. Just concentrate on drinking. Good girl."

He had to admit Razor did know what he was talking about. As soon as she'd figured out that he was serious and willing to back up any misbehavior with punishment, she'd become much more relaxed.

Secure. She felt more secure.

He just held her gently as she drank more. When the bottle was three-quarters gone and she'd stopped sucking, he pulled it away, feeling an odd sort of satisfaction.

He settled her into bed and slipped his arm away, standing.

She stirred. "Duke?"

"Yeah?" he replied gruffly.

"Thanks."

"No problem." He paused. It wasn't any of his business. . .but still he had to know. . .

"What happened today?" Something bad had happened for her to react this way. Didn't take a genius to figure that much out.

"Lost my job," she whispered. "Loved that job. Even if my boss was a pig."

Oh, poor baby.

She had to be so stressed.

"You'll find a new job."

"Won't give me any references," she mumbled. "Knows everyone, I'll be blackballed. All because I wouldn't sleep with him."

He froze. That motherfucker. "He fired you because you wouldn't fuck him? Sue the bastard for sexual harassment."

Or tell me who he is. . .I'll go have a chat with him. Teach him the way you treat a woman.

"Right. Like anyone will believe me. There's no point. Not sure what I'm going to do though. . .I'm so lost. . ."

She drifted off to sleep. He stood there for a long while, trying to convince himself to move. Standing there, watching her sleep was a little creepy. She would be fine. There was no reason for him to stay.

Finally, he managed to get himself to move.

But he didn't expect to sleep all that much tonight.

5

She was a dork.

Oh God. A giant, idiotic, ridiculous dork. She crawled into the fort she'd built and hugged Moody tight, closing her eyes. But her heart still raced, memories filling her mind.

Dork. Dork. Dork.

What had she been thinking? Why?

She was never going to show her face outside this house again. She guessed that was the silver lining of no longer having a job. She didn't have to go anywhere. Until she ran out of money, was no longer able to pay the mortgage and ended up living on the streets.

Maybe she should pre-empt that and call a realtor, put her house on the market. She could move, rent a small cottage by the sea and live out her days with twenty-five cats and a dog called Fido. Wouldn't that be nice?

Anything would be better than having to see Duke again. She groaned, pressing the palms of her hands against her eyes. Had she really tried to pull down his boxers? Oh no, please don't tell her she'd asked if he was going to spank her?

"This day can't get any worse, it really can't."

Usually a blanket fort would make everything better. She hadn't been able to create them when she lived with Greg; he'd have thought her ridiculous. But the day he'd left she'd called into work sick, the only time she'd ever done that, and spent three days in that fort.

Well, obviously she'd come out to eat and use the bathroom. She wasn't some sort of animal.

But today it couldn't work its magic. Even a blanket fort couldn't counter the absolute humiliation of what she'd done.

"This cannot be happening to me. He's not a Daddy. He can't be. He. . .he's too. . ."

Abrupt? Cold? Mean?

Rough, tough biker dudes couldn't be daddies, right? That just seemed crazy. And yet he'd said the right things last night. Well, sometimes.

He hadn't always gotten it right. But no one is perfect.

"You cannot be thinking that he is any way perfect, Sunshine River Bright." She winced as she said her full name. Her parents had a lot to answer for. Seriously.

"Oh man, did I call him a biker babe? What is wrong with me? Really? What. Is. Wrong. With. Me." She'd had a serious Daddy Dom addiction since she was nineteen when she'd signed up to this dating site that matched Daddies and Littles. Only, the Daddy she'd been paired with hadn't turned out to be a love match. Or a sexual match.

Her confidence had taken a serious hit when she'd discovered that Alan, the man she'd trusted, that she'd been falling for, that she'd thought might be a permanent Daddy to her Little, didn't find her sexually attractive.

Yeah. That had sucked.

And the reason he hadn't said anything straight away? Because his friend had started the dating site and he didn't want her to bad mouth it. He must have finally decided that she wasn't the type of person to do that. Or maybe it was just that he couldn't stand touching her any longer.

She'd been devastated. She guessed that had left her open and vulnerable to Greg.

A knock on the door startled her and she froze. Who the hell would be knocking on her door? There was no reason for anyone to visit. And she definitely was not answering. Whoever it was could go away because this fort was indestructible. It might even make her invisible.

Oh God, let her be invisible.

It was the only way out of this mess. For her to gain the power of invisibility.

"I want to be invisible. I want to be invisible. I want to be invisible."

"Hate to break it to you, little rebel, but a fort doesn't have the power to make you invisible. Especially not this fort. This is just a blanket over a table. It doesn't have a door or lights, did you even put down flooring?"

Fudge. What was he doing here? He wasn't here, was he? It was her imagination.

It didn't matter because she was invisible.

"Why is he criticizing my fort, though? That's just rude."

"Because the fort is crap. And you're definitely not invisible."

Temper overrode her embarrassment and she moved onto her hands and knees, sticking her head out of a gap to glare up at him.

"It is not crap!"

He just stared at her. Then held out his hand. "Come here."

"No!" She shot back into the fort, bringing her legs up to her chest and clasping hold of them. "I'm not coming out. Ever!"

"Ever is a long time to live in that crappy fort. You even got snacks?"

"Of course, I've got snacks!" Who climbed into a fort without snacks? Did he think she was an amateur?

"What sort of snacks?" he asked weirdly.

"Uh, why?"

"Seen your fridge and pantry, babe. You don't know how to do snacks for shit. Let me guess, raisins and carrot sticks?"

Close. Cheese, crackers and an apple.

"Everyone knows junk food is the only acceptable snack in a fort, babe. Even a crappy one."

Suddenly, one blanket was partially lifted, allowing light to flood through and she saw him crouching down.

"Why are you here? How did you even get in? The house was locked."

"Your locks are like this fort."

What did that mean. . .oh, so now he was insulting her locks as well?

"Did you just come in here to insult me?" she snapped at him. A low-grade headache was starting to thump in her temples.

"Came to take you for breakfast."

"I've had breakfast," she lied.

"Uh-huh, what did you have? An egg white omelet with some soy cheese?"

"There is nothing wrong with eating healthy! Better than eating pork rinds and. . .and Cheezits!"

Really? That's the best comeback you had?

"Weird combination, babe. But I'll try anything once. So, what did you have for breakfast?"

"Nothing, all right," she groaned. "I'm so crappy at lying."

"You shouldn't try to lie. At least not to me. That will just get you in trouble."

"Please don't," she whispered.

"Don't what?"

"Don't pretend something you don't feel. I know I made a

complete idiot of myself last night. I showed you a part of me that I've only ever shown one other person. And I still don't know why! I don't even know you."

"No," he agreed slowly. "But maybe you saw something in me that I didn't even know was there."

"What do you mean?"

"I'm not a Daddy Dom."

She froze. This seemed kind of cruel. It wasn't as though she thought he was.

Didn't you? Then why did you open up to him like you did?

She hadn't meant to. It had been almost beyond her control. She'd lost her job. It happened to people all the time. However, that combined with little food or water to drink all day and she'd kind of just dropped all her walls.

She'd never shown Greg her Little. Yet she barely knew Duke and her Little appeared easily.

Was he right? Had she sensed something in him?

"While I like being in control in the bedroom, I've never done any age play stuff. Never imagined it was something I would enjoy, being a Daddy."

"I'm. . .I'm really sorry I forced you to take care of me."

He barked out a laugh. "Babe, you're what? Five-foot-four and a hundred pounds?"

A hundred and twenty-five but it was nice he thought that. And why was he talking about her appearance? Did he not find her attractive either?

How much rejection could one person take before they broke?

"You're tiny. You can't force me to do anything. I didn't have to take care of you last night. I wanted to."

I wanted to.

I wanted to.

"You did?" she whispered.

"Even fucking rang a friend to find out how best to handle you. Not like I have much experience." He ran his hand through his hair. "Will you come out now?"

"I'd still rather wait until I'm invisible," she murmured.

He snorted. "Out, baby girl. Now."

Drat. His voice had that stern note she couldn't resist. The one that sent a shiver down her spine. She started to crawl out. As she grew closer, he stood and reached out with his hand, helping her up.

He stared at her. She noted that he hadn't shaved yet this morning. The slight scruff on his handsome face suited him. Made him look slightly more dangerous and sexier.

"How you feeling this morning?" he asked, letting her hand go. Damn, she missed that contact. His hand was large, warm and calloused.

Delicious.

"Umm." How to answer that? That she really wished a hole would open up and swallow her whole?

She stared down at the floor.

"Babe? What you staring at?"

"Hoping a hole will appear in the floor."

He sighed then reached out and gently grasped hold of her chin, tilting her face up. "Ain't nothing to be embarrassed about."

"Really? Has your memory gone faulty? Because I can remember lots to be embarrassed about." She frowned up at him.

"Hmm, and here I thought you were so quiet and shy."

"I am," she muttered. "Until someone insults my fort and snack-making ability."

"Babe, a two-year old could have done better." He looked at her fort, shaking his head. "Sad, really. How your education is lacking."

"You want to do better?"

"Another day. Go get dressed, babe. We're going for breakfast."

"I'm not hungry."

He folded his arms over his very wide chest. He was wearing a pair of worn blue jeans and a blue T-shirt. His dark hair was scruffy, like he'd just woken up, pulled on his clothes and walked over here.

Which he likely had.

"Babe, word of warning. I'm grouchy before I get in my morning coffee or three so you might want to hurry it up before I take you out looking like that."

She glanced down at the clothes she'd pulled on this morning. A pair of nearly see-through yoga pants and an old, paint-stained T-shirt. These were her housework clothes. She wouldn't be seen dead outside the house in them.

She glared up at Duke. "I just lost my job; I don't think going out for breakfast factors into my budget anymore."

There, that was a nice adult reason not to go out. Nothing to do with the fact that she could feel herself blushing every time she looked at him and remembered the way he'd held her in the shower. . .oh Lordy.

"That was a shit excuse. I asked you. I pay. Now get. Before I dress you myself and haul you out of here over my shoulder."

"Anyone ever tell you that you're stubborn and rude?" She glared up at him.

"Been called way worse. You're gonna need to up your game to actually insult me. Now go. I'm out of patience." He took hold of her shoulders and turned her towards the bedroom, landing a heavy smack on her ass.

She rubbed the sting, turning to gape back at him. It didn't actually hurt. But it was the first time anyone had smacked her bottom since Alan. Greg had been horrified the one time she'd suggested it to him, and he'd actually offered to find her a therapist to deal with her unhealthy desires.

Yeah, she hadn't mentioned it again.

She stared in disbelief at Duke who just watched her calmly, his arms crossed over his chest, his T-shirt tight across his pecs and a stern look on his face.

Okay. She guessed she was getting dressed.

6

He'd insisted they take his truck. Since she doubted whether he could actually fit into her car and she disliked driving anyway, she didn't argue. She just settled herself into the leather interior of his surprisingly spotless truck. Well, when she said settled, she'd attempted to heave herself up into the high seat and had ended up needing a boost in.

Like that hadn't been embarrassing enough, her body's reaction as he'd touched her had really been the icing on the cake. A shiver had run down her spine, blood pooling in her clit.

He pulled into the parking lot of a small diner not far from their neighborhood. She'd never eaten here before. But then she couldn't actually remember the last time she'd eaten in a diner. Greg would never have stepped foot in a place like this. The paint on the outside of the building was chipped and peeling. Inside wasn't any better. The floor was uneven, with unknown stains. The vinyl on the booth seats was peeling and everything just looked worn.

And it smelled absolutely delicious.

Duke surprised her by opening the door and letting her go in first. He'd also opened the truck door for her.

"Yo, Duke!" a friendly guy called from where he sat at the counter. Several other customers called out greetings as he placed a hand on the small of her back and led her to a booth in the back.

Don't react. Don't show him how much his touch affects you.

But she was pretty certain he already knew. He waited until she slid into the booth seat then instead of sitting across from her as she'd expected, he sat next to her. The roomy booth suddenly felt all too small and constricting. She scooted further into the corner, but he just followed her over, his thigh brushing against hers.

A cup of coffee immediately landed in front of him.

"Thanks Jo, you read my mind," he said warmly to the older waitress.

The thin, heavily-wrinkled woman with gray hair pulled back in a bun and twinkling blue eyes just smiled at him. "Lucky for me, you're a man of habit and you have simple tastes."

"Not sure that I wasn't just insulted. What do you think, babe?" He turned to her with a wink.

"I'm sure Jo knows what she's talking about," Sunny told him.

He leaned back. "In here two seconds and already I'm being ganged up on."

"You'll survive. Big, tough man like you." Jo reached over her, placing a menu down. It had been laminated, but looked like someone had attempted to chew one corner and there was a stain down the middle.

"Get you something to drink, honey?" Jo asked her.

"Sweet tea, please."

"I'll come back in a few to take your order." She strode away.

"You don't need a menu?" she asked.

"Nah, I always have the same thing."

That kind of surprised her. He didn't seem the predictable type. Then again, he also didn't seem the type to own a cute little house in suburbia. Or to take care of a neighbor who had gone into Little space.

She searched the menu for something remotely healthy. The waitress returned.

"Usual, Duke?" she asked as she refilled his coffee and placed Sunny's sweet tea down.

"You got it."

"And for you?" she asked Sunny.

She opened her mouth to ask for poached eggs on wholegrain toast.

"She'll have the pancakes with extra whip and syrup. Can we get some water too, please," Duke requested, picking up the menu and handing it back to Jo who quickly left. That woman was surprisingly fast on her feet.

"That wasn't what I was going to order." She glared at him.

He raised an eyebrow. "You don't like pancakes?"

"What? Yes, I like pancakes."

"Then what's the problem?"

"The problem is I was going to have eggs and toast."

"You're still hungry after the pancakes, you can have that," he told her.

"What? No, I can't eat that much." She stared at him aghast. She shifted around on the seat, feeling angsty. "You know that ordering for me like that isn't sexy."

"Who said I was trying to be sexy?" he drawled.

Shoot. Why had she said that?

"I just. . ."

"Baby girl, what's the real problem here?" He half-turned towards her, his forearm resting on the table. "You think I'm being a jerk. Wasn't trying to be but I'll take that on board. Not saying I'll change, of course."

She rolled her eyes at him.

"You really don't want the pancakes? I'll go change the order."

He moved along the booth. She reached out and wrapped her hand around his arm.

"No, wait. . ."

He stilled, watching her carefully.

"I like pancakes. I just haven't had them in years because. . ." Because why? Because she wanted to be healthy? Or because Greg wanted her to be thin?

"When I met Greg, I was bigger. I had curves." She missed having boobs and an ass. "He helped me with my diet. If I stray from it, then I'll put on weight again."

Except, it had been Greg that cared about that, right?

And Greg was gone, so why was she continuing on like he hadn't left?

Duke moved in closer, his scent wrapping around her. Leather and spice. "Babe, a man shouldn't try to mold his woman into something else to make him happy. That ain't a man. Not a good man. A real man wants his woman to be happy. With herself. With him. A real man wants his woman to be healthy. A real man makes a woman feel desired and safe. Secure in the knowledge that her man thinks she's fucking sexy no matter what. Being healthy is good, not saying pancakes every day is a great idea. Not saying you should immediately become a junk food addict. But some treats aren't a bad thing. You got to live a little, baby girl."

Her heart stopped for a moment. That was not what she'd been expecting him to say. And her insides melted. She took in a low breath. He was right. She nodded her head. "Extra whipped cream and syrup might have been overkill."

He smiled. Holy hell. That smile was lethal. "Who said that was for you?"

She rolled her eyes at him.

"How long have you known you were a Little?" He leaned back in the booth. How did he suck up so much space? And air? And her ability to think? Her mouth was dry and she reached out a shaky hand for the sweet tea, managing to spill some on the tabletop.

"Shoot," she muttered, reaching for some napkins.

"Here, let me." He grabbed the napkins and mopped up the mess. Then he wiped down the glass. "Drink up, babe. You're probably still a bit dehydrated."

She nodded then took a sip of the sweet tea.

"Not a coffee fan?"

"I am, but Greg didn't. . ." her voice trailed off at his frown. "Maybe we shouldn't talk about him."

"Might be best," he agreed. "You didn't answer my question."

"Noticed that, did you?"

He raised an eyebrow and just waited patiently. Crap.

"I've known for about six years. I, um, I like to read and I was always drawn to books with, ah, dominant men in them. Then I found these books about Littles and Daddies and it struck a chord with me, I guess. Do you think I'm weird?"

He grasped hold of her chin, turning her face. "Would I ask if I thought you were weird? Would I have helped you last night? I have some friends who are into the lifestyle. Even called one for help last night. Don't think he's weird. Not for that anyway. Other reasons maybe. . ."

He winked at her and she smiled, feeling more at ease. She knew a lot of people didn't understand the dynamic. Who thought it was wrong. That was part of the reason why she'd been worried about seeing him again. That he'd look at her like she was a freak. Or gross.

"You called someone for help?"

"Needed some advice, babe. Thought I was gonna end up taking you to the hospital."

"Thank you," she whispered. "For helping me."

He just gave a nod. "You ever been in a relationship with a Daddy Dom?"

She looked around but there was no one close by to hear their conversation. Not that she knew anyone here so she shouldn't care. Greg's opinions, his needs for peer approval, still had a hold on her. She needed to change that.

"Ah, yeah, kind of."

"Kind of?"

"Here you go." She looked up with a smile of thanks as Jo placed a huge plate of pancakes in front of her. In front of Duke, she placed a big plate of hash browns, sausage, ham and eggs.

Holy hell. Did he eat like that every morning?

"Dig in, babe. Then you can explain about this 'kind of' relationship."

She cut into the huge mound of pancakes and took a small bite. That tasted so good. They ate for a while without talking but it wasn't a weird sort of silence. It was pleasant. She couldn't remember the last time she'd sat with someone to eat a meal.

When she was full, she wiped her mouth carefully and watched him continue to work his way through his big plate of food. She felt guilty that she'd only been able to eat a third of hers.

"Feel free to talk while I eat, babe, I can multi-task."

She sighed. "You're not letting this go, huh?"

"Nope."

"You're stubborn."

"One of my better qualities."

"Fine. When I was nineteen, I joined this kink dating site that matched people up. I was matched to this older guy who was a Daddy. I thought we had something. He didn't. End of story."

He snorted. "Babe, you can't tell a story for shit. Lot left out of that."

"I don't see why this has to be all about me. Why am I doing all the sharing?"

"We're getting to know each other."

He hadn't seemed to want to get to know her before now.

They'd lived next door to each other for close to a year with barely exchanging a hello, but now he wanted to know it all?

"That implies you will actually tell me something about you."

He shrugged. "Nothing to tell. I own a tattoo parlor. I belong to the Iron Shadows Motorcycle club. Last night I rescued a Little who didn't have the sense to get her butt out of a hot car and drink some damn water."

There was a stern note in his voice that had her squirming. "I wasn't thinking properly. It was a bad day yesterday."

"You lost your job."

"Yeah." She poked at the leftover pancakes with her fork.

Duke pushed his empty plate away then grabbed the fork from her hand, putting it down and pushing her plate away too. He turned so he was half-facing her.

"That's a big problem?"

"Well, yeah." Of course it was.

"There are other jobs, baby," he said in a soft voice. "Was it worth risking your health?"

She rubbed at an imaginary spot on the table. "No."

He reached out and grabbed her chin, tilting her face up. "No, it wasn't. There are other jobs out there. I know it has to be frightening and your boss sounds like a jerk. Wouldn't mind having a little chat with him."

She shook her head. "Don't. Please. He's not worth it."

He narrowed his gaze. "Needs to fucking learn not to touch what doesn't fucking belong to him."

He did, but she didn't want Duke getting involved. "Please."

"Fine, I'll leave that for the moment. But, baby, you can't risk your health like that again."

"I panicked. I had to buy Greg out of his half of the house. I have a mortgage and bills and not much in savings, and it all got on top of me. I've never been fired in my life. I worked so hard and then it was just gone. I don't want to lose my house. I need the stability, of knowing I have somewhere to go. . ." she trailed off, feeling like she was going way off track.

"You all right with working nights?" he asked abruptly.

She just stared at him, confused at the change of topic. "What?"

"Nights? Can you work them? Can you manage a booking system? Does fourteen-fifty an hour with benefits work okay for you? If you work out then we can review that in a month."

"Wait. . .are you offering me a job?"

"Yep."

"Out of pity?"

He raised both eyebrows. "You in a position to reject it?"

She went red, feeling ashamed.

"Hey, look at me."

She raised her gaze up to his, feeling the sting of tears.

"Didn't say that to upset you. I need someone working reception. My last girl only lasted two months before she ditched and we've been handling things ourselves since. It's a pain in the fucking ass. But so is hiring someone who's gonna fucking bail again. Am I offering you the job because I know you fucking need it? Yeah. But I'm also offering it because you don't seem the type to run when the going gets rough. Guys who work for me, who come into the parlor, they aren't bad people but they can be rough round the edges, what I'm not sure is if you can handle that."

"I've worked primarily with men for the last two years. Believe me, none of them made concessions for the fact I'm a woman. I can handle working with guys. But you don't know if I'll be any good."

He shrugged. "That's why we'll review in a month. So?"

It still felt like a pity hire, but he was right. She had little choice and if it didn't work out then she'd at least have time to search for something else.

"All right, thanks."

He nodded. "You might not want to thank me until you hear the rules."

"Rules? What sorts of rules? Like client confidentiality?"

"Oh yeah, there's that. But that wasn't really what I was talking about. Rules for you."

She stared at him in confusion. "Rules for me?"

"Uh-huh. Babe, your car is a rust bucket piece of shit."

"Don't hold back, please. Speak your mind." She bit her lip. She wasn't sure what it was about him that made her lose that usual reserve. Maybe it was because he'd seen all of her, because she'd already dropped her shields around him and he hadn't run screaming from her.

"Always try to, babe."

"Okay, what does my car have to do with these rules?"

HE COULDN'T QUITE BELIEVE he was doing this. What was he thinking? Hiring his next-door neighbor? He hadn't even intended to hire someone for the front desk but he was getting sick of Rory's moaning.

But hiring his next-door neighbor? His neighbor who he'd held in his hands, half-naked. That had disaster written all over it.

Not only that, but the rules he was going to lay on her weren't normal. He was asking for a lawsuit. No way did he want her to equate him with her old boss which is why he was laying this out now.

"Thing is, find myself feeling rather fucking protective of you. Guess it's because of last night. Maybe because of who you are. Possibly because you're my neighbor but I'm guessing not since I don't feel this way about Yoga Barbie."

"Yoga Barbie? Oh, do you mean Paisley?"

He shrugged. "The one always walking around in a sports bra and pants so tight you can see the outline of her pussy lips."

She went bright red, her eyes wide. Jesus, she was such an innocent. Sweet and naive didn't have a place in his life.

Yet he still fucking wanted her.

Then she shocked him by bursting into giggles. "Oh God, you so can. Greg used to go on and on about what a perfect body she had and how I should ask her for tips on how to look as good as she does."

"Babe, think I've made it clear what I think about him, but in case I haven't, your ex is a douche."

"He sure is."

"I don't care about a lot of people. The club, the shop, they're basically my life. But I find myself protective over you. So there's gonna be some rules and I need to tell you upfront so you know what you're getting into. My tattoo parlor, I'm the boss, so it's my way. Got it?"

"All right, you want me to follow your rules, which are?"

"When it's possible, you ride into work with me. Less chance of someone running over you in that sardine can of yours."

She bit her lip. "My car isn't that bad."

He gave her a look, trying to ignore the effect on his cock that watching her mouth was having on him. Damn, he had it fucking bad.

"It is. You'll ride with me."

"All right. I'll pay you some gas money."

He snorted. "Hell. No."

"But that's not very fair."

"Don't care about fair, babe. Few things you should know about me right now. We're in my ride, I drive. We're in my ride, I pay the gas."

"All right, so if we're in my ride then I drive and I pay."

"Sure, babe, if that makes you feel better."

She narrowed her gaze at him. "Why do I feel like that's not a victory for me?"

"Maybe because I'll never be in your ride? Not only won't I fit. But like I said, it's a piece of shit. We'll work on getting you something better."

"I don't need something better."

He ignored her, making a mental note to ask around the club. Razor owned a mechanics shop; he would keep an ear out.

"All right, anything else?"

Ah, yeah.

"Shop opens at two. Closes at ten weeknights and six on Saturdays. Closed Sundays and Mondays."

"Okay. That's fine."

"Wasn't for the last girl. Cut into her social life."

She gave him a self-deprecating smile. "Well, I'm your girl then, since I have no life. So you open at two today?"

He nodded. "I go in an hour earlier to open up, set up stations. We can make that half an hour earlier now if you're helping set up."

"All right. You want me to start today?"

"Yep."

"I can do that. Anything else?"

"Yeah, place can get dangerous at night. I set up there because it's not far from the club, but there's some crime in the neighborhood. If it's dark out then your ass ain't out the door alone. Got me?"

"You don't want me outside on my own in the dark?"

"Yep. You need to go out to get food or go to your car if I'm not there, then you ask one of the others to take you. Got it?"

"Ah, yeah. I can do that. I'll bring my own food anyway."

"Let me guess, fucking salad?" he asked.

"Nothing wrong with salad."

"If you're a rabbit."

She rolled her eyes at him. Little brat. The urge to turn her over his knee, to pull those goddamn ugly jeans down over her ass and reveal what was likely plain cotton underwear struck him. Fuck. What was it about her that got to him? She wasn't his normal type, not by a long shot. Yet here he was practically panting after her.

Fuck. Clear your head, man.

"Anything else?" she asked.

"Not right at the moment. I'll let you know as I think of it." There would likely be more.

"All right. Thanks for the job, Duke. I appreciate it."

He just hoped they didn't both come to regret it.

7

Sunny snuck glances at him as he drove them to his shop later that day. They were going in early so he could show her the ropes. She'd packed a lunch, and yes it was a salad. She actually liked salads.

Or at least that's what she told herself.

"You didn't need to install the security lights and deadbolts."

He'd turned up an hour earlier than they'd agreed, with his tools and some security lights for outside along with deadbolts for both her doors. Which he'd proceeded to install, despite her protests.

She sighed. "It's going to be hard to teach me what to do if you're not talking to me."

Who knew biker babes could sulk?

"All I did was offer to pay you."

Another chilling look. Whoops. Things were getting icy. "Well, not pay you. Pay you back for the lights and deadbolts."

More cold silence. She sighed.

"It's not that big of a deal."

"It is," he told her. "I buy something for you then you don't try to pay me back. Just like if I take you out to eat, you don't pay for your own damn meal."

Yeah, she'd gotten schooled in that earlier at the diner when she'd tried to pull out her wallet to pay. He'd been upset over that too.

Seemed biker babes could be overly emotional about certain things.

Greg had always insisted that they keep things equal, financially. His reasoning was that too many couples broke up over finances so they should make certain to each pay their share. Which kind of made sense. Except he had earned a lot more than her, and insisted on going out for fancy dinners every week which she couldn't afford.

"Fine. I won't mention it again."

"You could say thank you."

She flushed bright red. *Way to be a bitch.* All she'd done was gripe at him, not once showing any gratitude.

"I'm so sorry. Thank you. I really appreciate it. I've never had anyone care about my safety before. I guess I'm not used to it."

He turned into a rough-looking neighborhood. She looked around. This was where his shop was?

"Your parents?"

"What? Oh," she said recalling what they'd been talking about. "They weren't really the type to notice anything I did. They were free spirits."

"That why your name is Sunshine Bright?"

She sighed. "It's worse than that. It's Sunshine River Bright."

"No shit?"

"No shit," she repeated.

"Damn, must have been a bitch growing up with that name. Kids tease you?"

"What do you think?"

He nodded. "They teased you."

"My parents aren't bad people. They're just more interested in communing with nature and getting high than what their daughter was doing."

"You don't seem the getting high and communing type."

"I'm not. I was like a square peg trying to fit into a round hole. I didn't understand them and they didn't get me. I like order and rules and to live in the same place for more than a few months."

He nodded as he pulled the truck into a space outside a white building that had *Ink Inc* written on the outside. That was cute. Although she wouldn't tell Duke that. He didn't look like the type of guy who would appreciate something of his being called cute. There was a small parking lot out front and on one side there was a small convenience store, on the other a Chinese take-out place.

"I usually park around the corner to leave these spaces for customers. Up a few blocks is Reaper's, the bar owned by the club. Our compound is behind it. Any reason you're ever in trouble and I'm not here, you can go there. I'll tell them all you work for me." He turned towards her, unbuckling her seat belt. "You'll be taken care of. Wait there."

She sat and waited for him to walk around to her door, knowing better than to get out on her own.

Another of Duke's infamous rules.

For a rough, tough biker dude he sure had a lot of rules.

He slid his hands around her waist then lifted her down. Definitely not normal employer-employee behavior. But then, Duke wasn't a normal sort of guy. And he wasn't like Ronny. She knew he'd never force anything on her. Trust had formed quickly after the way he'd looked out for her last night.

She was attracted to him. Even though the conversation in the diner was awkward and a bit terrifying for someone who had been hiding that part of herself for years, it also felt freeing to have it out there.

He knew. He wasn't grossed out.

"I'll get you a set of keys. But this one opens the front door. Don't ever go through the back, it opens out into the alley behind all of these shops. In fact, I don't want to catch you ever in that alley, all right?"

She looked around with a nod, noting a homeless man going through the dumpster outside the convenience shop. Sorrow filled her and she made a note to make extra food next time she worked in case he was still around.

Duke opened the door and showed her the alarm. Crap. Numbers weren't her thing. She'd have to write the code down and work on memorizing it. He led her through everything. He wasn't impatient, but it was also clear he didn't want to have to go over anything more than once.

None of it seemed too hard, though.

"It's up to you to keep the staff room clean and stocked," he told her. "Take the trash out each night."

"The dumpster is in the alley?"

"Yeah. It is. Just leave it at the back door and someone will throw it out."

She nodded.

"We have T-shirts and sweatshirts with the shop logo on it for you to wear. Got some spares in my office. Probably need to get some smaller sizes for you. That's it for now. You good?"

"I'm fine wearing whatever you have on hand."

The front door opened and a big, bald man stepped in. He was huge, muscular, dressed in a white T-shirt and dark blue jeans. Tattoos swirled their way down his forearms and over his hands. Another tattoo peeked above the neck of his T-shirt. It was hard to judge his age, but she guessed he was in his late forties.

"Yo, Duke, what's going on?" he rumbled.

"Madden, this is Sunny. She's our new front desk chick."

Chick?

"I prefer 'front desk person'," she said, sending Duke a look.

He just waved a hand. "Whatever. I got a client coming in soon. Need to set up my station."

Madden walked into the staffroom and she followed, watching him turn on the coffee machine.

"Oh, I should do that."

"No problem, darlin'," he said with a smile. "We're used to making do. Been a couple of months since Darlene ran off with her man and left us high and dry. Didn't think Duke would hire anyone else. You know him?"

"Um, yes, we're neighbors."

Madden raised his eyebrows. "Huh."

She wasn't quite sure what that *huh* meant. "So, um, as well as putting on the coffee is there anything else, I can do before we open?"

"Duke didn't give you much guidance, huh?"

"No."

"You'll pick it up," Madden said quietly.

"Fuck. I have got such a fucking headache," another man appeared in the doorway. His hair was pulled back in a man bun, the lower half of his face hidden behind a patchy beard. He was thin and a little hunched.

"Rory! You're late!" Duke barked. She jumped.

"Fuck, Duke, stop yelling," Rory whined.

Duke appeared in the doorway, frowning at the other man. "Pull your shit together and get to work." Duke walked away.

"Jesus, he's an uptight bastard. Thought working for a biker he'd be more easygoing. Parties and biker trash sluts, but no, he's all about work ethic and coming in on time," Rory muttered.

Her eyes widened and she stared over at Madden who was glaring at Rory. "That's your mistake then isn't it? Duke's a good boss, as long as you follow the rules."

Oh, so it wasn't just her that he had lots of rules for. Somehow, she was a little disappointed.

"Who're you?" Rory turned to her.

"Hi, I'm Sunny. The new front desk person." She looked over at Madden who just grinned as he poured himself coffee.

"About fucking time that Duke hired someone. I'm an artist not a fucking phone bitch."

Right.

"Make me a coffee. Cream and two sugars."

"Um, sure."

Madden leaned against the counter and she had to reach around him to get a coffee mug from the cupboard.

"Not that one," Rory barked. "The one with the bulldog on it. We got a lot in common, me and bulldogs."

"Yeah, both ugly as sin," Madden whispered to her.

"I don't know, I think bulldogs are kind of cute. Him, on the other hand. . ." she trailed off, slightly embarrassed. *You just started, Sunny. You should be trying to get on with everyone, not insulting them.*

But Madden just grinned and winked.

"Here you go." She handed Rory the mug.

He took a sip and nearly choked. "What the fuck? Have you never made coffee in your life? This is fucking shit."

She'd worked with men for years and she'd never had one be quite so rude and abrasive, at least not right off the bat. So she just gaped at him for a moment. Then she was suddenly facing a wide, muscular back.

Madden.

"I made the coffee, asshole. Don't like it, make it yourself."

"Not paid to make coffee. New girl, make a fresh batch and bring me a cup. I'm going to get my station ready." He stomped out.

"Was it something I said?" she asked, uncertain anyone had ever taken such an instant dislike to her.

"Nah, it's not you. Rory's got a problem with women. He's just a fucking jerk." Madden sighed. "It's gonna be a long fucking day."

8

Sunny parked her car around the corner from the tattoo shop and got out, opening the trunk to drag out the big bag of stuff she'd packed up. She'd been working here for nearly two weeks and this was the first time Duke had been unable to drive her in. Something about club business, which she knew not to ask about. He was very tight-lipped about anything to do with the club.

She carried her bag around to the entrance of the back alley.

"Marv? Hey, Marv, are you here?" she called out for the older homeless man who often hung around. But there was no one back here. Drat, she'd come out and look for him later. She turned around, only to find him standing behind her.

She let out a cry, dropping the bag.

"Marv! You scared me!" How the hell had he managed to sneak up on her?

"Sweet little thing like you shouldn't be hanging out in an alley."

God, now he sounded like Duke. He'd caught her going to throw the garbage out the other day and had a fit. She'd only been doing it because Rory had been bitching about having to do her work and she couldn't take it anymore. Mind you, Rory bitched about everything. Especially if it was to do with her. Nothing she ever did was right for him.

But she shouldn't complain. Other than Rory's moodiness and Duke's overprotective tendencies, she was really enjoying this job. Duke could be abrupt, but she was growing used to his manner. Madden was sweet, despite the fact he looked like he broke faces for a living. And most of the clients, while often scary looking, were surprisingly sweet and respectful.

Now if she could just get a hang of the damn ordering system, she'd be happy. She'd mucked up the last order she'd submitted. She could tell Duke was a little frustrated, but he'd been patient as he'd gone over it again.

Duke was bossy and protective, but like one would be to a kid sister. Not someone he wanted to drag into bed. Which was disappointing.

Her Little hadn't been out once since she'd come to work for him. Not even at home. It seemed like she'd retreated for a while.

"I wasn't hanging out; I was searching for you."

Marvin had long, scraggly dark hair. She was uncertain of his age, but she guessed he was probably in his sixties. He was slightly stooped with baggy clothes. She worried he didn't get enough to eat and always packed some dinner for him.

Duke wasn't particularly happy that she'd befriended him, and had made her promise she wouldn't be alone with the older man. But Marvin was harmless.

"Here, I brought you some clothes. My ex left them behind and I think they might fit you. I've washed them all." She was lying. Greg hadn't left a thing behind and he wouldn't be seen dead in the warm, flannel shirt and thick, down jacket she'd bought. While it was summer, it still got cold at night. So she'd bought

Marvin a new shirt and jacket, removing the tags and washing them.

"Your ex? What kind of fool would leave you?"

She shrugged. "He didn't think I was good enough for him, I guess. Greg wanted someone sophisticated and intelligent. Personally, I think he just wanted someone with more money so he could live the high life. . .and I can't believe I just blurted that all out."

Marv just gave her a gentle smile. "Thank you, sweet girl. That's so kind."

"I also included dinner and some cookies that I baked this morning. Are you sure you don't need any bedding? I have some spare stuff I was going to donate," she lied.

"No, no, I'm fine for bedding. You go on, and get to work. I have to make my rounds."

She wasn't sure what his rounds included, but she knew he liked to move around different places so she nodded and squeezed his hand. She walked to the front of the shop and unlocked it, heading to the alarm. She input the number, but the little red light continued to flash.

Had she gotten it wrong?

She re-entered it. More flashing red lights. Drat! Panic flooded her and she raced to her desk for the piece of paper she'd written the code on. The alarm started blaring as she searched through the top drawer. Where was it?

The phone on the front desk started ringing and she picked it up.

"This is Mason security," a calm voice stated. "Your alarm is going off."

That seemed like an idiotic statement. "Yes, I know! I can hear it!" Along with most of the block, no doubt.

"Are you in distress, ma'am?"

"Yes, I'm in distress! I can't find the damn pin number and the alarm is blasting my ear drums!"

Suddenly, the alarm stopped. She sighed with relief, slumping into her chair. "Thanks for turning it off."

"We didn't, ma'am."

She stood up, looking over the high back of her desk towards the door. A heavily tattooed, blond, surfer-looking guy stood there. Another sort of panic filled her until she realized he wouldn't know the alarm number unless Duke knew him.

"Thanks, bye." She ended the call.

"Forgot the alarm number?" the guy asked, leaning against the doorway and folding his arms over his thickly muscled chest. His hair was shaved at the sides and slicked back on top. His tattoos ran down each arm and she thought she saw glimpses above the neck of his T-shirt.

"Yes, Duke changes it every week and I just drew a blank."

He grinned. "Yeah, he's a real prick over security. I'm Ink."

"Oh. Are you a friend of Duke's?"

"Yeah. I'm a member of the Iron Shadows."

Her stomach bubbled with nerves for another reason. "Right. Well, thank you. Did you have an appointment today?" She didn't remember an Ink being booked in. She kind of thought she would. Then again, she couldn't remember a four-digit pin, now, could she?

"Nah, the security company called me. I was around at the compound."

"They called you?"

"Yeah, I own the company."

"You do?" She stared at him in surprise.

He grinned. "I don't look like the type of person to own a security company?"

"No, it's not that. . ." she trailed off because it was exactly that. His grin grew as there was a screech of tires behind him. "Here comes Duke. Don't think he's too happy."

Her eyes widened as Duke's black truck pulled up and he jumped out. His face was like thunder as he strode to the shop.

Not too happy was an understatement.

Ink stepped to the side to let Duke in, but didn't walk any further into the shop.

"Duke, hi!" she said cheerily. "I didn't think you were coming in until later."

Ink snorted. She looked around Duke's wide body to glare at him. He just winked at her.

She started as Duke moved around the desk. Oh sugar. He wasn't going to fire her over forgetting the pin number, was he?

"What happened? Are you okay?" He ran his gaze over her, as though searching for injuries.

"I'm fine. Why would you think I wasn't?"

He took hold of her shoulders, looking like he really wanted to shake her. Then he drew his hands away and took a hasty step back. "Because I just got a phone call that the damn alarm was going off!"

And he'd been worried about her? That was really sweet. And it made her feel awful.

"I'm all right. I just forgot the number for the alarm."

He gave her a slightly exasperated look. "Babe."

"I know. I'm sorry."

He ran his fingers through his hair. "Where the fuck is Rory? I told him to come in early and open up with you."

"Oh, ah, maybe he forgot."

Or maybe he was just a prick who'd rather watch her mess up than help her.

Duke grumbled something under his breath as he turned away. He seemed to notice Ink for the first time.

"What're you doing here?"

"Well, that's gratitude," Ink drawled, not seeming to take

offense at Duke's growly tone. "I rushed over here when the alarm went off to check on Sunny-girl here."

He knew her name? Oh, Duke had said he was going to tell everyone at the club about her. For some reason that thought made her blush.

"I'll just go start the coffee. Um, feel free to go about your business."

She waved her hands at them both. Duke gave her an incredulous look. "Go about my business?"

She bit her lip, feeling that blush growing deeper.

"I'll take some coffee, Sunny-girl," Ink told her.

Duke scowled at him. "She's not here to make you coffee. Besides, we've got a meeting."

"I thought you might want to move it here, so I texted Reyes while you were checking out Sunny." Ink grinned and she blushed at his innuendo. Duke had just been concerned that she wasn't harmed. Nothing more.

Duke grumbled some more. Then he turned and headed to his office. "Make a big pot of coffee, Sunny. And when Rory gets here, send him the fuck in."

Ink grinned at her as he walked past. "I take my coffee sweet and creamy, doll. Bit like you."

Wow. That was so cheesy. She just rolled her eyes before walking out to the back room to get everything ready. After putting her stuff in her locker, she took a moment to steady her nerves. She hated upsetting Duke. She didn't want him to regret hiring her.

She looked up as Rory strolled in.

"Coffee started yet?"

She clenched her hands into fists. *Be nice.* "Not yet. Duke wants to see you."

Rory narrowed his gaze. "What? Why? Isn't he supposed to be having some secret club meeting?"

She was pretty certain that Rory was jealous of Duke.

"It's been moved to here." She didn't say anything more, just made a pot of coffee before heading out to the front room again.

Where was that bit of paper with the pin number on it? She got down on her hands and knees to start searching around. She didn't want to admit to Duke that she'd lost it, she was in enough trouble with him as it was.

Ah, there it was. She spotted a piece of white paper beneath the desk and started crawling under the open space, grabbing it just as the buzzer indicated someone was coming through the door. She started wiggling back.

"Hello, down there."

She sat up, misjudging where the surface of the desk was and bumping her head.

"Owie!" she muttered without thinking, reaching up to rub the sore spot while staring up at a large guy wearing a black, tight tee, and worn blue jeans.

To her surprise, he crouched down so they were nearly face-to-face.

"Ouch, that looked like it hurt," he said with surprising sympathy for such a cold-looking man.

"I'm okay." Aware of how unprofessional she was acting, she tried to scramble to her feet, only to bump into her chair and send it flying across the room on its wheels.

"Oh, whoops." She turned back to look at the man with a grimace. "Um, hi, I'm Sunny, can I help you?"

"Hello, Sunny," he replied. "I'm Reyes. I'm a friend of Duke's. He back in his office?"

"Ah, yeah. He's a little busy right now." She winced as she heard Duke yelling at Rory. She moved over to get the chair, wheeling it back behind the desk. Reyes leaned against the counter, seemingly in no rush.

Reyes raised his eyebrows. "Seems like he's upset."

She sighed. "I forgot the darn pin number for the alarm again. I wrote it down on a piece of paper, but it went missing." She held up the piece of paper she still held in her hand. "It must have fallen under the desk. Although I swear, I put it in the drawer."

She rubbed her throbbing head again.

"Still hurts, little one?"

She dropped her hand. "Oh no, it's fine." Last thing he cared about was her sore head.

Reyes' face grew cold and she bit her lip in consternation. What had she said?

"Lying is naughty. Did your Daddy never teach you that?"

"Ah, well, my dad didn't teach me much of anything. Well, other than how to roll a joint properly." Her face went bright red as she realized what she'd said. "And that probably wasn't something I should have told you."

"He smoked drugs?"

"He smoked everything," she muttered.

Reyes gave her a concerned look. "I wasn't actually talking about the man who fathered you."

Then who was he talking about. . .oh, did he mean that he thought that she had a Daddy? That she was a Little?

You are a Little.

But how does he know that? Was he a Daddy Dom?

Duke let out a string of swear words that had her blushing and Reyes frowning. "Duke needs to calm down. Who's in there with him? I've known him a while now, he doesn't often get worked up."

"Rory and Ink. Rory was meant to open with me. He's probably annoyed because he had to come in here when he was meant to be meeting you guys at the club."

"Hmm, somehow I doubt it's that."

There was the sound of a door slamming and Rory stormed out, giving her a dirty look as he strode towards her. "You bitch, this is your doing."

Oh. Awesome.

Reyes cleared his throat, and Rory glanced over at him, paling as he took in the much larger man.

"There a problem here?" Reyes asked coldly.

"Hey, Reyes, didn't see you there." Rory attempted a smile. "How's it going man? I've been meaning to ask you what you thought about me and my friend, Horse, becoming prospects?"

"Horse?" she murmured.

Rory shot her an annoyed look. "Yeah, because he's hung like a fuckin'—"

"Enough," Reyes snapped at Rory.

Goosebumps raised on her skin. Even she could see how angry he was, although she wasn't sure why. "It's a no. For both of you."

Rory's face grew red. He glanced from her to Reyes, obviously embarrassed.

"I'll just go check on the coffee," she said quietly, turning away.

"Nice to meet you, Sunny," Reyes said to her.

"You too."

He said something quietly to Rory, but she didn't hear what it was and when she returned to the front desk, he was gone. She was just walking over to switch the sign to open when several more men stepped inside.

The first man was older, with hints of silver in his black hair. He whistled as he walked into the front room, stopping as he saw her.

"Well, hello there, darlin'," he drawled in a southern accent.

Ooh, she always loved that accent.

"Hi," she murmured.

Two more men stepped in behind him. One was huge, towering over the other two. He looked younger, closer to her age. His hair was long, down to his shoulders. The third man was the scariest looking. He was bald, with a scar working its way down his neck but it was the complete lack of expression on his face that made him truly terrifying.

"I'm Razor," the older man told her with a smile. "The tall guy behind me is Jason and the bald, scary-looking guy is Spike."

Spike and Razor? Holy hell.

"Hi, I'm Sunny." She smiled back.

"You sure are," Razor said weirdly.

Jason smiled at her. Spike didn't even look her way, he just turned and walked towards Duke's office.

"Don't mind him," Razor told her. "He's grumpy today."

"He's grumpy every day," Jason added.

"Yep." Razor winked at her. "We'll see you later, Miss Sunny. Be good now and drink your water."

That was kind of a weird thing to say, but she shrugged it off as Rory's first customer of the day arrived.

DUKE PACED UP and down his small office, unable to sit still.

"Something happen?" Razor asked as he took the last remaining seat. Spike leaned back against the door and Jason stood in the corner. Ink sat on the edge of his desk, his leg swinging and a shit-eating grin on his face.

Reyes was in Duke's chair behind the desk. That bastard always had to be in a position of control.

"Duke just had a fright. He's now working through his delicate emotions," Ink stated.

"Fuck you," Duke growled.

Razor smiled, his too-knowing gaze taking in Duke. "This have anything to do with Miss Sunny? She's looking good. No adverse effects from a few weeks back?"

He was aware of everyone staring at him. Everyone except Reyes who was staring at something on his phone.

"What makes you think that was about Sunny?"

"Well, unless you've met two Littles in the past fortnight, I thought it was a fairly safe guess she was the one you were calling me for advice about."

"Fuck. Do you ever stop running your mouth? That was private," Duke snapped.

Razor's grin widened. "So it was Sunny you wanted to know how to deal with."

"Sunny is a Little." Ink gave him an interested look. "And you needed help handling her? She seems pretty sweet to me."

"I didn't need help handling her," Duke started. Fucking nosy bastards. "We're not here to talk about my private life."

"So she's part of your private life too?" Ink asked.

"That's none of your fucking business," Duke bit out.

"Grouchy today, aren't you?" Razor commented.

"I don't know. He seems a little frustrated to me," Ink added. "He needs to relax. You know what helps me relax—"

"I don't need to get fucking laid," he snapped, knowing what Ink was going to suggest. "And if I was going to get laid, it wouldn't be with Sunny. She's my employee and neighbor. She's not a fucking one-night stand kind of girl." Unlike the women Ink slept with.

"Can we please stop talking about the fact that Duke needs to get laid and get on to business?" Reyes spoke up for the first time. The rest of them grew silent. Although Ink sent him a sly look.

Fucking bastard.

"We had another warning from the Fox," Reyes stated. He turned his phone around, showing them an image of a Fox's head that had been spray-painted onto a wall. "One of the prospects found this on the outside wall of the compound this morning."

"Fuck, he's getting ballsy," Duke commented.

Reyes tapped his fingers against his desk. "There was nothing written there but it's pretty clear he's showing us he can get to us anytime he wants."

"We need to know more about this fucking asshole," Jason stated.

Spike nodded. "He's an enigma. Nobody knows who he is. You get in contact with him by leaving a message via voicemail. You can only get the phone number from one of his former clients. Then he decides whether to call you back or not."

"Did you have any luck getting the number?" Duke asked.

"Yeah. Called him yesterday and left a message. Haven't heard back. Then he leaves this. Pretty obvious he doesn't want to fucking chat. We can't underestimate this guy," Spike warned.

A headache throbbed in Duke's temple. This was the last thing they needed. They'd just gotten rid of Bartolli's hold on the club when Reyes had killed him. Now this.

"Could he have been in league with Bartolli?" he asked quietly. "Worked with him?"

Reyes continued to tap his fingers, looking thoughtful. "Bartolli's dead. If he hired the Fox for some reason then why would he still be on the job? And Bartolli is unlikely to have hired him when he had us to do his dirty work."

"Do you think the senator hired him?" Jason asked. "As protection?"

Spike frowned. "Don't think it would be for protection. But maybe to find out who was blackmailing him. Senator Robins likely doesn't know the person behind it is dead."

Reyes nodded. "We got anything more on the senator? Or the girl in the photos that were being used by Bartolli to blackmail him?"

"Other than his holiday home in Maine where's he's been these last few days, the senator doesn't own any other property that I can find," Jason told them. "Neither does his wife. And I can't find who the girl was."

"The senator would cover his tracks," Ink said slowly.

Reyes stared out the window in Duke's office that led out to the back alley. Duke glanced out to see that homeless guy, Marv was pulling on a jacket that looked brand new. He wondered where he'd gotten that.

Reyes turned back around. "She must have come from somewhere."

"Still want to know how Bartolli knew what the senator was up to," Duke commented. "Did he have a tie to the senator?"

"Or the girl," Jason suggested.

"Maybe he supplied her," Spike rasped. "Or knew who did."

"Do we still want to keep going?" Reyes asked. He looked each of them over.

"Don't see how we can fucking give up now," Ink commented even though he'd been arguing against stopping a fortnight ago. "Would be a fucking itch we couldn't scratch."

"The senator should be back tonight. Duke, you and Ink take first shift. Oh, and I told Rory that he and his friend, Horse weren't being accepted as prospects."

Duke nodded. He'd expected as much. But now he had to listen to Rory whine about it.

"Thank fuck, can't stand that weasel, Rory," Ink stated.

"His friend was worse." Razor looked ill. "The fucking sick shit that came out of his mouth, especially about women. He's fucking lucky I didn't take a blade to his tongue."

There was a reason Razor had earned his nickname.

Reyes stood up and they all knew that meant the meeting was over. Ink stood with a grin.

"Sorry to drag you away from that sweet thing out front," he said slyly to Duke. "But if you're not interested, guess you won't mind me asking her out."

"You'll stay the fuck away from her!" Duke snapped, enraged at the idea of Ink hitting on Sunny.

Ink grinned. And Duke knew he'd given the other man the reaction he'd been looking for.

Razor walked past him and tapped his shoulder. "Give it up, man. We all know you want her. It's only a matter of time until you give in."

Duke sighed. Wonderful. Now he got to spend the night listening to Ink gloat. He'd rather be fucking tortured.

9

"Sunny, go get me some dinner from the sub shop from up the road," Rory demanded, walking into reception. She sighed. Less than two hours to go until closing. She could last that long without killing him, right?

It might just take a miracle.

"Your next client isn't due for half an hour."

"So? You're just sitting there on your fat ass doing nothing. Get up and get me some food. I've got other things to do."

She had to hold back a wince at the fat ass dig. It was too close to what Greg used to say to her. Although even he hadn't used that nasty tone of voice.

Things to do? Right, like sneak out the back and smoke a joint. Yeah, she knew exactly what sort of important things Rory had to do. He only snuck in a joint when Duke wasn't around. Unfortunately, Madden was in with a client.

"It's dark out."

"So what? Are you scared of the dark?" he mocked. "Go get me a meatball sub and hurry the fuck up."

She clenched her hands into fists and stood up. "I'm not your slave."

"After what you did today, you fucking well are," he snarled.

"What are you talking about? I didn't do anything to you!"

"You couldn't even open the shop without fucking it up! Just like everything else you fucking do around here. You're a mess. You're hopeless. You can't even get a simple stock order right. Duke's only keeping you around because he feels sorry for you. And now, because of your fucking incompetence I've gotten a verbal warning and lost my chance to join the Iron Shadows. Getting me a sub is the least you can damn well do for me."

She was pretty sure she wasn't the cause of either of those things. But the look on his face, one of hate and fury, was starting to scare her. Suddenly, going to get him a sub didn't sound like the worst idea in the world. It wasn't like Duke was going to find out, he had disappeared a while ago. And the sub shop was only a block away. Wasn't much that could happen.

"I'll need some cash."

He scowled but reached into his pocket and pulled out ten dollars. She snatched it up and stormed out, without bothering to grab her jacket or phone. Something she regretted as soon as she was out the door. But she just hugged herself as she strode around the corner to the sub shop.

She'd dealt with her fair share of jerks over the years. But Rory was next level. He actually scared her.

You need to tell Duke.

Right, and just add to the hundred and one reasons why he should regret hiring her? No, thank you. She'd just have to avoid Rory as much as she could.

Yeah, that was a solid plan.

Fifteen minutes later, with the sub in hand, she hurried into the shop. She had the distinct feeling of being watched and it creeped her out enough that she'd very nearly broken into a run.

As she stepped in the door, she didn't see him at first. She kept her face down, trying to shake off the last of her nerves and she bounced right into him.

"Oomph!" The sub squished between them then fell to the floor.

Whoops.

Big, rough hands grasped hold of her shoulders, steadying her before she could fall on her ass. She was wearing a short-sleeved black T-shirt with the shop logo on it and black pants. A shiver raced through her that had nothing to do with the chill still clinging to her bare skin.

She raised her head slowly when he said nothing. Her gaze roamed over his own black T-shirt, which fit him much better than it did her. Then over his chin. He hadn't shaved in several days and it only added to his appeal. When she reached his eyes, her gaze stopped.

His blue eyes were burning.

"Uh-oh," she muttered.

One dark eyebrow rose. That's when she noticed the small tic by his right eye.

Double uh-oh.

She forced herself to smile.

Duke shook his head. "Oh no, don't even think about it."

"Think about what?"

"About trying to smile your way out of this."

She frowned. What was he talking about? "I don't try to smile my way out of stuff."

"You sure as shit do. But this time, I'm not letting myself get distracted."

She had no idea what he was talking about. She glanced back down at their feet where the sub lay in a mess of meatballs and tomato sauce. Shoot.

She attempted to step away. She needed to clean that up before a customer arrived. Shit. Rory was going to be grumpy about this. She sighed. She really didn't feel like dealing with a Rory tantrum right now.

"Where do you think you're going?" he rumbled.

"I've got to clean this mess up."

"No."

She stared up at him. "No?"

"No, you're not cleaning it up until you explain what the hell you were thinking?"

"I just went to get a sub, Duke," she said tiredly. What was the big deal?

"No, you didn't just go get a sub. You disobeyed a rule. What was your rule, Sunny?"

"I wasn't to go out alone in the dark."

He turned her to face the large windows that looked out onto the parking lot. "And is it dark outside?"

"Yes."

"And were you out alone?"

"Yes," she bit out.

"Then your ass should have been safely inside this building, shouldn't it? Not out getting yourself dinner. Since when do you eat meatball subs, anyway?"

She bit her lip as he turned her back around to face him. She thought about telling him who the sub was for, but at the end of the day it was still her decision to leave the shop.

"Sorry," she told him. "It won't happen again."

"Not good enough, Sunny. If I can't trust you with your own safety. . ." he trailed off.

What? Would he fire her?

Nausea bubbled in her stomach. She couldn't lose her job.

"Sunny! Sunny! Hey, what's wrong?"

"I. . .umm. . .are you firing me?"

He sighed and to her surprise, drew her into his chest for a cuddle. That was unexpected. Nice, though. In fact, it was just what she needed right then. His big hand cupped the side of her face.

"Jesus, your skin is freezing. Where the hell is your jacket?"

"Oh, um, I forgot it."

He heaved out a sigh. "What am I going to do with you?"

"Hopefully not decide that I'm more trouble than I'm worth."

He drew away from her, placing his hands on her shoulders as he stared down at her. "Sunny, you are definitely not more trouble than you're worth. But you are in trouble. You broke a safety rule. That comes with punishment. Not being fired," he added hastily, no doubt seeing the way her face crumbled. "When's the next customer due in?"

"Um, about five minutes." And Rory hadn't had any dinner. Shit.

"All right. This was meant to be your dinner?"

"Ah, no. It wasn't."

He just stared down at her until she sighed. "It was Rory's."

His face tightened.

"But it was my decision to go out and get it so you shouldn't blame him. I don't think he knows that whole no going out at night rule."

"He will soon," he said ominously. "Don't worry, I'll take care of Rory. You've eaten?"

"Yeah."

"What?"

"Oh, um, a salad."

He shook his head and muttered something. "Clean this up. Then after the next customer is here, put the closed sign out. Then get your ass into my office. We're going to discuss your misbehavior further."

Yay. That sounded like fun.

FIFTEEN MINUTES later he was still sitting at his desk, wondering what he was doing. He'd torn into Rory and had fun doing it. Lazy fucker could get his own dinner from now on.

He shook his head. On the surface, hiring her made no sense. She was terrible when it came to anything to do with numbers and she couldn't even follow the rules he'd given her.

And yet, he couldn't imagine walking into the shop without seeing her smiling face. He actually enjoyed taking her to and from work most days. Liked that she didn't try to fill the quiet with useless chatter. The greatest surprise was how much his clients liked her. From rough truckers to bikers to college students.

They all liked Sunny. She just had an innate sweetness that drew people to her. It could also make her a target for someone trying to take advantage of her. And Duke took protecting her seriously. He told himself it was just because she was his neighbor and employee.

Truth is that it was much more than that.

He couldn't stop thinking about her. Every night, he went to bed tired, but hard as a board and he usually ended up jerking off while thinking about a pair of pale blue eyes and a gorgeous smile.

No matter how much he told himself that getting involved with her was a bad idea, that she wasn't his type, he still found himself wanting her. Thinking about her.

He leaned back in his chair. He figured he had a choice about what he did now. And what he chose to do could change the course of everything.

Either he treated her as he would any employee, which was laughable since his other employees didn't have rules like she did.

Or he dealt with her as he would a disobedient sub. As a naughty Little. He'd been doing some research into the lifestyle and the more he read, the more he was tempted to explore these feelings he had for Sunny.

Thank fuck the senator hadn't returned home from his vacation house tonight or he wouldn't have known about her breach of the rules.

There was a knock on the door and he took in a deep breath, letting it out slowly. Time to figure out which path they were going to take.

"Come in," he called out.

She stepped inside, looking nervous.

"Shut the door behind you."

She shut the door but stood just in front of it. Her dark-blonde hair was pulled back in a hideous bun at the nape of her neck as usual. Fuck, his fingers itched to pull that bun apart. Her face was pale, her eyes wide and he didn't like it. She was still wearing just a T-shirt. He couldn't believe she'd gone out without a sweatshirt or jacket. The temperature had dropped to fifty-three degrees. Damn woman was going to get sick.

"Come sit down, Sunny." She looked like she was about to fall over. He didn't like how frightened she appeared.

She stepped forward and sat across the desk from him.

He tilted his head, studying her. "Are you scared of me?"

She startled. "What? No?"

"You sure? You look like you'd rather be anywhere but in here."

"I'm worried you're going to yell at me," she whispered.

He frowned slightly. "Why would you think that?"

"Well, I heard you yelling at Rory earlier."

"Rory is on his last leg with me. I'm tired of his bad attitude and lazy work ethic. I've tried talking with him. Today, I lost my temper. Doesn't happen often, and I'm sorry you had to hear that."

She looked surprised then gave him a slow nod.

He leaned forward, resting his forearms on his desk. "We do need to have a chat about where we go next, though."

"What. . .what does that mean?"

He stood and came around to sit on the desk in front of her. "It means that you've got two choices here."

"Choices? About what?"

"About our relationship."

"We have a relationship?"

"Not yet. Maybe not ever, not if you don't want. Thing is, I'm attracted to you. I didn't think I was a Daddy Dom, that it would interest me. But over these past two weeks, you're all I've been able to think about. Touching you, kissing you, dominating you. Being a Daddy to your Little."

"It. . .it is? You'd want that?"

"Yeah, baby girl. I want that. What I need to know is if you want it too? If you want to explore this attraction between us. If you even feel it as strongly as I do."

Her hands were twisted in her lap. "I do."

"Yeah?" A huge weight lifted off his chest.

"But. . ."

Shit.

"You're my employer and I'm worried about. . ."

"About a personal relationship interfering with our professional one?"

"Yeah."

"Well, that's what I meant when I said we have a choice here. First thing I need to tell you is no matter what you decide, you still have a job here. This has nothing to do with your employment. I'd get in a fuckload of trouble if it did."

"Okay," she murmured, looking a little confused. He didn't blame her; he was feeling slightly confused about all of this himself.

"You decide you don't want to explore this attraction then things will be strictly professional. Like with Madden and Rory."

"All right and the other choice?"

"We start seeing each other out of work. Figure out this attraction between the two of us. I explore my Daddy side with you."

"Right," she said quietly.

"You decide on that route and there is likely to be more rules. The lines between employer and employee will blur."

"Which means what, exactly?"

"Well, if you go that route then I'm going to punish you for breaking a safety rule just now." He was not happy with her.

"Punish me?" her voice squeaked.

"Yep."

"How?"

He longed to reach out and touch her, to reassure her that they could do this. That this is what she wanted.

"Well, for a start I'd have you go stand in the corner and think about what you did wrong and all the ways you could have been hurt."

Her breath caught and her eyes grew wide.

"And then after some time to contemplate that, I might have you come and place yourself over my lap for a spanking."

She just stared up at him. He braced himself for her refusal. For her to tell him where to stick his suggestion. She licked her lips.

"They might hear."

"What?"

"The others might hear you. . .spanking me. I don't want them to hear. It makes me uncomfortable. I have to work with them and I would be embarrassed."

It was his turn to stare at her. She wasn't refusing his proposal outright. In fact, she seemed to be totally accepting of his right to punish her, it was the fact that others might know that she objected to.

He cleared his throat, trying not to look too eager even as his cock pressed against his jeans painfully.

"That's fair enough. Any punishment would wait until we were somewhere private or it would be quiet."

She blushed but nodded slowly.

"So you're agreeing to exploring these feelings we have?"

A blush filled her cheeks. "I. . . I think so." She ran her hands down her thighs nervously.

"You think so?"

"I don't quite. . .I don't quite know what you want from me. What will I be to you? What will we do? How will it work?"

"We can adjust as we go along, but I'm thinking you'll let me take you on a date tomorrow night."

"A date?"

His lips twitched. "That's what normal people in a relationship do, yeah?"

She smiled. "Yeah. But I wouldn't exactly call us normal."

"Normal is overrated."

"Are you sure about the Daddy Dom stuff? Because I can suppress that side of me. Truth is, my Little hasn't come out since that night you found me in my car."

He frowned, not knowing if that was normal or not. "How often does she come out?"

She shrugged. "Well, she often appears when I'm tired or emotional. And most Saturday mornings."

"Saturday mornings?"

"Cartoons," she whispered.

That was cute.

Did he really just think something was cute? Christ, he was a hard-ass biker, he didn't think things were cute. Except for her. She was most definitely cute.

"I don't want you suppressing your Little, baby. I've done a bit of research into Daddy/Little girl relationships and I seem to have a Daddy side. When it comes to you, anyway. Even if I didn't, I would never want you to hide a part of yourself from me to please me."

"I did with Greg."

"What have we agreed about Greg?"

"Greg is a douche," she said obediently.

"That's right."

She licked her lips, drawing his attention to them.

"What about if things don't work out? What about my job?"

"I won't fire you because of our personal relationship. If need be, I'll help you find another job."

She thought that over. She liked working here. Was she willing to risk her job in order to date Duke?

Except it wasn't just dating, was it? He was offering her everything she'd ever wanted. A man who cared about her, found her attractive—although why, she didn't understand—and wanted to be her Daddy.

Was a shot at happiness not worth a job that she'd just started? She could find another job.

She might not be able to find another Duke.

"So, what do you say, Sunny?"

"I say yes," she replied.

He grinned. Oh Lord, his smile was to die for.

"That's my brave girl."

She had never thought of herself as being all that brave before.

"Come here," he demanded huskily.

She stood and he reached out, grasping hold of her hips to bring her between his thighs. He was sitting on the edge of the desk, his long legs spread out in front of him. The warmth of him made her gasp.

He drew her tight against him. "I thought I told you to put on a sweatshirt."

"I don't. . .I don't have one with me and if I put on my jacket, I'm gonna be cold when I go out later."

He grumbled at that. "I can see I'm going to have to watch you closely. I don't want my girl getting sick because she's not properly dressed."

His girl.

Holy hell.

Even if he wasn't interested in being her Daddy, she still would have said yes because Duke was like catnip. Irresistible and addictive. If she could rub herself over him without looking like a complete weirdo, she would.

He cupped her ass as he held her and she buried her face in his neck. This was heaven. His arms were solid around her. Not too tight but not too loose either.

"Just right," she muttered.

"What was that?"

"Oh, nothing. Sometimes I talk to myself. I think it's because I'm alone so much."

"You're not alone any more, baby girl."

No, she wasn't. And it was a huge relief. She hated being alone. She was lonely. Starved for touch, affection.

"You sure you know what you're agreeing to here? I might not have a lot of experience being a Daddy, but I'm pretty sure I'll catch on quick. I like being in control. I'm probably going to be stricter with you than you'll want, but I look after what's mine."

The possessive words maybe should have sent alarm bells ringing. She barely knew him after all. But she wanted to be his. She was so tired of making every decision herself. Even when she was with Greg, she'd handled most of the day-to-day stuff.

She was tired. She was lonely. Her Little wanted a strong Daddy to protect her. To coddle her when she needed it. A Daddy that cared about her enough to give her rules and enforce them.

"I know what I'm agreeing to."

He grabbed hold of her ponytail and gently tugged her face back. Then he kissed her. It started off light, in direct contrast to the hand he kept firmly wrapped in her hair, holding her still.

A shiver of pleasure ran up her spine.

She loved how he took charge, but wasn't an asshole. How she wasn't in charge, but she still knew she could say something and he'd stop immediately.

He was arrogant but not a jerk.

His tongue slid along her lips. She opened her mouth to his silent command, letting him dip his tongue inside to play with her. She groaned and he deepened the kiss. He became more demanding. His touch more heated.

He grasped hold of her hips then slid his ass backwards, pulling her with him so she straddled his hips, kneeling on the desk as he continued to ravage her mouth. Her pussy was pressed up against his crotch and she could feel his hardness even through the denim of his jeans.

She rubbed her breasts against his chest, wishing she could feel his mouth around her hard nipples, tugging and suckling.

With a groan, he drew back, grasping hold of her face between his hands when she would have followed him.

"Easy, baby girl. Here isn't the place to take this any further."

Her heart was racing. She stared around, forgetting where they were for a moment.

His office. Work.

Right, bad idea to continue this. Bad, bad idea. But oh, she wanted to.

Duke grinned at her and she groaned as she realized she'd said that out loud.

Jeez, Sunny way to act cool and sophisticated.

Hmm, probably that ship sailed a while ago anyway.

"Damn, baby girl. I've been wanting to do that ever since the night I came home to find you mowing my lawn."

She frowned. "Why were you so grumpy that night?"

He sighed and cupped the side of her face. "For one, I'd had a bad day and I just wanted to be alone and have some peace and quiet."

"Oh." She winced; she hadn't even thought about the fact that she might be disturbing him.

"For another, I thought you'd opened my mail."

"I didn't!"

"I believe you, Sunshine."

She rolled her eyes at her full name.

"And lastly, I'm a pretty private person. I have the club and the shop and that's it. I don't like people in my business, on my property who I don't know."

She nibbled her lip. "I didn't even think about that, I'm sorry."

He ran his thumb along her bottom lip, freeing it. "And now, I'm also upset because you went onto someone's property, by yourself, without knowing who I was. I could have been dangerous. I could have hurt you. Not acceptable, Sunny."

She winced. "Is that a rule?"

"It most definitely is. One that will result in a harsh punishment if you break it."

"But we weren't together then, so I can't be punished now, right? And besides, it was your property and you're not any of those things."

"That's beside the point. But I'm not going to punish you for that."

"I don't think it will be a problem in the future, I don't anticipate trying to mow anyone else's lawn."

He narrowed his gaze. "I won't always be around to watch you. So I want you to start thinking first before getting into these situations. Don't do anything that might put you in danger, because I'm not going to be at all happy if you do."

"Jeez, that seems to cover a lot."

He just raised his eyebrows. "Just keep yourself safe and we'll both be happy."

"I'll try."

"Good. There will be more rules. We'll deal with those later. For now, we have your punishment to take care of."

"But. . .but you just said you weren't going to punish me," she protested.

"For coming onto my property alone," he explained. "But you broke another rule, didn't you? And you definitely knew about that rule."

She pouted. "Couldn't we just start the whole punishment thing from now? Like a do-over, now that I know there is actual punishment for breaking the rules rather than just suffering through your disappointment."

He grinned at her. "Suffering through my disappointment?"

"I'm sure that's enough of a punishment, right?"

"Nice try, but no. I want you to go stand in the corner. Nose touching the wall, legs spread slightly and ass pushed out."

"You. . .you're joking, right?" She could hear the high squeak in her voice.

"I'm not. And if you want to prolong your corner time then keep on arguing with me. Actually, before you do, put this on." He walked behind his desk, reached into a box and picked up a sweatshirt with the shop's logo on it.

With a small squeal, she moved into the corner. Her cheeks were bright red. She couldn't believe she was doing this. Yet at the same time, a part of her was pleased. Not about the corner time. She hated corner time.

But the fact that he cared about her safety. And he was willing to back up his words with actions. It made her feel secure. Taken care of.

And wasn't that just what everyone wanted?

She found her mind drifting slightly as she stood there. For someone who had never done this, he sure was finding his Daddy side quickly.

He was a natural.

"Baby girl, you can come out of the corner now."

She turned and walked out right into his arms. He held her tight.

He officially gave the best hugs.

He kissed the top of her head then drew her over to his desk. "Right, little rebel. I have some paper here for you. I'm going to go see whether the guys are all finished. I want you to write, one hundred times, 'I will not disobey Daddy.' Understand?"

She gaped up at him. "You're giving me lines?"

"Yep. Problem?"

"Um, I've never done lines before."

"First time for everything. And maybe this will help remind you to obey me. I'll be back soon. Make sure the writing is legible, you get extra lines if it's not."

Extra lines! That didn't sound fair.

She scowled down at the paper as he left the room. Well, this sucked. She was thinking she'd rather take a spanking. The image of her lying over Duke's lap, his hand smacking down on her bare ass filled her mind.

She squirmed at the thought, feeling aroused and nervous. Maybe she shouldn't think about that right now.

She started her lines, having to roll up the sleeves of the huge sweatshirt he'd given her to wear.

She wasn't sure how long he'd been gone, but when he returned, she glanced up immediately.

"How you getting on, baby girl?"

"Okay. I guess. Are you sure I have to write this a hundred times?"

"That sounds like whining. Whining gets you extra lines as well."

Her jaw dropped open then she quickly snapped it shut. Fine. No whining either. Darn it.

"Keep going, baby girl. I just came in to tell you that the guys have finished up and left so I'm going to shut everything down and clean up. I want you to stay there until I come back. Unless you have to go to the toilet?"

"Ah, I'm good at the moment."

With a nod, he turned away and she settled back in to write freaking lines.

This is really not how she'd expected her night to end up.

Not that she was complaining. And she definitely was not whining.

10

"I can drive," she insisted.

"No, I don't want you driving home in the dark."

"I've done it plenty of times before."

"Yes, but you weren't mine then."

A little shiver crossed her skin. Christ, was it messed up that she already liked being his? When she hardly even knew him? Sunny had never felt important to anyone before. She wasn't important enough for her parents to remember to feed her or send her to school. She hadn't been important enough for Greg to wonder where she was when she came home three hours late, having had a flat tire as well as a dead battery on her phone. He hadn't even called her. Not once. So yeah, being important enough to have someone worry about her driving in the dark, even if it was a little overprotective, it did things to her.

"I can't just leave my car here. What if I need it tomorrow?"

"Do you?" he countered.

"Well not that I know of, but I might."

Sounded lame, even to her.

"You need to go somewhere tomorrow; I'll take you since we're spending the morning together."

"We are?"

"That a problem? Got other plans?"

She let out a laugh then reined it in. She was pretty sure sleeping in then watching cartoons in her pajamas didn't count as plans. But he didn't have to know how pathetic her life was. "Ah, no. I don't. Do you?"

"Babe, I'm the one who just suggested we spend the morning together. So, no."

"Oh, yeah."

Way to act like a dork, Sunny.

"Come on, I don't want you standing out here in the cold." Since she was still wearing the large sweatshirt with her coat over the top, she was in more danger of overheating than being too cold.

"It's not that cold out, it's still summer."

"Babe, it's nearly autumn. Temps drop at night. And you're just a little thing."

"What if something happens to my car while it's parked out here?"

He snorted. "I don't think we'd be that lucky."

She rolled her eyes at his dramatics. Her car wasn't that bad. Although sitting next to his massive truck, it looked pretty pathetic.

"Oh, there's Marv," she said, spotting the man on the corner. "I don't like him being out in the cold."

"You were just trying to tell me that it's summer," he said dryly.

"Can I ask him if he needs a ride to a shelter?"

"Baby, I—"

"Please, Duke." She grabbed hold of his arm pleadingly.

He leaned in, his mouth brushing her ear. "Stop arguing about your car and you can offer the old guy a ride."

"Deal." She grinned up at him and he shook his head.

"You won't always get your way, little rebel."

She turned towards Marvin, feeling pretty pleased with herself since she'd been about to give in to his demands to drive her home anyway. Duke gave her a heavy slap on the ass as she moved, making her jump with a squeal.

Marv paused and turned back. She scowled up at Duke, but resisted the urge to rub her sore bottom, not wanting Marv to know what he'd done.

"Marv! Can we give you a ride to a shelter?"

"Oh no, sweet girl, I don't like those places. Too crowded." Marvin gave Duke a sharp look. "You okay, Sunny?"

"Oh yes, I'm fine. Duke's just giving me a ride home."

"Well, you get on inside. Little thing like you shouldn't be out in the dark and cold, thought I saw you before running around on your own but I know that wouldn't be right, now would it?"

She blushed at his scolding. "I won't do that again. Promise. Duke already told me off."

Marvin grunted. "Good. You find a good woman like yourself, Sunny, you don't let anything happen to them. You guard them like a treasure, isn't that right, biker?"

"It is," Duke growled back.

Marvin shuffled away as Duke led her to his truck. He walked her around to the passenger side, opening the door and lifting her in. He even fastened her seat belt. She flushed as his arm brushed against her nipples, having to bite back a gasp of pleasure.

Holy hell.

~

DUKE PULLED up outside his house and turned off his truck. The inside cab light came on as he undid his seat belt. He turned towards her, taking hold of her chin.

"Much as I want you to spend the night in my bed, I know it's too early for that."

She let out a small noise. "Yeah, I think so."

"How do you usually spend your Saturday mornings?"

"Ah, well, I. . ." she stuttered over her words, clearly embarrassed about something. He remembered her telling him how she liked to watch cartoons.

"You watch cartoons, right?"

"Yeah. Well, I used to. Like I said, my Little hasn't been around lately."

"We'll see what we can do to change that. Maybe she just misses having a Daddy."

"Maybe," she said quietly. "I um well. . .I. . ."

"Babe, spit it out," he said with amusement.

"Sorry. When we're. . .when I'm Little can I call you that?"

Satisfaction filled him. It surprised him how much he really wanted that. Maybe he did need this in his life. Or maybe it was just Sunny he needed. She was like a breath of fresh air when he'd been locked in a stale, dark hole. "Yeah, baby. You can call me Daddy anytime you like." He kissed her gently.

"Oh yeah, even in front of your friends?" she teased.

"Even in front of them. Who do you think I rang the other night when I needed advice?"

"Oh, it was one of them? So they know about me?"

"Don't be embarrassed, sweetheart. They don't think either of us are weird or crazy, I promise. I called Razor. He's a Daddy Dom. So is Reyes."

"Reyes?"

"Yep. You met him?"

"Ah, yeah. He seemed nice."

Nice? Really? Now his suspicions were raised. "Did he just?" he murmured. "I'll have to have a word with him."

"About what?"

"About you being mine."

She shifted around on her seat. "He was nice to me. He wasn't interested in me."

"Reyes doesn't talk to people outside the club unless he wants something from them or needs to threaten them with something."

"That seems rather anti-social."

"Right. But he talked to you."

"Well. . .umm. . .that might have more to do with the fact that I was crawling around on my hands and knees and then when I tried to sit up, I banged my head."

"You banged your head, baby?" he cooed.

"Yeah. Right here." She patted the top of her head and working on instinct, he pulled her close and kissed her head.

"There, Daddy's kisses will make it all better." Yeah, he was really shocking himself with how easily this all came to him. How right it all felt.

She cleared her throat. "Feels much better."

"I'm still gonna have a word with Reyes. Like I said, I'm a possessive bastard."

He waited for a complaint, for her to tell him that he was a Neanderthal.

But she just nodded. "All right."

Damn was this girl built just for him? And she'd been living next door. All that wasted time. . .and then he'd nearly ruined everything by behaving like a dick to her.

"Let's get you inside and into bed. Little girls shouldn't be out this late." Not that he could do much about that. Plus, he liked that they shared the same work hours. "In the morning, I'll come by with some breakfast. What time do you wake up?"

"Oh, um, about eight, I guess. But you don't have to bring breakfast, I can make something."

"No offense, but egg white omelets and hummus ain't my idea of breakfast."

"I can make you a normal omelet," she countered.

"Not tomorrow. Maybe another day. I feel like spoiling my girl."

"Spoiling me?" There was a note of uncertainty in her voice. Had no one ever spoiled her before? Just done things for her for the fun of it? Hell, Duke wasn't really the spoiling, coddling kind but like with everything else, with Sunny it was all different.

"Spoiling you. Get used to it, baby girl. Because I have a feeling that I'm going to want to do it often." He squeezed her thigh. "Wait there. I'll come around and get you."

Climbing out of the truck, he used that moment to let the air cool his overheated skin. Seemed like most of the time he was around her, he wanted to touch her, to have her close. She was a sweet treat he'd never tasted before. But damn, he wanted more.

He opened her door and frowned as he saw she'd already undone her seat belt. Doing it up earlier, he'd felt how hard her nipples were as he'd brushed his arm against them. Heard her small gasp of pleasure.

He wanted more of that.

Slow. She isn't here to ease an itch.

She was more, so much more. He lifted her down and shut the door to his truck. He was grateful he'd gone for the bigger model now. Gave him a good excuse for having to lift her in and out.

Not that he needed an excuse any longer.

He slipped his arm around her waist, pressing her into his side. Her coconut scent teased him as they walked towards her place.

"Keys, baby girl," he demanded, holding his hand out. The security lights came on immediately, he noticed happily.

But then he saw the way she'd frozen. He glanced down to see her chewing on her lip.

"Sunny, do not tell me you left your keys under a damn flower pot again," he growled.

"Um, all right, I won't tell you that."

He groaned as she didn't move. "Which one?"

"The pink pansies."

"Babe." It was a scolding and a plea for more information all wrapped up in one word.

"Over here." She moved to one of the numerous pots and lifted it up, picking up the keys.

He held out his hand and she handed them over. He undid the lock then opened the door and stepped inside, shutting it behind her.

"Stay here, while I check the house over."

"Why?"

"Sunny, you keep your key under a fucking pot on your front porch, anyone could use it to sneak in here and hide, ready to attack you."

"Nobody is going to do that," she scoffed. "They'd have to know I kept the key there. And why would they wait to attack me? Wouldn't they just steal my stuff?"

Christ. He was starting to realize how naïve she was.

"Baby girl, some fuckers don't just want to steal shit. They want to hurt people. Sweet little thing like you, they'd like to do a whole lot more. They could watch you. Follow you home. Lie in wait so they could fucking beat and rape you. Then they could steal from you, while you lie on the floor bleeding to fucking death."

He was aware of the silence behind him as he switched on the lights and stalked forward. He turned around to see how pale she looked.

With a groan, he turned back and cupped her chin in his hand, raising her face. "That's not going to happen to you. Because I won't let anything bad happen to you. Ever. But you got to help me out here and be sensible. Don't leave your key out for someone to find. Don't forget to lock the deadbolt."

He moved away. "Let me check the house. Although any

asshole with brains would be long gone by now. Wait right here." He pointed at the floor in front of his feet. "Do. Not. Move."

Moving quickly, he searched through the house but saw no signs of any disturbance. When he returned, she'd taken off her jacket and sweatshirt but was still standing where he'd left her. The tension inside him unraveled slightly.

Reaching out, he took hold of her hand and led her over to the plain moss green sofa. It was worn-looking and not at all what he thought Sunny would choose. She was definitely a girly-girl.

He sat on the sofa, but instead of letting her sit beside him, he drew her onto his lap. She sat there stiffly, as though not sure what to do. He widened his legs slightly so she slid down further then he pulled her in against his wide chest, rubbing his hand up and down her back until she relaxed.

"Been a while since you were cuddled, huh?"

"I don't think I've ever been cuddled like this."

What? What about her husband? Or the guy she'd been in a relationship with before that? Hadn't he been a Daddy Dom?

"The douche never held you on his lap?"

"Oh no, Greg would have thought this was undignified. He wasn't very affectionate."

That fucking bastard. He tightened his arms around her.

"And the Daddy Dom you were involved with?"

"Oh. . .well. . .umm. . ."

"Sunny," he told her gently. "You can tell me anything, baby."

"Anything?"

"Anything," he reconfirmed. "I promise you I can handle it all. There shouldn't be stuff you keep back. Little girls shouldn't keep stuff from their Daddies."

"He didn't want me sitting on his knee."

"Did he give you any sort of affection? Hug you? Kiss you?" Tell her she was beautiful? Because she was, you could see it once you looked more closely.

"He said I had to earn affection. I guess I never did much that deserved a cuddle."

"I'll kill the fucking bastard." He'd hunt him down and teach him a lesson on how to talk to women. Hell, she'd barely been a woman. At nineteen, she'd just been a young, impressionable girl.

"I'm better off without him or Greg anyway."

"Damn straight you are," he growled. "And any time you want a cuddle, you tell me. You don't fucking earn it."

She started to giggle.

"What is it?"

She leaned back to wipe her eyes. "Nothing."

"Oh no, you don't, let me know the joke." He tickled her until she was dancing around on his lap, fighting to get free.

"No! No, stop! I'll pee!"

He stilled and helped her sit up, raising an eyebrow expectantly as she fought to calm her breathing. "It's nothing. It just struck me as odd that, out of the three men I've been with that it's the rough, tough biker that gives me the most affection. I guess most people don't look at bikers and think they'll be cuddly teddy bears."

"No one said anything about me being a teddy bear, brat," he snarled. "I can be dangerous and still like to cuddle."

Her gaze warmed as he stared down at her, studying her face.

"Thank you," she whispered.

"For what?" he asked, surprised.

"For this. Even if. . .even if tomorrow you decided you didn't want anything more to do with me than what you've already given me it's. . .I'm starting to see that I deserve more than I had with Alan or Greg. That I can have more."

God, and he'd barely given her anything at all. A little time and attention and she thought it was everything.

He cupped her chin in his hand. "Well, luckily, I have much more to show you and I'm not going anywhere." He gave in to the urge that had been riding him for days and leaning in, kissed her. At first, he kept it soft and light, gentle. Giving her time to pull away if she didn't want this.

But when her hands wrapped around his neck and her mouth parted beneath his, he deepened the kiss, taking command, running his tongue over hers. His cock, already hard from having her ass cradling it, grew even harder. Fuck. His balls were tight and sore.

Definitely gonna need a cold shower when he got home.

Forcing himself to pull away from her, he stared into her cloudy green eyes.

"Wow," she murmured.

Yeah. Wow. He cleared his throat. "I need to get home and you need to go to bed."

She nodded, looking a little disappointed at that.

"I'll be back tomorrow."

"Okay, yeah."

"And baby girl?"

"Yes?"

"We need to have another chat about safety, I think. But I want you to know that if I ever catch you leaving your key under a flower pot or anywhere outside, then I'm taking a paddle to your ass."

Her eyes grew wide. "A paddle?"

They hadn't had a talk about limits and safewords. It had been a long time since he'd had a chat like that. He hadn't properly played with a sub for years. When he was younger, he'd gone to a BDSM club a few times, but the club scene wasn't for him. He didn't sleep around much, not any longer, and any of the women he did fuck were experienced. A bit of light bondage and spanking was something they both enjoyed. But this was different.

"Paddle a hard limit?"

"Um, I don't know."

"Think about it. If it is, I'll come up with something equally as bad. I'm serious about your safety, Sunny. I'm not letting any harm come to you."

He'd do whatever it took to keep her safe.

11

He knocked on her door the next morning, holding a box of donuts.

She opened the door almost right away, making him bite back a smile as he wondered if she'd been watching for him. He frowned slightly as he saw what she was wearing. He'd expected her to be in her pajamas. For her to look all cuddly and sleepy this morning.

Been looking forward to it actually. He'd had to rub one off in the shower last night after kissing her, but it hadn't helped get her out of his head. But what he'd really been looking forward to this morning was spending time getting to know her better, especially her Little side.

"Come in." She licked her lips nervously, staring from the donut box to him.

He closed and locked the door behind him. He caught the faint scent of bleach in the air and looked around the house. Having been in here last night he could tell she'd recently cleaned the place. Not that it had been dirty before, but now it looked extra shiny clean.

There wasn't much stuff around. No clutter, no photos on the walls or throws on the couch. That surprised him. She seemed the type to like pretty, girly shit like cushions and throws.

Why had she cleaned? And gotten dressed?

Nerves? Embarrassment?

He walked in to find the T.V. wasn't even on. This wouldn't do. He wanted to make her more at ease with him, not nervous.

"Where's the PJs, little rebel?"

Her cheeks flushed red. "Oh, well, I just thought. . .I don't know, I felt a bit silly wearing them when you're dressed."

He placed the donuts down on the coffee table and turned back to cup her cheeks between his hands. "I was looking forward to seeing you in them, your hair all messed up from being in bed, your eyes sleepy as you curled up next to me and watched whatever passes for kids' T.V. nowadays."

"Oh, you did?" She gave him a surprised look.

"Yeah. Sunny, I don't need you to change yourself for me. All I want is for you to be you. Because who you are is perfect. Now, go put on a pair of cute pajamas while I find something for us to watch, yeah? And bring me out a hairbrush too."

~

Because who you are is perfect.

Nobody had ever said anything like that to her before. She doubted they'd even thought it. Because in no way was she perfect.

She liked that he thought she was, though.

Now she felt bad about getting up early to shower, dress and clean the house. She hadn't really thought he was serious. That he'd truly want to just sit and watch cartoons while she lazed around in PJs, without even doing her hair.

Turns out, she'd been wrong.

She pulled off her baggy jeans, top and bra and changed into one of her favorite pairs of pajamas. She had a few. They were her one indulgence. These ones had a lightweight, three-quarter pants with a T-shirt top. They were pale pink and written on the front of the top was, *On Saturdays We Wear Pajamas.*

She picked up her hairbrush and made her way back into the living room. He took up almost all the space on her small sofa. He'd opened the box of donuts and was flicking through channels, finally stopping on the Nickelodeon channel.

He turned to look at her, offering her a small smile as he read what her top said. Then he held out his hand.

"Come sit between my legs, little rebel, and I'll brush your hair."

She'd already brushed her hair and tied it back, but she didn't argue. She noticed he'd placed a pillow on the floor for her to sit on. He must have grabbed it from the spare room.

"This show all right?" he asked as she settled in and he pulled her hair out of its bun.

"Oh, uh, yeah."

He paused behind her and she turned to look up at him. He was staring down at her with a firm look.

"Sunshine River, I know we haven't had much of a talk about expectations, but one thing I expect from you is honesty. Even if it's just a small thing like what T.V. channel you want to watch. Understood?"

His voice sent a shiver across her spine. One filled with anticipation and a slight bit of trepidation. She'd gone to bed last night with her clit throbbing. For the first time in ages, she'd actually brought herself to pleasure with the vibrator she'd bought after Greg left.

It had been the best orgasm she'd ever had. Which made her wonder how amazing her orgasm would be with Duke. She just hoped he wasn't going to be disappointed.

If it even got to that stage.

"Sorry," she told him.

"Sorry, Daddy," he said firmly.

They were diving straight in then. Not that she was complaining. "Sorry, Daddy." She gave him the channel she usually watched.

"Was that so hard to tell me? Was it scary?"

"No, Daddy. I just..." She nibbled on her lip.

"You what?"

"I guess I'm just used to doing what other people want."

"You mean those two douches you were with made you put them first when it should have been the other fucking way around," he said bluntly.

Yeah, she guessed that was a fair assessment.

He switched the channel and she turned, trying to watch it without feeling self-conscious. Kind of difficult, though, when she couldn't see his face. Was he bored? Was he still looking forward to this? It wasn't exactly exciting.

Then he started brushing her hair in long, slow strokes. Oh, that was heavenly.

"Who knew you were hiding all this beautiful hair," he murmured. "Jesus, baby. This stuff is thick and gorgeous."

She blushed. Did he really think that? But she was learning that Duke wasn't the sort of guy who said things he didn't mean. He certainly didn't believe in beating around the bush.

"It's a damn crime to keep this pinned back all the time."

"It gets in my way," she explained leaning her head against his thigh and giggling at something on the T.V.

"Hmm, maybe we should compromise. At work, you can wear it how you like, but when we're at home you wear it down. Or in pigtails. That would look cute. You got any hair ties?"

"You know how to do pigtails?" She stood and looked down at

him skeptically. He was wearing another tight T-shirt; this one was dark blue and his biceps were straining against the material. His jeans were dark and worn at the knee.

He shrugged. "Man's gotta learn sometime."

"You just keep surprising me," she muttered as she walked past him, aware of his grin.

She brought back some hair ties and settled in as he played with her hair. A couple of times, he pulled at it a little sharply, but she ignored it as she watched another cartoon. She found herself relaxing more, giggling a few more times as one of her favorite programs came on.

"There. Done," he said with satisfaction in his voice. "You want to sit up here with me?"

She nodded and he pulled her up onto his lap. His strength took her breath away. "Like the pajamas."

"Thank you." She gave him a shy smile. "I'm sorry I got dressed. I guess I didn't think you meant it when you said you wanted to hang out with me."

"I try to never say things I don't mean. Life's too short for bullshit."

She nodded, relaxing into him. "Yeah. It is."

He ran his hand up and down her back then leaned over to snatch up a donut. "You had breakfast?"

"No." She looked at the box of donuts. Her mouth watered at the smell.

"Not gonna tell you what to eat. So long as you're healthy, and I already know you eat way healthier than I do. But I did choose one with pink icing and sprinkles I thought you might like."

Pink with sprinkles?

Boy, did he already know how to speak her language.

"I guess one donut won't hurt," she said, standing up to get the pink donut. She sat back next to him on the sofa, her donut in hand. She took a nibble of it and hummed with enjoyment.

"Good?" He grinned at her; his own donut already gone.

"Oh yeah."

"Everything in moderation, baby girl," he told her, bringing her in against his side. "Except for me. Because you want me in big doses."

"Oh, I do, do I?"

"Yep." He winked down at her and she found herself smiling at him. Thing was, she was pretty certain he was right. More of him was exactly what she wanted.

HE FELT her settle in next to him. He smiled as she giggled at something on the T.V. He didn't really know what she was laughing at since he spent most of the time watching her. Sitting there in her pink pajamas, with her hair in pigtails, she looked absolutely fucking adorable.

He had the thought that he could do this every Saturday for the rest of his life. Not something he would have thought a few years ago. Saturday mornings were for sleeping in after a night getting wasted and laid.

Not for sitting on the sofa eating donuts and cuddling his woman. Yeah, times had changed.

She let out a bark of laughter. He turned to the T.V. to watch some show about a family of pigs. Weird. He frowned slightly as the girl pig said something.

"What is this show? I don't think you should be watching this; she seems to be a bit of a brat."

"Daddy!" she protested.

He smiled at how that just slipped out. He hadn't wanted to push. But damn, it felt good hearing her call him that. "It's just a T.V. show."

"Can't have my girl getting ideas about talking back to me. Of course, my girl would end up with a red bottom for doing that."

She squirmed next to him. Oh yeah, she liked the idea of that. Being bratty might get her a fun trip over his knee. Something he figured they'd both enjoy. But breaking the rules and putting herself in danger, that would get her a real punishment.

They still needed to have a chat about her limits. But he'd wait until later. Right now, he was enjoying this time with her.

She turned to give him an exasperated look. "Daddy, you can't spank me all the time."

"Why not? I have plenty of muscles, my arm won't get tired." He flexed his arm, showing off for her like a complete idiot.

What has happened to you, man?

"I wasn't worried about your arm," she told him, her eyes riveted on his bicep.

"Oh, you were worried about your little bottom and your ability to sit. Some spankings you might like. But break the rules and you won't be sitting comfortably. Those punishments, little rebel, you will not like at all."

She cleared her throat as he cupped her cheek. He shook off his need for her and turned back to the T.V. *Go slow.*

"How did we get onto this conversation? Oh yes, the pig who is a bad influence."

"Daddy, you're being silly."

"Oh, silly, am I?"

She nodded her head.

"They just don't make cartoons like they used to. What happened to Bugs Bunny and the coyote?"

He looked over as she rolled her eyes at him. "They're old, Daddy."

"They are not. I used to watch them as a kid."

"Uh-huh, cause you're old."

"Excuse me, young lady," he said with a mock-outrage. "I'm young and handsome."

She peered up at his hair. "I can see a few grays coming through, old man. Maybe we should get you some hair dye for those."

"You take that back! I do not have gray hairs!" He leaned over to tickle her and she started to laugh, trying to push his hands away. She kicked out with her feet. Gathering her up, he settled her on her stomach over his lap.

"That sort of insult will result in a punishment."

"No, Daddy! No!" She kicked her legs against the cushions of the sofa.

He slowly slid her pants down, hoping she wore panties underneath. Last thing his control needed was to be presented with her bare ass.

He'd guessed right. Underneath she wore white cotton panties with Saturday written all over them. Jesus, she even wore the right panties on the right day. Such a little rule follower.

She'd grown stiff over his lap and he couldn't have that. This was about making her more at ease with him.

"Hmm, what do you suppose the standard punishment for sassing your Daddy should be?" he pondered as he rubbed her bottom.

"Um, a cuddle and a new Barbie!" she suggested.

A Barbie, huh? He wondered if that's what she enjoyed playing with? He'd have to find out. He was all too aware that he had nothing prepared for her Little at his place.

"Nope. Wrong answer. I'm thinking ten spanks."

"Ten!"

He continued to rub her ass. "You've been spanked before?"

"Oh yes, Alan used to spank me."

"Just his hand? Or other things?"

"Just his hand." She tensed.

"Easy, baby girl. This spanking is just fun. The paddle is for something far more serious, like putting yourself in danger. I'm just getting an idea of your limits."

"I've never been paddled before so I'm not sure. Definitely no cane."

"No cane," he agreed. "And during sex?"

"You want to use a cane during sex?" she squeaked.

He had to laugh. "No, baby. Have you got any limits during sex?"

"Um, no humiliation or calling me names," she said quietly.

His hand stilled. Yeah, he could have figured that would be one.

"No blood play."

"Bondage?"

"I. . .yes, bondage is good."

He noted the way she pressed her thighs together. Yeah, she liked the idea of being tied up.

"Anal?"

"I. . .umm. . .think I'd be all right with trying anal."

"That's enough to start with. We can talk more later."

Go slow.

"And you can say your safeword whenever you like. What would you like to use?"

She looked around at him, her eyes wide, her face flushed. He worried for a moment that she was scared of him. But then she licked her lips and he realized there was a little trepidation but also a lot of arousal too. "Red."

"Good. Keep it nice and easy. Turn back around, baby girl. Now, where were we? Oh yes, how many spanks have you earned for sassing Daddy? At least ten."

He landed his hand against her panty-clad bottom. Holy fuck, that was so hot. Her little ass clenched. Thank God he hadn't pulled down her panties because he was all too tempted to part her ass cheeks and take a peek at the puckered entrance beyond.

Calm. Slow. Fuck.

Another two spanks. He heard her let out a little gasp of air. He wondered what he'd find if he pushed his hand between her legs and cupped her mound. Would her heat sear him? Would her panties be slick with moisture? He was betting yes.

Several more spanks landed and he paused, rubbing her ass.

"What a naughty little girl, calling Daddy old. Not too old to give you a spanking, though, am I?"

"No, Daddy," she agreed in a quiet voice, her breath hitching as he massaged her warm bottom.

"Spread your legs," he demanded.

She let out a small groan but pushed her legs as far apart as they'd go with her pajama pants around her thighs. He couldn't resist, he ran his finger over her slit. She still had her panties on, but as he'd expected the cheap cotton was soaking wet.

Fuck. Yes.

He had to force himself to pull his hand away. He gave her several more, rapid spanks. Then before he was tempted to do anything more, he quickly pulled up her pajama pants and turned her over his arms, holding her tight against him.

"Daddy?" she asked, squirming on his lap.

Nope. He couldn't let her keep doing that.

"Have you ever ridden on a bike, baby girl?" he asked to distract them both.

"You mean a motorcycle?"

He grinned. "Well, I wasn't meaning a bicycle. I assumed you've ridden one of those before."

A funny look crossed her face before she looked away. That almost. . .that almost looked like shame. He gently grasped hold of her chin, raising her face. "You've never ridden a bike?"

"A motorbike? No. I've never known anyone who owned one until now."

He gave a small shake of his head at her attempt to deflect. "A bicycle. Have you ever ridden a bicycle?"

She let out a small, frustrated puff of breath. "No."

"Why not?"

She shrugged. "No one ever taught me."

No one had taught her?

"Your parents? Grandparents? Friends?"

"I didn't have grandparents. My dad's parents died before I was born and my mom didn't talk to her parents. I never even owned a bike."

Jesus. He hugged her tight. They were going to have to change that. But not right now. She tried to climb off his lap, but he kept her there, not ready to let her go.

"All right, so you've never been on a motorcycle?"

She shook her head.

"Wanna go for a ride on the back of mine?"

Her eyes lit up with excitement that quickly dulled. "Are you sure? I mean, what if I do the wrong thing? What if I make us fall off?"

He grinned. "Baby, you're not going to do the wrong thing, I promise. You'll pick it up, it's a piece of cake."

"That's what you said about doing the orders at the shop and look how that worked out."

He set her on her feet and then stood, giving her ass a sharp tap. "Go get dressed. Tight pants or jeans, and a long-sleeved jacket. It can get cold and you want your skin protected from the elements. You might want to rearrange your hair too. Probably pigtails and a helmet don't mix."

~

HER HAIR WAS A MESS. She burst into giggles as she finally took a look in the bathroom mirror. She was glad she hadn't gone outside looking like this. Not that she'd ever tell him that. She didn't want to hurt his feelings when he'd tried so hard.

She rolled her eyes at the idea of hurting Duke's feelings. The guy was hard as rocks.

On the outside. On the inside though. . .yeah, there was definitely a softer side to him. She'd already gotten dressed, now she redid her hair so it hung down her back in a braid. Maybe she could do something different with her hair. And maybe she should get some new clothes. Everything she wore was a few sizes too big. She'd long ago lost interest in shopping.

He said he doesn't want you to change yourself for him.

Yeah. But this would be for her. Because she wasn't entirely sure she was happy with the Sunny staring back at her. A knock on the front door startled her out of her thoughts and she gathered up her stuff, putting some cash and her ID in her back pocket in case they stopped.

Then she opened her door.

Oh shit. He looked fine. He wore the same jeans, but he now had his leather jacket on. It was black with patches down the arms.

"All ready? Where are your gloves and scarf?"

She eyed him suspiciously. "Are you sure I'll need them?" It was a nice day out. He seemed to have an obsession with keeping her warm. Not that she was complaining too much. She liked that he cared.

"Yes, you will. Now go grab them, baby girl."

She loved the way he called her that. It made her feel special. She picked up a pink scarf and matching gloves then locked up and placed the keys in the zip-up pocket of her jacket. He gently patted her bottom.

"Good girl."

For someone who said they'd never been a Daddy before, he sure did come by it naturally. She walked with him down the driveway to where he'd parked his bike.

It was gorgeous. It shone in the sunlight, chrome and black.

"What sort of bike is it?"

"This is a Harley-Davidson VRSC."

Right.

"Does it have a name?" She bounced on her toes excitedly.

He gave her an incredulous look. "Hell, no. Here, I have a helmet for you to wear."

Hmm, she thought she might call it Princess Moonbeam. Yeah, that sounded like a great name. She wouldn't tell Duke that, though.

"You'll sit on the back here." He patted the seat. "Your feet go here." He showed her the two small lips on either side that her feet could rest on. "When you're on, hold me nice and tight around the waist and just lean with me, all right?"

"All right. There's nothing else I need to do?"

He grinned. "Just hold on and enjoy the ride, babe."

She rolled her eyes. "I bet you say that to all the girls." She could feel herself blushing as he laughed. She couldn't quite believe she'd said that.

"Only the special ones." He winked at her.

He placed the helmet over her head and did it up.

"All right?"

She nodded. It was a little weird. Heavy, bulky and it dulled her hearing. But better safe than sorry. He took the scarf from her hands, putting it around her neck and tying it then tucking it under her jacket. Then he helped her with her gloves.

She couldn't remember the last time someone had helped dress her. When she was a baby, she guessed.

He didn't use a helmet. She frowned at that. As he climbed on the bike, he took off the kickstand. She got on behind him and made sure her feet were in the right place. Then she wrapped her arms tentatively around his waist. Damn, he was so wide she could barely manage.

He grasped hold of her wrists and gave her a tug so she was firmly plastered against his back, her arms tight around him.

Oh wow.

Then the bike started up, the vibration pleasant underneath her.

She was starting to really see the appeal of this.

12

She climbed off the bike, her legs almost giving way beneath her.

"Easy, little rebel." A firm hand wrapped around her arm, steadying her. She didn't care. She looked up at Duke, aware of the huge smile on her face.

A smile he couldn't see because of her helmet. He pulled off her gloves and helmet. She didn't care that her hair was probably a mess and that she no doubt looked like a crazy person; her grin didn't fade.

"That. Was. Awesome!"

He laughed. "Liked that, did you?"

"Liked it? I loved it! It was so peaceful. I felt so free." She ran her hand along his bike. "Maybe I should get one of my own."

He took hold of her hand, squeezing lightly.

"I can see I've created a monster. Not sure I want you on your own bike, though."

She pouted. "Why not?"

He drew her close, his arm around her waist. He held her helmet in his other hand. "Because I like you tucked up behind me, your arms around me, your little pussy snug against my ass."

Her breath caught. She looked around the parking lot of the diner they'd pulled into but nobody was nearby. She licked her lips. If he could talk naughty, then so could she.

"I liked that too."

She had no idea how to talk dirty. She wasn't even sure what he said was considered dirty or whether she was just so inexperienced it seemed that way to her. He cupped her cheek with his hand. "Oh, I can tell you liked it, babe." Leaning in, he kissed her. He tasted delicious. Almost smoky even though she knew he didn't smoke. Which had surprised her. Seemed she had a few stereotypes about bikers that had needed revising.

He drew back.

"Do you have a gun?" she blurted out.

He raised an eyebrow. "Uh, that's kind of out of left-field."

"Sorry." She blushed. "I was just thinking I had a few misconceptions about bikers and I was wondering if you had one."

"I do. But I keep it at home for protection." He straightened. "Come on, let's go have some lunch. This place has the best burgers. Then we better get home and get ready for work. I hear your boss is a real hard ass."

"Hm, I'd agree with that," she teased, glancing down at his ass.

He chuckled and she blushed. He let go of her to hold open the door to the diner for her. Something Greg would never have done, despite his lectures to her on the proper way to act.

What a douche.

She nearly blushed again as she thought that. Duke was becoming a bad influence. But in a very delicious way.

She followed him into a booth. This place was similar to the last one they went to.

"Have you eaten at all the diners in the local area?" she teased.

"I can't believe you haven't," he deadpanned back.

She snorted. "Greg wouldn't have been caught dead in a place like this. Only fine-dining, five-star restaurants for him."

"And is that what you enjoy too?"

"What? You mean restaurants where I had to put on spanx just to fit into the ridiculous outfit he would pick for me, which meant I could hardly breathe, let alone eat and then I got to spend the night watching him eat hundred dollar appetizers made of foam, while I could barely afford the breadsticks? And he would point out all the women in the room and how successful and poised they were? Yeah, no thanks."

She'd been trying for light-hearted which was obviously a fail when he frowned. "He did what? He checked out other women? He made you pay for your meal? When you were married?"

She shrugged. "Greg liked everything to be even financially. But he made a lot more than me and he could be really petty about it. I don't miss any of it, to be honest. Sounds silly, but it wasn't until he was gone that I realized how utterly miserable he made me."

"Asshole."

She nodded, smiling as the waitress dropped off some menus and told them the specials.

"I can vouch for the double beef burger," he told her.

She raised her eyebrows. "You do know we just ate breakfast?"

"That was hours ago. And it was just donuts. That's really just a snack." He grinned at her.

"How do you stay so fit?" she asked with a tinge of jealousy. He was sitting across from her this time, which she'd kind of been disappointed by, until he started rubbing his foot up and down her leg.

She'd never played footsies with someone before. It was surprisingly stimulating.

"You think I'm fit, huh?"

God, why did she have to blush so much? She glanced down at the table.

He reached over and tilted her face up. "I'm very. . .active."

Her blush deepened even as she grinned at him. He grinned back and tapped her nose. The waitress came over to take their orders. The double burger for him and grilled cheese for her. She wasn't really hungry.

He slipped out of the booth and leaned down to kiss the top of her head. "Going to the bathroom. Stay here."

She just shook her head at his bossiness. She was staring outside when she felt someone come up to their table. She glanced over to see a man standing close, and staring at her strangely. He had long, greasy hair and a nose ring. A scar ran through his right eyebrow.

"Um, can I help you?"

"You're here with him? Duke?"

She frowned. She hadn't seen him earlier when they'd come in. He nodded over to the helmet. "Saw his hog outside."

"Oh, right. Do you know him? He should be back any minute." She hoped. This guy was a little creepy.

"No. I don't want to talk to him. You his old woman?"

"What? Uh, no." Old woman? Didn't that mean wife or girlfriend?

He narrowed his gaze at her then grunted. "I don't like liars." Then he turned around and left.

Well, that was strange.

When Duke returned, he paused at the counter and asked their waitress for something. With a smile, she handed over a piece of paper and some crayons. He strolled back to Sunny, placing the paper and crayons in front of her, this time sitting in her side of the booth.

"What's this?" she asked, staring down at the child's menu. He turned it over, on the other side was a picture of a gorilla holding a banana to color.

"Thought you might want to do something while we wait, baby girl."

She looked up at him in embarrassment. "Won't people think I'm weird?"

"What do we care what people think?"

She froze for a moment. When had she not cared what people thought? All through school, she'd never brought anyone home for a playdate because she didn't want them meeting her parents. Then she'd tried to live up to Greg's expectations. Seemed like she'd always cared.

But she didn't have to now.

She reached for the menu eagerly and Duke let out a quiet chuckle as she started to carefully color between the lines. She was concentrating so hard; she didn't even realize the food had arrived.

"Food, baby girl."

"In a moment." She stuck her tongue out as she carefully colored the gorilla's belly.

A fry was waved in front of her face then pressed to her lips. She opened her mouth automatically, letting out a small moan of appreciation at the greasy, salty taste.

Duke leaned in to speak quietly in her ear. "That's a really cute picture. You're very good at sticking to coloring in the lines."

She preened at that. She was, wasn't she?

"But I want you to eat your lunch now, please." The 'please' was said very firmly and she knew he was serious. Especially when he pulled the picture away and replaced it with her plate of food.

"I'm not hungry."

"You barely ate breakfast. I want to see half of that gone. You can finish this off later."

She sighed but reached for half of the grilled cheese. Yum. When was the last time she'd eaten this?

"So how come your parents never taught you to ride, baby girl?"

She shrugged. "Too busy getting high and partying, I guess. And then spending the next day coming down from that high. We spent the first five years of my life in a commune. Those were actually the best years because even if my parents were shit at least there were other people around to feed and clothe me and who actually cared."

She stopped to take a sip of her root beer float. She didn't know what had possessed her to order it. She hadn't had one in years, but damn, it tasted good.

"What happened after they left the commune?"

"I think we got kicked out. My parents didn't exactly contribute anything. We travelled around a lot. My dad got odd jobs but never stuck at anything long. When I was thirteen, I got a fake ID so I could get a job. At least then we got to stay in one place because I made sure the rent was paid."

WHAT THE FUCK? At thirteen she was paying the goddamn rent? Her fucking parents ought to be shot. He was getting more of an idea about her now. Her parents had neglected her and she'd had to take on a lot of responsibility at a young age.

Maybe that was part of the reason she was drawn to age play. As a way to have a childhood she'd never had. A way to be free from all the worries that had been weighing her down from a young age. He stared at the picture she was coloring. It was perfect. She didn't cross over the lines once and everything was the right color. The trees were green, the sky blue.

He'd have felt better if she'd made a mess. Colored the sky purple and the clouds orange with black polka dots.

Seemed like she'd spent her childhood taking care of her parents. But when had anyone looked after her? Certainly, seemed like that douche, Greg, hadn't. All he'd done was teach her that she had to be perfect or she wasn't good enough.

Screw that.

If nothing else, he was going to get her to stop coloring in the lines all the time.

He finished off his food and picked up a crayon. "Mind if I help you finish, little rebel?"

"Sure," she said suspiciously.

He started to color the banana pink.

"Hey!" She grasped hold of his hand, sending a spark of heat along his skin. "That's the banana."

"Yeah, so?"

"So it should be yellow."

He leaned in and kissed her ear. "Not everything has to be perfect to be right, baby girl. Maybe the banana wants to be pink for a change."

Christ. Why did he have to go touching her? Now he'd grown even harder. He hadn't been this horny since he was a teenager.

She raised her eyebrows. "A pink banana?"

He shrugged. "It's a party banana. It wants to rebel against society's rules."

A smile crossed her face. "A rebellious banana? I didn't realize bananas had feelings."

He sighed. "A misunderstood fruit."

She giggled. "You're silly, Daddy."

Oh, there was her Little. Good. This might be the perfect time to find out a few things about her.

"What's your favorite thing to play with, baby girl?" he asked, keeping his gaze on the picture.

"Umm, playdough."

"Playdough, huh?"

"Yep. I like making things."

"Anything else?"

"I like coloring."

"And you're very good at it," he praised.

"I like reading too. My favorite story is *Alice in Wonderland*."

"The one with the rabbit and the tea party?"

She giggled. "Have you read it, Daddy?"

"Don't think I have," he said gravely.

She gave an exaggerated gasp.

"Obviously a terrible oversight."

She nodded solemnly, giving him a shy look. "You're easy to talk to."

"I am?" He'd never considered himself much of a talker. He liked to get on and get stuff done.

"I'm not very good at talking to people usually. Maybe that's why I like plants so much. Especially pretty flowers."

"I couldn't tell," he deadpanned.

She giggled again. He liked that sound. A lot. "Maybe we should plant some flowers at your house, Daddy."

"I don't know. I'm not very good at remembering to take care of plants. They tend to die on me."

"But I can do it for you." She bounced on her seat with excitement. Then he watched as a shutter came over her face. The child-like look of joy left her face. "I mean, obviously since I live next-door. I wasn't implying anything—"

"Shh, little rebel." He put his finger over her lips. "You're fine. You don't have to explain or worry you said the wrong thing."

She gave him an incredulous look as though she didn't ever not worry about what she said. Which could be the case, except maybe when she was deep in Little space.

"Come on, we need to get to work." He left some cash on the table, giving her a stern look when she reached for some money.

Little brat knew the rules.

He helped her out of the booth and she turned to get the helmet, bending over and waving her ass at him.

Fuck that was tempting.

He tucked her under his arm, liking the way she fit there as they strode towards the door.

"Oh, I think a friend of yours was here before," she told him as they made their way to his bike.

"A friend of mine?"

"Yeah, well, this guy came up to me while you were in the bathroom. He asked me if I was with you. Said he'd seen your bike out in the parking lot."

"What was his name?"

"He didn't actually say. He was a little weird, especially when I said you would be back if he wanted to wait."

He paused and took hold of her arm, not liking the sound of that. "What did he look like?"

"Um, long, brown hair. A ring in his nose. Kind of greasy looking."

He sighed. He knew who that was. "Horse. He's a friend of Rory's."

"Oh. He's Horse?"

He noticed a small blush on her cheeks. "You know about him?"

"Um, yeah, Rory might have mentioned him the other day when he was asking Reyes if he'd decided whether they could join the Iron Shadows."

"Fucking idiots. Rory is a dick and Horse has a few screws loose. Stay away from him, okay?"

She nodded. "I will. Why do you employ Rory if you don't like him?"

"Because he's a talented artist. Brings in a lot of clients. But I think he's a shithead and I don't want to spend any more time with him than I have to. Come on, little rebel."

He plonked the helmet on her head, making certain it was done up before he swung his leg over his hog. He liked the way she felt plastered against him. He couldn't remember the last time he'd had someone on his bike.

But it felt right in a way nothing had in a long, long time.

"Reyes, what's up?" Duke answered his ringing cell as he sat behind his desk. His last client for the day had just left and he needed to sort some paperwork.

"Need you to meet me at the club. Got a lead on the girl in the photos. I want you to come with me to talk to some contacts I have. Where I'm going, always good to have eyes on your back. Spike is across town doing something. The senator is back, so Razor and Jason are watching him."

"Right. Fuck." He was meant to take Sunny home. He ran his hand over his face. "I'm supposed to be taking Sunny home once the shop closes."

There was a note of silence. "She can't drive?"

"Her car's a piece of shit. She comes in with me most days."

"That so?" Reyes drawled.

"I'll organize something. Be there soon." He hung up before Reyes could question him any further. Shit. He hated not taking her home himself.

"Sunny?"

She looked up as Duke made his way towards her. There was about another hour until they got to close up and go home and she was feeling fatigued.

She couldn't believe that Duke had spent time with her Little. It had been sweet the way he'd done her hair and watched cartoons with her. Then he'd listened to her talk about her past at the diner over lunch. Even helping her color.

"Everything okay?" she asked, noting Duke's frown.

"I have some club business to do. I don't think I'll be back in time to give you a ride home."

Disappointment filled her but she just nodded. "That's fine, I'll take an Uber."

"You'll what?" he asked, gaping down at her.

What had she said that was so weird? Oh, maybe it was the money thing. He was a bit funny about her spending her own money. She was going to have to have a talk with him about letting her pay her way more. She didn't want to leech off him.

"I'll take an Uber. I have an App. Don't worry, I'll wait inside until they come."

She felt proud of herself for remembering that. Although that meant she'd have to set the damn alarm. Maybe Madden would wait with her until the Uber came.

"You're not taking a fucking Uber."

"Duke, shh, Rory has a client."

"Don't give a fuck. If a bit of swearing puts them off then they're not our sort of client."

Well, she guessed that was pretty accurate. She'd heard all sorts of colorful phrases and words since she'd started working here.

"What's wrong with taking an Uber?"

He opened his mouth. Closed it. Then he shook his head. "I do not know where to begin. How about how unsafe it is getting into a fucking car with a stranger?"

"Ubers are perfectly safe. Lots of people take them without an issue."

"Well, you are not most people and you will not be taking one. Someone will be here before it's time to lock up to take you home."

"And how do I know this someone is safer than an Uber?"

He leaned in so they were eye-to-eye. "Because I will be choosing who that person is and it will only be someone I trust with your safety. Not a damn fucking stranger."

"I've taken an Uber on my own before, Duke."

"Don't expect to take one in the future. Not unless you want to sit uncomfortably the next day."

"Duke!" she protested.

"You tell her, son!" a deep voice rumbled from out the back.

She went bright red, glaring up at Duke who still remained stern. He pointed at her. "Wait here for who I send. Do not try to disobey me on this. It's a safety rule."

And he was very big on safety rules.

"Fine. But I think you're overreacting."

He grasped hold of the nape of her neck and pulled her in to kiss her. Hard. "You're mine now, little girl. That means you have to put up with me being overprotective and bossy."

"I won't always give in," she warned.

"When it comes to safety, you will. Or I'll be wielding that hairbrush of yours in an entirely different way."

He stepped back, leaving her standing there, swaying slightly.

"I'll call you tomorrow." Then he strode out of the shop without a backward glance. As though he knew she was going to do exactly as he'd ordered.

Damn man. Entirely too arrogant for her peace of mind.

She rubbed her ass. He wouldn't use her own hairbrush on her, would he?

13

She stood nervously outside the door to Duke's house the next day. She wasn't sure she should be here. What if he was still asleep? What if he'd had a long night? Doing club business. What exactly was club business?

She bit at her lip.

Go home, Sunny. Wait for him to call you.

That was something the old Sunny would have done. She'd never dare make a move. She always let other people call the shots. But while Duke far outweighed anyone else in her life for dominance and bossiness, she also knew he didn't want a puppet he could maneuver into doing what he wanted.

She'd let Greg, and to a certain extent, Alan mold her into what they wanted. Growing up, she'd had to take on an adult role young.

She'd never really gotten to be herself. Whoever that was.

So she'd spent half the morning moping, waiting for Duke to call and telling herself not to bother him. Now it was mid-afternoon and she was done waiting.

Which was why she was standing at his front door, a basket of freshly baked blueberry muffins in her hand. She just needed to find the courage to ring the bell.

What if he rejects you? What if he doesn't want to see you?

No. He liked her. He'd made that clear. She had to stop listening to her insecurities. She pressed the doorbell, hearing it ring. There was a long moment of silence. Maybe he wasn't at home. His truck was here, though.

Had she turned him off somehow?

Then the door opened and he stood there, dressed in a pair of sweats and a tight black sleeveless top.

Hello biceps.

She swallowed; her mouth dry as neither of them said anything. Then she held up the basket.

"Muffins."

He raised an eyebrow. Why wasn't he saying anything? Now she felt like a complete dork. He hadn't wanted to see her. She'd done something wrong. She put the basket down by their feet.

"Enjoy." She turned to flee, tears stinging her eyes.

Then a hand reached out and wrapped around her arm. "Wait."

She turned back to find him staring at her in puzzlement. There was something else in his gaze. Something dark. Intense. He looked stressed. Even standing there with a bottle of beer in his hand.

He was drinking already? Not that she was a prude or anything. It was his day off; he could drink if he wanted. He rolled his head from side to side as though trying to stretch tight muscles.

"Where you goin', babe?"

"Um, well, I wasn't sure if you wanted company. I mean, you said you'd call me, not that it matters that you haven't," she said hastily. "But I thought you might want something to eat. . .see I made muffins and I made too many and I. . ." she squeaked as he wrapped an arm around her waist and hauled her inside the house. Then he leaned down and snagged hold of the basket of muffins. He kept her tight against his side as he kicked out to shut the door.

Then he half-carried her into his living room. There wasn't much in this room. Just a big sectional, two recliners and a huge T.V. mounted on the wall. The layout of the house was exactly the same as hers, with the addition of a large deck out the back. There was a game playing on the T.V. so she guessed he was just relaxing. Doing guy stuff.

And you interrupted.

"You didn't have to invite me in," she told him. Not that he'd actually invited her.

He just grunted then drew her along into the kitchen. He opened the fridge and silently pulled out some butter and two more beers.

"Oh, I don't want a beer thanks," she said as he offered her one. "I don't drink much."

He gave a nod and put one back. Then he split open some muffins and slathered them with way too much butter. She bit back a remark about healthy fats.

He took a huge bite then wrinkled his forehead. "What's in this?"

"Um, blueberries."

He shook his head and crooked a finger at her. "Come here."

She moved a step closer. "I, ah, added some bran to make them healthier. You know, keep you regular."

He raised an eyebrow at that.

"Well, not you, I mean I made them for me too. Not that I meant I needed. . .I just mean, bran is healthy and I. . .shit I need to stop talking now."

His lips actually twitched, lightening the dark look on his face.

"Closer." He crooked his finger at her again.

She thought she was plenty close enough, but she took another small step. He grasped hold of her hips and pulled her in until their lower halves were pressed together.

All right, so he'd wanted them that close.

Then suddenly, he lifted her so she was sitting on the counter and settled himself between her legs. Her breath caught as her pussy brushed against his firm stomach, her breasts pressed against his chest, her nipples pebbling immediately.

"Fuck, you're beautiful."

She knew she wasn't. But it felt good to hear the words, to see the desire in his face.

"I'm not," she murmured.

He tugged at her ponytail, the small spike of pain increasing her arousal. She raised her face so she was looking into his. "Nope. That's not allowed."

"What?" Her breathing quickened as he lowered his mouth so it was inches from hers.

"No speaking badly about yourself. If I say you're beautiful it's because I mean it. Not a man who says things he doesn't mean."

And she appreciated that more than she could say. Even if she couldn't see what he saw in her.

"Fucking beautiful. Sexy. Deliciously sweet." He leaned in those last few inches and took her mouth with his. This was not like any of the kisses she'd experienced before. This was hard. Hot. Primal.

He was devouring her.

This was no quick peck. No brush of the lips. This was all-in, raw. Hungry.

She loved it.

She wrapped her arms around his neck, trying to get closer, to find her way inside him. He abruptly drew away, stepping back. She sat there, panting, her body licked with flames wondering what just happened.

"Why did you stop?" The demand in her voice surprised her.

He leaned against the opposite counter, staring at her like he was a man starving and he wanted to feast.

Well, she was here for the taking.

"Because that wasn't meant to happen."

"Why not?"

He turned away, running his hand through his hair. "My control is shot today. You shouldn't have come over."

Ouch. That fucking hurt. She dropped her gaze and slid off the counter. "Sorry. I'll go."

"No, wait. Fuck! I didn't mean it like that." He stepped forward and caged her between his arms as he rested his hands on the counter behind her. "Sunny, look at me."

She kept her gaze lowered, not wanting him to see the tears in her eyes.

"Sunny. Look. At. Me."

Nope. No way. Nuh-uh.

"I'm going to start counting," he warned.

She raised her gaze to glare at him, her temper overriding her determination to hide her hurt feelings from him.

"Just because you start counting doesn't mean I'm going to do what you say." She stomped her foot on the floor then looked down at the limb in question in amazement. Had she really just stomped her foot?

"Are you having a tantrum, little rebel?" he murmured.

"No," she sulked. "I want to go home."

"No, you don't."

"You're not the boss of me!"

He grinned. "Ah, but honey, that's exactly what I am."

She frowned up at him.

His face sobered. "I'm sorry if I hurt you, Sunny. I didn't mean to. I misspoke."

She felt her temper drift away at the regret and worry on his face. "Are you all right?"

His face lightened. "Oh, Sunshine River, what the hell did I ever do to deserve you?"

She blushed slightly at those words.

He cupped her face with his hand. "So sweet. Always thinking of everyone else. But who looks after you?"

"I can look after myself."

"Of course, you can," he said, surprising her. "You're smart and strong and resourceful. But I like taking care of you. It makes me feel needed and useful and strong."

"You're all those things," she whispered. "And more. You're much stronger than me."

He smiled down at her. "My Sunny. She makes everyone around her feel good, but she doesn't see how truly amazing she is."

Her blush deepened.

"I've spent all morning resisting the urge to call you. To go to your house, throw you over my shoulder and carry you back here where you belong."

"So why didn't you? I mean, the whole caveman routine is a bit overkill, I'd have come willingly."

He ran his thumb across her cheek. "Ah, but deep down I'm a caveman at heart."

"Would have given the neighbors something to gossip about."

"There's my little rebel."

She shook her head because she was pretty much the opposite of a rebel. She'd followed the rules all her life. And look where it got her.. .maybe she should have thrown them out the window a long time ago.

"Why didn't you come get me?"

"Because I'm not good company today. I had a damn shitty night. Got barely any sleep. I didn't want you around me today, not when I'm like this. And it seems I was right since I hurt you just now."

"You didn't mean to." She wrapped her hand around his wrist. "You don't have to be perfect for me all the time, Duke."

He snorted out a laugh. "Well, I can guarantee that won't be the case. I'm far from perfect."

She wasn't so sure about that. She was pretty sure he was perfect for her.

"I can deal with dark and intense Duke. He's not so different from bossy and grouchy Duke," she teased.

He shook his head. "Like I said, don't know what I did to deserve you, but I know I don't want to let you go."

"So let me stay with you today." She reached up and brushed his hair off his face. "We don't have to do anything. I'll sit and watch the game with you and drink beer."

He raised an eyebrow. "Do you even know who's playing?"

She grinned. "Baby, I don't even know what sport it is."

He leaned his head back and burst into laughter before crouching down to swing her over his shoulder. He slapped her ass as she squealed.

"Come on, little rebel. You can sit on my lap while I give you a sports lesson."

"I hope there's not a quiz at the end."

"Oh, there is and every wrong answer gets you a smack on the ass."

Well, for once it seemed like her lack of sports knowledge was going to come in handy.

14

"I'm really sorry, I don't know how I mucked up the stock order again." Sunny ran her fingers through her hair, tugging at the pony tail she had it pulled back in today.

Agitation filled her. How did she keep getting this wrong? It was ridiculous. And embarrassing. She needed to get this stuff right, otherwise she was just a liability.

He's only keeping you around because of your relationship.

This last week, it felt like Duke had been putting some distance between them. He was still attentive. Still affectionate, particularly when her Little surfaced. But she'd been retreating too. Uncertain whether this was still something he really wanted.

Shouldn't he have done more than just kiss you by now?

Unless he doesn't find you attractive. Maybe you've gained weight. Maybe you embarrass him.

Shame and self-doubt ate away at her until she was practically shaking as she stood across from Duke. He was frowning as he stared down at the order.

Idiot. Idiot. Idiot.

"You should fire me," she blurted out.

He glanced up from the piece of paper, that slight frown still on his face. "What?"

She twisted her hands in front of her. "You should fire me. I made a mess of the ordering system. For a second time. I mean, what kind of an idiot messes up something that simple?"

"Sunny, you're being too hard on yourself," he stated, putting the paper down and studying her intently. "Come here."

She shook her head. Then she wrapped her arms around herself. "You shouldn't keep employing me just because we're. . .ah. . .we're friends."

His frown deepened; his puzzlement clear. "We're not friends."

Ouch. That hurt.

"Right. Right." She nodded. "We're neighbors."

He narrowed his gaze. "We're a damn sight more than neighbors, Sunshine River. Now get your ass here. Right the fuck now."

She still shook her head, standing her ground. What was she doing?

"This isn't about the order," he stated.

"Yes, it is. I'm a fuckup. . ." she trailed off. Whoops. She hadn't meant to say that.

"You're a what?" he asked in a low voice.

She just shook her head.

"Right. We need a chat. Because it seems there are a few things you're keeping from me. I'm going to give you until the count of three to get your ass around my desk or I'm going to come and get you. And, little rebel, you will not like it if I have to come get you."

That dark note sent a shiver of longing up her spine. She wanted the protection of a Daddy, the cuddles, the love. However, it also seemed she enjoyed having boundaries, being dominated. Taken in hand.

"One." He stared at her. She fidgeted, not knowing exactly why she wasn't moving.

"Two." Did she want him to come for her? Seemed so. Because she wanted a punishment? Maybe.

"Three." Oops. Time was up. And as he rose, regret settled in her gut. His face was easily read in that moment. And the man was not happy. At all.

"Wait, I'm coming," she said hastily.

"Too late, little rebel." He stalked around the desk.

Maybe she'd best get back to work. She stepped towards the door. "I think I'm needed out front. Madden's next client is probably—" she squealed as he picked her up and carried her to the sofa. "Duke!"

"Nope," he told her gruffly then he sat on the sofa with her on his lap. Face-up, thankfully. He held her as she fought to get free. "Settle down, little rebel. Before I settle you down."

"And how are you going to do that!"

He leaned in, brushing his mouth against her ear. Another shiver raced through her. For an entirely different reason. Her clit throbbed. "You really want to know how I'd stop this budding tantrum?"

"It's not a tantrum."

"That's exactly what it is. Somehow, we went from discussing the mucked-up order to you calling yourself names, claiming I should fire you, which is ridiculous, and then calling yourself my friend and neighbor."

She stiffened. "I'm sorry you don't want to be my friend."

"Sunny, we're a damn lot more than just friends. At least I thought we were. Was I wrong?" He stared down at her, his anger gone and confusion in its place.

To her horror, a tear dripped down her cheek. "Do you find me attractive?"

"What the fuck?" He shook his head. "Damn, women are confusing. How does you messing up the stock order have anything to do with me finding you attractive?"

"I just. . .I. . .you haven't done more than kiss me and I was worried that I'm not. . .that you've been turned off. . .I just. . ."

He blew out a breath then leaned his head back on the sofa. "Damned if I do, damned if I don't."

"What?"

"Baby girl, I was trying to go slow. I wanted you to feel comfortable with me, for your Little to be comfortable with me, before we moved onto anything more. You don't have a lot of experience and I can be demanding. I didn't want to scare the fuck out of you."

"I started worrying that I was doing something wrong."

He sighed and tucked her in against him, resting his chin on her head. "I've never had a relationship like this, babe. Where I need to care for someone else's emotional needs as well as their physical ones. Get what I'm saying?"

"Sort of." Not really.

"I'm saying I should have communicated this shit better, but I don't want to be too fucking blunt and send you running for the hills. I want you, Sunny. I fucking want you so much that I go home every night with a hard-on that doesn't seem to ease even when I jack off, thinking about you. I want to tie you to my bed and keep you there all night, exploring every inch of you, fucking you into oblivion then starting all over again. I want to bury my face between your legs and stay there for hours, seeing how many times I can make you come. I want you on your knees in front of me, sucking me off. I want to sink my dick into your pussy and claim you. All of you. I want to take you over my knee and spank your butt then plug it before I fuck it. I want all of that and more." He leaned back and gently grasped hold of her chin, raising her bright red face up so he could stare in to her eyes.

"What I do not want is to do any of that before you're ready. Because once I get you in my bed, I ain't fucking letting you go, Sunshine River. Not that I'm planning on letting you go anyway. But because you're important, I wanted to get the relationship part of this right first. Because you're important, I didn't want to just stick my dick in you at the first opportunity. Because I want more with you than I've ever wanted with anyone in my life. I could go down to the club now and find pussy, Sunny. What I can't find is you."

"I. . .I. . ." Holy shit what did she say to that? His words were raw and honest. And they washed away the insecurities that had been plaguing her.

Tears dripped down her face and he groaned. "Damn it, baby girl. Say something. That wasn't meant to make you cry. I didn't mean to upset you."

"You. . .you didn't upset me."

He wiped away her tears. "Where's a fucking tissue when I need one?"

She snorted out a laugh. "They were probably on the stock order I messed up."

"Hold that thought about the stock order, because I'm coming back to that. We're going to have a little chat about you calling yourself names."

To her surprise, he shifted her slightly on his lap then drew off his T-shirt.

"What are you doing?" she squeaked as he drew her back against his warm chest. Sugar. He was so ripped. She hadn't realized someone could have abs like that unless you were a professional athlete or gym junkie.

Her hand twitched with the urge to explore. Then he held his T-shirt up to her face, wiping her tears. "Duke, don't! Your T-shirt."

"Got others," he said, sounding unconcerned. He held the shirt to her nose. "Blow."

"No! I can't do that. I'll go to the bathroom."

"You're going nowhere until I'm certain we're both on the same wavelength. Blow. Now, baby girl."

She knew she was bright red, but she blew her nose into his shirt. Gross.

But he just balled it up and threw it on the ground.

"I'll take it home and wash it."

He sighed. "Sunny, I'm not worried about the damn shirt. Tell me you understand why it seemed like I pulled back from you."

"I get it now. You were going slow because I. . .because I mean something to you. I guess I got tearful because no one has ever treated me like I'm important. Like I really mean something to them."

"Well, you do. You need me to tell you that every day, I fucking will." He tucked a strand of hair behind her ear. "I want all of you, Sunny. Not just the parts of you that you think I might want. You understand me?"

"Yeah. I'm sorry. I guess I'm still a bit shy about letting completely go. Worried about getting hurt or rejected."

"I'll get all your trust once you see that you can be yourself completely. That I don't want to change you because you're already fucking perfect."

"You say the nicest things," she said with a sigh of pleasure.

His chest moved as he laughed. "You might not say that in a moment." He twisted his fingers in hers. She stared down at his darker tan. The rough calluses rubbing against her smoother skin. Made her think about his fingers touching her in other places.

"I think I might like where your mind just went, but we're still taking this as slow as I think you need."

She turned her head to protest and he gave her a stern look. "We're not hurrying into anything, Sunny. Not until I'm certain you're sure."

She was sure. But she knew she wasn't going to win this argument. Not quite yet.

"You're in trouble, little rebel."

"Me? Why?"

He snorted. "Where shall we start? For calling yourself an idiot? A fuckup? For trying to tell me I should fire you? For not coming to me, even when I gave you a count. For future reference, Daddy expects you to come immediately when he counts."

Uh-oh.

"Well, I don't think I should get in trouble for calling myself an idiot and fuckup because clearly I'm both of those things."

She squeaked as he turned her over his lap. This time, she was facedown. Not a good position for her to be in.

"Duke! We're at work! You can't do this here."

He sighed and rubbed her ass through her pants. "I can't spank you at work, while there are people here. However, I think this is a good position for you to be in while you listen to me."

"I really should get back to the front desk."

His hand rested on her ass. God, she hoped no one came in. Why hadn't she locked the door?

Because you thought he was pulling you in here to scold or fire you and you figured a quick getaway was vital.

"First of all, you are not an idiot or fuckup. You messed something up. It is not the end of the world. We all do it."

Sunny didn't. She hated making mistakes.

"I know it's hard on you because you like to get everything right and you obsess if you don't. We need to work on getting you to be less hard on yourself. You're allowed to make mistakes, Sunny. No one ever died because of a messed-up stock order. You need to stop punishing yourself. Especially since that's my job now."

She shot a look over her shoulder at him, to find him grinning. He thought he was so smart.

He rubbed her ass. "Talking or thinking about yourself like that is never going to be something I'll tolerate, little rebel. That's earned you a trip over my knee when we get home."

She sucked in a breath.

"I want you to think about everything you're good at because tomorrow you're going to write me a list of everything positive about Sunshine River Bright."

She groaned. "Can't the spanking be enough?"

"Nope."

"I don't like homework."

"Don't like the time, don't do the crime. I don't like hearing you talk about yourself like that, because my Sunny isn't an idiot or a fuckup. So she messes up from time to time. Isn't one of us that doesn't do that. Just means you're human."

"Greg always wanted me to be perfect."

"Well, we both know what Greg was, don't we?"

"A self-involved douchebag whose opinions and thoughts mean nothing."

"That's right. Greg wanted his version of perfect Sunny. Me, I just want Sunny. All of her." He helped her stand, placing her on the floor between his open legs, staring at her.

"Trust me?"

"Yes," she replied without hesitation.

"Good. Tonight, I want you to spend the night at my place. Nothing is going to happen so don't even think about trying to jump my bones," he warned.

She rolled her eyes even though that thought may have occurred to her.

"But I want to wake up with you in the morning. I want Saturday morning cartoons and breakfast and doing your hair."

Yeah. There, she wanted that as well.

"Of course, there's no cartoons until your homework is done. And you might be lying on your tummy to watch cartoons rather than sitting."

She groaned. Awesome.

He stood and hugged her tight. "You mean so much to me, Sunny. I know I'm not the best with emotions and crap, but if you're thinking negative thoughts, if you're worried about anything, tell me. Can't fix what I don't know about."

"I'll try," she whispered back. He then turned her and slapped her ass. "Good. Now get back to work before your boss gets grumpy."

"He's always grumpy," she said seriously. "I think he needs to get laid."

She dived out of there as he took a threatening step towards her, giggling. She stepped into the break room to get some coffee, coming to a stop as she saw Rory there.

"There's no creamer," he barked.

"There should be. I restocked it a few days ago."

"Not the kind I drink."

Great. Awesome.

She forced herself to smile at him. "All right, I'll get you some." She'd pick up some of the stuff she'd messed up on the stock order and pay for it herself. That would make her feel better.

"Good. I'm tired of having to tell you all this, Sunny. I mean, I know this is all hard for you to learn so maybe you should write it down or something."

His voice was condescending. Such a jerk. But he never did anything so bad that she felt she should say anything to Duke. Rory was a good tattoo artist, he brought in a lot of business.

Whereas she did not.

Rory walked away and she strode out to reception to check the bookings. She spent the next thirty minutes answering emails and welcoming Rory's customer before she had a block of time where she could get away.

It would soon get dark, so she knew she better go now. She strode towards Duke's office and knocked lightly.

"Come in," he growled.

She put her head around the door, noticing he was on the

phone. "Can I borrow your truck? I need to get some stuff for the break room."

He frowned, but she wasn't sure if it was at her request or from whatever someone on the call was saying. She stepped forward and snatched up his keys. He put his hand over the receiver of his phone.

"Give me ten and I'll take you."

She gave him an exasperated look. "I'll be fine, Duke. Unless you don't trust me driving your baby? I promise to bring it back scratch-free."

He narrowed his gaze. She'd never driven his truck. As he'd told her, if his ass was in the vehicle, he was driving it. But she was pretty sure she could get it down to Walmart and back safely. She was starting to think she might as well get rid of her car as it never seemed to leave her garage anymore.

"Fine. Go. But don't be long and drive carefully. I don't want any scratches on *you*."

Warmth filled her and she smiled at him before retrieving her wallet from her locker and rushing out. They'd parked around the corner. Duke preferred to leave the spaces out front for customers, although she'd noticed Rory always took one right out front.

The ass.

As she came around the corner, she peered at Duke's truck in confusion. Why was it lopsided? Then she noticed a dark figure crouched next to the truck on the pavement. Dressed in a black hoodie and dark jeans, he almost blended into the shadows.

Then a loud scratching noise hit her ears and she gasped as she realized he was running something along the side of Duke's truck, leaving a deep gouge in the paintwork.

"Hey! What do you think you're doing? Stop that!" she yelled. Without thinking, she raced towards him. "Get away!"

The figure turned, but instead of racing off as she'd half-expected, he grabbed hold of her and shoved her back into the alley. He pressed her against the wall and that's when she saw the knife that he held up high in the air. He was going to stab her! She screamed in fear.

Then to her shock, the person in the hoodie was suddenly pulled away from her.

She gasped in a breath, marveling as Marv stood there, glaring down at her assailant. The other man quickly stood, still holding his knife. His face was hidden in the depths of his hood.

"Marv, run!" she yelled, terrified.

She was grateful for his help, but she didn't want him getting hurt.

"Sunny! Sunny, where are you?" a voice roared.

The guy in the hoodie seemed to freeze for a second, before turning and racing out of the alley just seconds before Duke reached the entrance.

"What the fuck? Sunny!"

"I'm here!" she managed to call out. Duke raced into the alley, his face filled with worry and rage.

"Get away from her," he yelled at Marv.

She jumped in front of Marv, holding her arms out to her side to protect him.

"Duke, stop! It wasn't Marv! He didn't hurt me. He helped me!"

Duke reached for her. "What the fuck happened? I was coming after you and saw the truck damaged, your bag on the ground and you gone."

"I'm all right. I promise." She stepped forward and pressed into him, craving the comfort of his arms around her. Fuck. She was trembling so bad; she could barely stand up.

"What. Happened?" he gritted out, but he pulled her carefully against him, holding her tight.

"There was a guy crouched by your truck when I came out. He was dressed all in black. I noticed your truck was on a lean and then I saw him start to scratch your truck. I yelled at him to scare him off, but he just grabbed me and shoved me into the alley. That's when I spotted the knife. He was looming over me. I think he was going to stab me when Marv dragged him away from me. I thought he would hurt us both but he heard you yell and took off."

He started swearing loudly and colorfully. "You're sure you're not hurt?" He drew back to run his hands over her. "Did he get you with the knife?"

"No, no, I promise I'm fine," she reassured him. "Marv, are you all right?" She looked around Duke to the other man.

"I'm fine, but you should have run away from that guy rather than at him," Marv said in a scratchy voice.

"You ran towards him? Jesus, Sunny, what the fuck were you thinking?"

"I was thinking that I'd scare him away, not that he'd turn on me," she replied, glaring at Marv.

"Got little sense of self-preservation. She needs more watching over, boy," Marv told Duke.

"Marv! You're meant to be on my side."

"I am, sweet girl. I'm trying to keep you safe and alive. I won't always be around to rescue you. And not sure this old body could have done much more to protect you."

"You did a great job, Marv. Thank you." She tried to step away from Duke to hug the old man, but Duke wouldn't let her go.

She nudged him in his side and he glared down at her. "Can you let me go?"

"No," he snapped.

She sighed.

Marv chuckled. "Quite right, too. You were mine, sweet girl, I wouldn't be letting you out of my sight for a long while. I'd also make sure you didn't sit down for a week."

She groaned. "Don't give him ideas."

"I don't need them, but I do agree," Duke said. "Come on, I want to get you inside where I can check you over properly."

She sighed. "Thanks again, Marv."

Duke gave him a short nod and guided her out of the alley. She shuddered as they passed his truck. The scratch down the side was deep and the two tires were fully deflated.

"We need to call the police. That guy will be long gone by now, though and I didn't see his face. It was hidden by his hood. I'm so sorry."

He simply grunted and led her into the shop. Thankfully there was no one in the front room, she wasn't feeling up to dealing with anyone right then. He led her into his office and over to the sofa.

He sat down and pulled her onto his lap, just holding her. She held him back, her arms around his neck.

"Fuck. Fuck," he muttered in a low, shaken voice. "He had a goddamn motherfucking knife."

"I know," she whispered.

"And you ran toward him. You ran towards a man holding a goddamn knife." His voice had grown harder. Sharper.

Uh-oh.

He drew her back so he could look at her. She dropped her gaze from the rage blazing in his eyes.

"What the fuck were you thinking, Sunny! You don't ever, ever run towards the person holding a weapon."

"I didn't know he had a knife!"

"But you saw him marking up my truck. You knew he wasn't up to any good."

"I thought he'd run off!"

"Well, you were wrong. He could have fucking hurt you! What you should have done, and what you will do if anything like that fucking happens again, is turn on your heel and get your little ass back to safety. Back to me!"

He shook her lightly. "Nothing can happen to you. Do you understand me?"

She might have been annoyed at his grouchy orders if she

couldn't see the fear on his face. The idea of something happening to her had really shaken him.

Because he really does care about you.

"I'm sorry," she whispered. "I wasn't thinking."

"Well, start," he snapped then he let out a long breath and ran his fingers through his hair. "Sorry. I just. . .I can't believe you were fucking attacked. In fucking daylight and if that old, homeless guy hadn't been there..."

He was almost shaking and she gathered him into her arms. "I'm all right, Duke."

"You're sure?"

She was shaken up but overall, she was fine. She nodded. "I'm sure. I'm sorry. I won't do anything like that again."

He held her until they both stopped trembling then he stood and laid her on the sofa. "I want you to rest." He moved over and gestured for her to lie down.

"Duke, I've got to work. I'm not tired."

He just raised an eyebrow. All right, so her adrenaline rush was fading and she was a little sleepy.

"I've got to make some calls about the truck and then we're going home." He picked up the blanket that sat on one arm of the sofa and lay it over her. Then he brushed his lips across her forehead.

"Rest, little rebel. I'll keep you safe."

She knew he would. She never felt as safe as she did when he was near.

15

It was close to ten by the time they left. She'd actually fallen asleep which had surprised her. Turns out, she'd been more tired than she'd thought. So sleepy, unfortunately, she'd forgotten to pee before they got in their borrowed truck. She didn't know where the truck had come from or when Duke had his towed, she'd slept all through that. This truck wasn't as big as Duke's behemoth. It was a double cab with bench seats. As they paused at some lights, she took a moment to study him under the streetlights. His jaw was tense, his hands tight around the steering wheel. He'd been very intense since she'd been attacked and she wanted to do something to help ease his worry.

She was all right. But somehow, he didn't seem ready to believe that.

But just as she was about to move, her bladder made itself known again.

Sugar.

She crossed her legs and fidgeted around. Duke turned to look at her. "Everything okay?"

"Umm."

Jeez this was embarrassing. *Just tell him, Sunny. Not like he doesn't pee.*

"Sunny?"

"I've gotta pee," she blurted out.

"Be another ten minutes until we get home, can you wait?"

"Oh, I really wish I could. But my bladder doesn't like car rides."

"It doesn't like car rides," he said slowly.

"Yeah, see, I always pee before I get in the car 'cause otherwise I need to go and I find it really hard to hold on and. . .are you laughing at me?" she asked suspiciously, seeing his shoulders shake.

She was glad to see him smile. Even if it was at her expense. "I'm not very good at hanging on at the best of times and the motion of driving just seems to make it worse. Can we please stop somewhere?"

"Of course, we can, baby girl. I'm sorry for laughing at you."

"It's fine. I know it sounds ridiculous. I'm a grown woman, I should be able to hold on."

"Hush," he murmured. "You are who you are." He put on his indicator and pulled into a park with a public toilet. "Let's hope it's open or you might have to pee in the bushes."

Pee in the bushes? Was he insane? Her bladder was an indoor sort of bladder. She did not pee outside.

He came around as she undid her seat belt. He lifted her down and took hold of her hand. She shivered slightly even though she was wearing one of his sweatshirts that went down to her knees. He led her inside the women's bathroom. The light came on automatically. She glanced around. Not as terrible as she'd imagined.

"Wait here," he commanded then proceeded to check each stall.

"I don't think anyone would be peeing in the dark," she said dryly.

"Not taking any chances with your safety." He stood back and waved her forward. "Go pee, baby girl."

"Um, aren't you going to leave?"

"Nope."

"Duke!"

"I'm not leaving, Sunny. I thought you were busting or do you need some help?"

"No, I don't need any help! I've been toilet trained since I was two. But my bladder is shy. I can't pee with you in here."

"You're gonna have to, because I'm not leaving you alone." He folded his arms over his chest.

"Look, I get you were worried about me today. But nothing happened. It was just a fluke encounter. I'm not going to be attacked while peeing."

"I'm going to start counting, Sunny and if you don't get your butt into one of those stalls, I'm going to pull down your pants and sit you down myself."

She scowled at him.

"One."

With a mutter, she stomped her way into the furthest away stall.

"Just for your information, I think your habit of counting sucks."

"So noted," he said dryly.

She heard the sound of water and realized he'd turned on a tap. Whether to help her get over her embarrassment or to hurry her along, she didn't know. But it did help. She quickly peed and got redressed. She gave him another glare as she washed her hands.

"You're acting crazy. That guy is long gone. He was probably just high on drugs and looking for money or something. I'm perfectly safe peeing on my own."

He drew her into him, holding her against his chest. "Until I can close my eyes and not think of all the ways I could have lost you today, until I can go five minutes without my heart racing with fear as I think about the fact that he could have stabbed you, that I could have lost you, you're going to have to put up with a bit of overprotectiveness, okay?"

Her breath stuttered out. He really had been terrified. Couldn't she put up with a bit of overprotectiveness to give him peace of mind?

There was only one answer.

"Okay."

He let out a deep breath then lightly patted her ass. "Good girl. Come on, let's get going. You need to get to bed."

She'd slept for close to two hours on his couch so she wasn't feeling all that tired but she just nodded. He led her out of the bathroom and they'd both just gotten into the truck again when his phone started ringing.

He swore under his breath. Then he answered the call. "What?" He listened to the other person, then swore again and looked over at her. "Fine. I'll be there in fifteen. I'm bringing Sunny with me."

Bringing her where?

"No, she didn't see his face. Dressed all in black. Nothing distinguishing. Yeah, not a bad idea. I'd feel better with more security there. And at her house, can you arrange a security system and alarm? Great, thanks. Bye."

"Where are we going? Who was that? Why are you getting a security system put into my house?" she asked as soon as the call ended.

"To Reaper's. Ink. 'Cause you'll be safer."

"I'm not unsafe, Duke. That guy wasn't after me."

"We don't know what he was after. Maybe it wasn't random. Maybe it was an attack on me and you got in the way."

"That's a lot of maybes. And what is more likely is that it was just a random attack. Unless there's some reason you think someone would want to get at you."

"Made a lot of enemies over the years."

"What sorts of enemies? Who are they?"

He shrugged.

She sighed. "I don't need a security system."

"You're a woman living alone. You should have one anyway."

"I can't afford one," she admitted.

"You're not paying for it. I am," he said firmly.

"You are not," she replied, equally as firm.

"Am."

"Duke!" she protested.

He slid her a look. "You're gonna let me do this, Sunny. Need to keep you safe."

She threw her arms up into the air. "I know you're a protective guy. You warned me about that. But doesn't this seem like a wee bit of an overreaction to you? I'm fine."

There were a few beats of silence. And just when she opened her mouth to ask him why they had to head to the club, he spoke.

"Lost my family when I was eight."

She closed her mouth.

"Car accident. I was staying at a friend's house for the night. They'd just dropped me off. I had a little sister. Lost all of them. Gone. Just like that. No chance for a goodbye. No opportunity to tell them I loved them."

"Oh, Duke." She reached over to grasp hold of his thigh. It tightened under her hold then relaxed. "I know it doesn't mean much, but I'm so sorry."

"My friend's family took me in. They were good to me. But it wasn't ever the same. They couldn't replace what I lost. Think that's one of the reasons I was drawn to the club. The sense of family and camaraderie. Hasn't always been a safe place. Not with

Smiley, the guy who ran the club before Reyes. But the guys there are my brothers. They were all I had. Until you."

He'd lost his family. He couldn't lose her. She closed her eyes. She got it now.

"Let me put in the security system, baby girl. Let me sleep better when you're not right there beside me."

"Okay," she whispered. "I wish I could have known them."

"I don't remember too much of them anymore. My dad, he liked to pick my mom up and twirl her around and she'd just laugh. She had the best laugh. They were happy. They loved us."

Her heart bled for the little boy who'd gone from living a life full of love and laughter to being alone. At least his friend's parents had taken him in and he hadn't had to go into foster home.

"I'd take you home but I don't want you there alone," he explained. "And I'm needed at the club for a meeting."

"It's fine," she told him, even as she felt a little nervous at the idea of going inside the club's bar. But Duke would be with her and part of her was slightly curious as well.

They drove in silence but she kept her hand on his thigh. He parked his borrowed truck outside the bar.

Duke took tight hold of her hand as they walked towards the entrance. "You stay next to me at all times and you listen to what I say, understand?"

"Why? Is it dangerous?"

He stopped and turned to look down at her. "Little rebel, do you seriously think I'd take you anywhere that was unsafe?"

Well, when he put it like that...

"No. But why do I have to stick close to you?"

"Because I don't want any of these fuckers getting any ideas about you. You're mine."

Wow. That had to be about the most Neanderthal statement ever.

She rolled her eyes. "They're hardly going to fall on me like a pack of wild hyenas."

He just snorted. "They might be my brothers, but I don't trust them not to attempt to steal you away from me."

"I'm not that much of a prize," she said dryly. In fact, remembering what she was wearing, her baggy jeans and his over-sized sweatshirt she suddenly wasn't keen at all on going inside. "Are you sure I can't wait out in the truck?"

"Baby girl, I don't know what you see when you look in the mirror, but I see someone who is gorgeous on the inside and outside. And believe me, anyone who looks closely will see what I see and they'll know that if they got hold of you, then they'd have all that light shining so bright inside you to themselves. And no other asshole is having that light. It's fucking mine."

How could he say something so sweet with one breath and then something so outrageous with the next? She just shook her head. He was completely delusional. She wasn't gorgeous and there was no light shining from her.

But it did feel nice that he thought so.

He opened the door and walked in, pulling her close behind him. The noise hit her first. And the heat. There were a lot more people in here than she'd expected. Then again, it was a Friday night. Just because she didn't have a life didn't mean other people sat at home in their PJs and gave themselves manicures.

The bar was old and dark, with the scent of beer and leather heavy in the air. There were tables and chairs off to one side and pool tables and more seating to the other side. They weaved their way through, people calling out to Duke as he moved through, towards the long bar that took up most of the back wall. There was a single door to the right of the bar.

Duke nodded at people but didn't stop, veering off towards the door.

"Duke!"

She looked over at the familiar voice and saw Ink striding towards him. He looked more serious than she'd ever seen him look before. Duke's life as part of the Iron Shadows was a bit of a mystery to her.

"Hey, man, we were just headed out the back," Duke said to him.

Ink gave her a small smile. "Hey, there Sunny-girl."

"Hi, Ink, how's it going?"

"Not wonderful."

She frowned at that and Duke squeezed her hand. "Anything I can help with?"

Ink looked a little surprised then he smiled. "No, babe. But it's sweet you'd ask. I heard you had your own trouble this afternoon. Shouldn't you be home, resting?" Ink gave Duke a chiding look.

Duke growled back at him. "I'm not leaving her home alone."

Ink nodded. "Understood. I'd feel the same. But she can't come back with us. Reyes will have a fit."

Duke's jaw grew tense. "I'm not leaving her out here alone."

"Leave her with me, I'll keep the wolves at bay."

Sunny turned at the female voice and her mouth dropped open as one of the most beautiful women she'd ever seen swayed towards them. She wore a tight, white, sleeveless top, high-waisted black jeans and a wide belt with a large silver buckle and dark boots. It all looked simple, but combined with her dark hair and lush lips and high cheekbones she was simply breath-taking.

"I don't know, Jewel," Duke said hesitantly.

Her name was Jewel? How awesome was that?

"You're beautiful," Sunny said.

The woman stilled and stared at her for a moment then a smile graced her lips. "I think we'll get along fine, Duke. Run along."

"I'm Sunny." She held out her hand and Jewel took it with another grin.

"Hi, Sunny, I've heard about you."

"I can't believe your name is Jewel. That totally suits you."

"Yeah, I can see your name suits you too."

"It's caused me all sorts of issues growing up."

"Get that too," Jewel commented. "Come on, I'll buy you a drink."

"Cool. How do you get your hair so straight and shiny?" Sunny asked, about to follow the other woman.

A throat cleared behind her and a large arm wrapped around her waist. "Forgetting something?"

"Oh, right, sorry." She turned and placed a kiss on Duke's cheek. "Have fun at your meeting. Don't rush, I'll be safe enough with Jewel."

The other woman slipped her hand in Sunny's and tugged her gently over to the bar. Just as she was about to slip onto a bar stool, a loud whistle filled the air. Everyone in the bar suddenly stopped talking and turned to look at her.

She blushed bright red and glanced up at Duke who stood beside her, his arm back around her. He'd been the one to whistle.

"Listen up. This is Sunny." He pointed at her. Actually, pointed at her. Her mortification grew. What was he doing? She looked over at Jewel, noticing the huge grin on the other woman's face.

"She's mine. Anyone touches her and they're dead."

A series of grunts and nods accompanied that statement.

"Now, you'll be safe." He kissed the top of her head and strode away with Ink, who sent her a wink over his shoulder.

"He didn't just do that, did he?" she asked Jewel, feeling slightly dazed.

"Oh, he certainly did. He just claimed you in front of the entire bar."

"It was completely caveman, wasn't it?"

"Yep," Jewel agreed, signaling the bar man.

"I suppose I should be upset about that."

Jewel shrugged. "Up to you. Personally, I like my men as possessive as fuck. Not jealous, petty-minded little fuckers, but the type of guy you know will have your back, no matter what. Who'll fuck up anyone who harms you. Who you can call to bury the body and they'll just ask if you want a shovel or some acid?"

Sunny gaped at the other woman who grinned and winked. "Joking."

Sunny shook her head. Somehow, she wasn't so sure. "It is nice having someone who cares about me. I've never really had that. I've always been the person looking after everyone else."

Jewel nodded. "I get what you're saying. What's your poison?"

"Uh, beer please." She wasn't much of a drinker, but she figured in this sort of bar, beer was a safe choice.

Jewel ordered them both beers and when they had them, she linked her arm with Sunny's, and led her off to a quieter corner. The guys sitting at a table, jumped up to give them their seats. Jewel nodded her thanks.

"That was nice of them," Sunny said as they sat. "I have to say, I think I had some misinformed stereotypes about how bikers would behave."

"That so?" Jewel drawled. "Well, some of them have manners and some of them are pigs. Like most men. You get the good and the bad. Plus, Duke just claimed you in front of everyone and no one wants to go up against him. He's a tough bastard."

"My Duke?" *As though there is going to be another one, Sunny.*

Jewel grinned. "The one and only. Didn't think I'd see the day he fell for a woman. I've known him for years and I've never seen him with the same woman twice. Not that he's a player or anything. He doesn't jump on anything with a skirt, he just never seemed interested in commitment."

She ran her finger down the moisture that had gathered on the outside of her bottle of beer. "We haven't exactly talked about commitment."

But she knew he was serious about her and she felt the same about him.

Jewel snorted. "What do you think that statement just was? That was basically a wedding ring to these guys."

She blushed. "It was?"

Jewel nodded. "So I hope you're serious about him. Because Duke's a good guy, one of the best. I don't want to see him hurt."

Sunny stared at her for a moment. Hurt Duke? That was the last thing she'd ever want to do. "He's the best thing that's ever happened to me and the thought of hurting him makes me feel ill. The thought of being without him. . ." she shook her head. "I don't even want to think about it. It's hard to think we've only known each other a few weeks. I shouldn't feel this intense about him already, right?"

It was nice to have someone to talk to about this. She'd just met this woman, but she felt instantly at ease with her.

"If it's right, it's right. Doesn't matter if you've known them six minutes or six years. Don't go messing it up just because it doesn't stick to society's timelines."

"You're smart. And beautiful. I wish I was more like you."

Jewel threw her head back and laughed. Around them, men stopped and stared, their admiration for the dark-haired woman apparent. But Jewel didn't look at any of them. Her attention was fully on Sunny.

"Sorry, that probably sounded weird. I've never had a friend before, not that I'm saying you have to be my friend or anything," she groaned. "Stop me anytime you like."

"Now why would I do that? You're seriously entertaining."

Sunny just shook her head. "I'm a nutcase, is what I am."

"Babe, seriously, you do not want to be like me."

Sunny sighed. "You seem so confident and together."

Jewel leaned in. "A little secret, because even though we've just met I feel like I can trust you."

Sunny nodded. “I feel the same.”

“It’s all a freaking act.”

“Really?”

“Yeah, babe. I give people what they want to see. Even if I don’t feel it on the inside.”

On instinct, Sunny reached over and grabbed hold of her hand. “I’m sorry you have to pretend all the time.”

Jewel smiled sadly. “Me too.”

“I also wish I could dress like you.” Sunny looked down at herself with a grimace.

Jewel narrowed her gaze. “You don’t like your clothes?”

“Everything in my wardrobe has been there for years. It doesn’t fit me properly. I don’t feel like I’m me in these clothes. I think maybe I’ve been hiding too.”

“I’ll take you shopping.”

“What? Really?”

“Yep. We can go this weekend if you like.”

Sunny grinned. “That would be awesome, if you’re sure it’s not too much trouble.”

Jewel took a sip of beer. “I wouldn’t have offered if it was. And truth is, I don’t have a lot of friends myself.”

Sunny leaned in, looking around to make sure no one else was close enough to hear her. “Can I ask you another favor?”

“Sure.”

“I need to know how to seduce Duke, have you got any tips?”

Jewel blinked. “Seduce him?”

“He’s taking things slow. He doesn’t think I’m ready for sex.”

“Oh, the whole I’m going slow for your sake deal.”

Sunny nodded. “So any suggestions?”

“Blow job.”

Sunny gaped at her. Then she smiled. “Really? You think that will work?”

"Babe. Not a man alive who can resist the woman he loves going down on him."

He'd said nothing about love, but he did care about her. A lot. Only thing was, were her blow job skills up to it?

Well, there were videos to help with that, right?

"Jewel, you're a very smart lady."

"I know."

~

"Do you know what just happened out there?" Ink asked Duke as they stepped into the back area of the bar and headed towards Reyes' office.

"No fucking idea."

"Jewel just walked up to Sunny and took to her like they were long lost friends. For the first six months that she lived in the compound she wouldn't even speak to me, but she just offers to babysit Sunny like that." Ink stilled. "Do you think Sunny will be all right?"

Duke had to smile. "Sunny will be fine. She has that effect on people. She's sweet and genuine and people see that."

Ink studied him for a moment. "You've got it bad for her."

"You were just there; did that seem like I'm all in or not?"

"Oh, that was definitely a declaration of ownership. You'll be lucky to go home with your balls tonight."

Duke shook his head. "Sunny will be fine with it."

"You're a lucky man, you bastard. She got any sisters?"

He frowned. "No. She has no one."

"Well, that's just changed, hasn't it? She's got all of us now."

Yeah. She did since he'd just declared she was his in front of the entire club. She'd be treated like his old woman now, respected and protected. And it eased something inside him. Knowing that he'd be giving her his family.

They stepped into Reyes' office. Razor, Spike and Jason were already there. Along with Reyes, who sat behind his desk, staring at his laptop.

"What's going on?" Duke asked, taking a seat at the side of the room. "Could we not have talked over the phone? I need to get Sunny home to bed, she's had an eventful day."

Reyes raised his gaze to his. "No idea who messed up your truck?"

"No." And that really pissed him off. Not the damage, he could care less about that. But that Sunny could have been harmed.

"Could it have been the Fox?" Reyes asked him.

Duke narrowed his gaze. "There was no calling card. That's the Fox's thing, right? To leave some indication it was him?"

"Usually, yeah," Spike rasped. "But he was interrupted by your missus."

Duke didn't deny she was his. They'd all hear about his declaration out in the bar soon enough. He frowned, thinking that through. If it was the Fox and Sunny had been so close to him. . .he sucked in a breath. Fuck! The danger she could have been in made him want to get up right now and find her, tuck her away and never let her out.

"Easy, man," Ink said. "She's surrounded by her people. Probably nowhere that she'd be safer."

"Don't underestimate the Fox," Spike told them. "Bastard could be sneaking amongst us and we'd never know. He's got a reputation for getting places other people can't."

Ink glared at Spike. "Are you trying to give Duke a heart attack? Christ, he's not going to let the poor girl pee on her own now."

That had basically been the case earlier so he couldn't argue that.

"Good," Spike grunted. "If it was the Fox she encountered she needs watching like a hawk."

"How likely is it that it was the Fox, though," Ink argued. "This guy is an assassin, why the fuck would he be involved in petty shit like keying Duke's truck?"

Reyes grunted. "It's a good point. Unlikely to be the Fox."

"Jewel has her," Ink told him. "She's safe for the moment."

"Jewel has her?" Reyes asked, shock clear in his usually emotionless voice.

"Yep." Ink grinned. "Think she's taken little Sunny under her wing."

"But Jewel hates people," Jason said with confusion.

"She likes Sunny," Ink drawled. "Everyone likes Sunny. Such a sweet *little* thing. Daddy Duke, such a nice ring to it," Ink mused, tapping his tattooed fingers against the desk.

"Can we get on with it? I don't like being away from her."

Reyes nodded. "My contact called me earlier. Turns out that girl who was found last weekend is the same girl in the photos. She was a runaway. They're trying to piece together what happened to her once she arrived here."

"Fuck," Duke muttered. Having the girl turn up dead had sent him spiraling last weekend. Which is why he'd been trying to stay away from Sunny, until she'd walked over with a basket of muffins. "Fucker killed her."

"Raped and murdered," Reyes confirmed in a cold voice. "Then in the early hours of this morning, Jason followed one of the senator's bodyguards. And he caught him meeting with this guy."

The senator was loaded and he had two bodyguards that went everywhere with him.

Reyes turned around his laptop to display a photo of one of the senator's bodyguards handing an envelope to a fat, middle-aged white man with a serious comb-over.

"Who is he?" Duke asked.

"Arnold James Francine. Or Frankie to his friends and the devil to the women he pimps out."

Duke sat up straighter. "He was meeting with a pimp?"

Reyes nodded. "And paying him off by the looks of it."

"So this could be the guy supplying him with the girls?" Razor asked with a scowl.

"Looks like it," Reyes said.

"Even better, Frankie has ties to Bartolli," Jason told them. "His son is married to Fergus Bartolli's niece."

"So Frankie could have told Bartolli he was supplying a US Senator with young girls, Bartolli decides to blackmail the senator, uses us to do it so it doesn't get back to him and Frankie isn't identified as the leak," Duke surmised.

"That's what we're thinking."

"Think we can get to Frankie?" Ink asked.

"I'll talk to Grady. Think he knows Frankie," Spike said quietly. "I'll see if I can get a meet set up."

Reyes nodded. "Sooner rather than later. Meanwhile, let's keep on this bastard. This could mean a new girl is coming in. It's our chance to nail him."

They all nodded and started to leave. "Duke, wait a minute," Reyes called out.

Duke stilled, giving him an impatient look. He needed to get back to Sunny.

"I've got her," Ink said quietly.

Duke gave him a nod of thanks and waited until the door was shut to speak. "What's up?"

"You told Sunny about any of this?"

He ran his hand over his hair. He felt torn about this. Reyes wanted this kept quiet between the six of them. There were still men in the club who had been loyal to Smiley and weren't entirely loyal to Reyes. He got it. But at the same time, he didn't like keeping things from Sunny.

"Not yet," he told him.

Reyes gave a sharp nod. "Figured as much. You should tell her."

Duke raised his eyebrows in surprise. "Wasn't expecting you to say that."

"Haven't been around the two of you much, but the others have. And I see the way you are when you talk about her. You don't even like her out of your sight."

"She was attacked today." But he nodded. He didn't like her out of his sight.

"You're in deep. We know that. The Fox might know it too. She deserves to know what's going on so she can be careful."

"I'm watching her closely." Except he hadn't today. "You think he could target her?"

"Not saying that. We haven't heard from him in a while. No way of knowing if he's even still around. But I know if she was mine, I'd want her to be informed. And I'd want her protected. Probably more than she'd be comfortable with." Reyes smiled darkly. Duke knew the other man's need for control ran even deeper than his. Any woman of his would be suffocated in his protection. Which might be why he was single. It would take a special woman to understand he wasn't being an asshole, that he needed it.

Duke got it, because he had some of that inside him. "I don't think I can do surveillance on the senator anymore."

Reyes nodded. "Think that's wise. Rest of us are single. But we need to keep Sunny safe. Tell her what you need to and let us know if you need our help."

This is what he'd been searching for when he'd first joined the Iron Shadows. Someone to have his back and to know he'd always have theirs.

"Yeah. Thanks, man."

"It doesn't even need to be said," Reyes replied. Something

dark filled his face. “She really ran towards the asshole with a knife?”

“She didn’t realize he had a knife, but yeah.”

Reyes shook his head. “I take it she won’t be sitting well tomorrow.”

“Or maybe for the rest of the week,” Duke said darkly.

“Good,” Reyes grunted, turning back to his laptop.

Duke was used to his abruptness and he had somewhere else he wanted to be anyway.

16

"What do you need from your place for the night?" Duke asked her as he pulled into his driveway. "PJs, toothbrush, Moody, anything else?"

She blushed a little at the mention of Moody, but she wouldn't sleep well without him.

Although, maybe she should use tonight to work on taking Jewel's advice. She wasn't certain about her blow job skills. Sex hadn't been something Greg had wanted much of and he'd been her only sexual partner.

Duke escorted her over to her place, making her wait while he checked the house over.

"Make sure you get your hairbrush," he told her.

She found a bag and packed up her pajamas, a spare set of clothing, her hairbrush and other toiletries. Lastly, she grabbed Moody.

"Ink's guys are coming tomorrow to put a security system into your place."

He settled his hand on the small of her back as they walked to his house. He unlocked the door and turned off the alarm.

"All right," she told him.

"No argument?" He sounded surprised.

"Would it make any difference if I did?" she asked dryly.

"Nope. Put your stuff away, I'm going to run you a bath, I want to make sure you really weren't injured."

"I'm fine, Duke."

He ran his hand over his face. "Yeah, well, I need to make sure of it myself. Won't be able to sleep until I do. I need to take care of you tonight, Sunny. All right? Tomorrow, we'll deal with your punishment."

Well, that was something to look forward to.

She put her stuff in the bedroom and grabbed her toiletries, taking them into the bathroom as he ran her a bath.

"Right, little rebel. Let's get you undressed." He reached for her clothing.

"I can do that myself."

"Little girls don't undress or bathe themselves. They could slip and drown or hurt themselves," he explained.

"Oh, umm." This was the first time Duke would see her naked, even though he'd showered her, she'd still had her underwear on and she'd been kind of out of it.

He grabbed hold of her chin tilting her face up. "If you can't do this, I'll leave you alone. But I'd really like to take care of you. I need my little rebel right now."

No way could she say no to a request like that.

She took a deep breath and let it out slowly.

"Don't you have any bubbles, Daddy?" she asked, looking down at the plain bath. "And what about toys?"

He tugged off her sweatshirt then reached for her T-shirt. She had to work hard not to be embarrassed about standing there just in her bra. Her Little and adult sides warred against each other as he reached for her jeans. This wasn't quite how she envisioned him seeing her naked for the first time.

"I'm afraid I don't. I seem to be very underprepared for having a baby girl to take care of."

"You could use some stuff from the kitchen as toys," she suggested.

"Good idea." He pointed at the toilet. "Go potty and I'll go grab some things. Do not get in the bath."

Go potty? Eek. He didn't just say that, did he? But she did need to go. She was just finishing up when he returned and blushed bright red as he walked in. But he didn't say a thing, just moved to the bath as she washed her hands. She left off her pants but kept her panties on, not quite ready to strip completely.

He dropped some things in the bath then crouched in front of her. Taking hold of her panties, he started pushing them down her legs. Sugar. She was so glad she'd shaved this morning. Everywhere.

"Hold onto my shoulders to step out of them," he instructed. He tossed her panties onto her pile of clothes then stood and reached around to undo her bra.

Wow. He was quick. She wondered how many times he'd done that. Then all thought fled as he whipped off his T-shirt. Oh God, he was gorgeous. She vaguely remembered seeing him without his shirt on that night he'd taken care of her. But seeing it now, with a clear head, she could really appreciate it.

He swung around to turn off the tap and she got a good look at his back. Yum. She reached out and ran her fingers over his tattoo.

"This is amazing." His entire back was covered. It started with an eagle at his shoulders, its huge wings expanding out. It looked so realistic, like it was going to fly straight towards her. But under the eagle was a woman looking up to it and rays of light shone down on her face.

It was gorgeous. Beautiful.

He turned and cupped her face between his hands, lightly kissing her forehead. "Thank you." He lifted her into the bath. His strength made her breath catch. He settled her on her bottom and knelt beside her. He'd already put some plastic cups, a sieve and whisk into the bath. Her toys, she guessed.

"Do you need your hair washed?"

"Yes, please. If you don't mind. I left my shampoo and conditioner in the shower." He rose and got them. Then he untied her hair and reached for one of the cups.

She picked up a sieve and started to play. He ran the cup of water over her head and she let out a small cry. "Daddy!" She wiped at her face, blinking her eyes.

"Don't like water in your face?"

"No," she sulked.

"Look up at the ceiling." She pushed her head back as he used his hand to keep the water from going in her face.

He worked shampoo into her hair, massaging her scalp and she let out a sigh of pleasure, feeling herself relax. He rinsed out the shampoo and she played with the toys again. By the time he'd finished washing her hair, she was too busy playing to worry about being naked in front of him.

He didn't speak as he washed her back, inspecting every inch of her for injury. He lightly rubbed her shoulders and she let out a murmur of pleasure.

"One arm out, baby girl."

She gave him one arm at a time to wash then he moved the cloth over the front of her body.

"Daddy, you're in the way," she complained.

"Enjoying yourself are you, baby girl?"

"Yep. I'm going to whisk up all the water." She poked out her tongue as she concentrated on using the whisk. Then he ran the cloth over one breast and she sucked in a breath as it crossed her nipple, sending a spark of pleasure through her blood.

"Just keep playing. Pretend I'm not here," he murmured.

Yeah. That was pretty impossible. But she didn't look at him as he washed her other breast, all too aware of the flush of arousal on her face. He moved down her tummy, towards her pussy. She bit down on her lower lip, but he slid the cloth down one leg to her foot, pulling it slightly out of the water to wash between her toes.

She giggled at the sensation.

"Someone has ticklish feet." He ran a finger along the sole of her foot.

"Daddy!" She kicked out, trying to loosen his hold, and ended up splashing water into his face. She burst into giggles before placing her hand over her mouth, worried he'd be upset.

But he just wiped his face and grinned at her. "Knew taking off my shirt would be a good idea."

"Sorry, Daddy, but you did tickle me."

He nodded. "Serves me right."

She smiled at him.

"Right, baby girl. Stand up so I can wash your pussy and bottom."

"What?" she asked, gaping at him.

"Stand up and I'll finish washing you."

"I can do that." She reached for the cloth.

"Nope. Daddy's job." He pulled the cloth away and raised his eyebrows at her.

Oh. Heck.

He stood and held out his hand and she took it, letting him help her stand up.

"Legs apart, baby girl. That's it. We need to make sure you're all nice and clean." He wiped the cloth between her folds, pulling the lips of her pussy apart.

She looked up at the ceiling, holding onto his shoulders for balance.

"Now, turn around and bend over and grasp hold of the side of the tub."

She let out a small whimper.

"Good girl, come on now. I don't want you getting cold."

She shuffled around and grabbed hold of the lip of the bath. Oh sugar. She couldn't believe she was doing this.

"Widen those legs. That's it. Good girl." He washed each cheek. Then spread her cheeks and wiped the cloth between, rubbing it over her puckered entrance before he pushed it slightly into her bottom hole.

"Daddy!"

"Shh. Just making sure you're all clean." His voice was husky. With desire? Her body was heated, arousal coursing through her.

Was she brave enough to suggest taking things further tonight?

"You can stand back up, baby girl." He held her steady then lifted her out of the bath and wrapped a towel around her. He dried her before wrapping her in a dry towel. He picked her up in his arms and carried her out to the living room.

She smiled. She loved the feeling of being picked up and held. It made her feel so small, so cared for. He set her down on the sofa before leaving and returning with her hairbrush. He put a cushion down on the floor.

"Let's get this hair dry and get you into bed," he said as she sat between his legs and he started brushing out her hair. She leaned her face against his leg as he patiently combed out the knots, gradually she relaxed, her mind drifting.

"Come on, baby girl. Sleep time."

She let out a murmur of protest. She didn't want to move. But she should have realized she didn't have to. He picked her up in his arms and carried her to the bedroom. He dressed her in her pajamas.

"Where's Moody gone?" he asked her once she was in all tucked up in his bed. It was so much comfier than her bed.

"He's in my bag."

"Poor monkey, he won't be able to breathe,"

He handed her stuffed monkey over and she held him tight,

closing her eyes with a yawn. Duke sat next to her, rubbing her back with gentle strokes. "Good girl, off to sleep you go. That's it. Just relax. Here, suck your thumb if you need to." He took hold of her hand, raising her thumb to her mouth. She latched on and drifted off to sleep.

The knife glinted as it was raised into the air. It was coming towards her. The dark face glared at her.

He was going to hurt her.

She opened her mouth but no noise came out. She was going to die. The knife started to slowly descend. She tried to fight but she was frozen, locked in place.

She couldn't move. She was going to die and she couldn't fight back.. .couldn't scream...

"Wake up! Sunny, wake up!"

She opened her eyes with a gasp to find herself sitting in someone's lap. A soft light shone in the room. She shook, sweat coating her skin. The scent of leather and man surrounded her.

Duke. She was safe with Duke.

"Fuck, baby. Fuck." He kissed the top of her head, holding onto her tight as he rocked her back and forth. "I woke up to you thrashing around and then you let out this scream that made my blood go cold. Christ. Fuck. Scared the shit out of me."

"Sorry. Sorry," she muttered as she grasped hold of Duke. "I was frozen in my dream. I couldn't make a sound and the knife was coming towards me." She gulped back a sob. "There was no face, just this dark, gaping hole. It was terrifying."

"It's all right. You're safe. I have you. I'm not going to let anything happen to you." He held her for a long time, murmuring soft words to her that she could barely make out, but still soothed her.

"Thirsty," she muttered.

He picked up of a bottle of water. She reached for it, but he held it to her mouth himself, sliding her back a little so she was reclined. She was too tired to protest; she just took a few sips as he held her like a baby having a bottle.

Finally, she pulled away from him, feeling slightly embarrassed. "I've got to go to the bathroom. I need a shower."

"It's still early, you should go back to sleep."

She shook her head. "I don't think I can."

"All right, baby girl. You go shower and I'll make us some pancakes for breakfast." He tilted up her chin. "You're safe with me, Sunny. I know I didn't protect you yesterday but that won't happen again."

"It wasn't your fault."

Determination filled his face. "It won't happen again."

17

She settled on the couch after eating the pancakes and drinking several cups of coffee. Duke walked into the living room, carrying her hairbrush.

Was he going to brush her hair? His face looked awfully serious as he studied her. And then he switched off the television.

Uh-oh.

"How you feeling, little rebel?"

She sat up straight. "I'm all right."

"Sore? Anything hurt from yesterday?"

She shook her head. "You inspected every inch of me. I'm not even bruised."

He nodded solemnly. "You remember the punishment you're owed?"

She froze then turned to stare at him. "P-punishment?"

He raised his hand up and started ticking things off with his fingers. "You threw a tantrum over getting the stock order wrong. Called yourself names. Ran at the man with a knife rather than away from him."

"I didn't know he had a knife," she muttered.

"You knew he had something he was using to scratch up my truck. You should have turned back and run to me. If Marv hadn't been there. . ." he trailed off, looking ill.

"Yeah, I know," she whispered.

"Like I've said before, babe. Your safety, number one priority to me. You risk it, you'll wish you hadn't once I get my hands on your butt."

Oh. Awesome.

"Okay, little rebel?"

"Not really."

He leaned his elbows on his legs as he studied her. "Come here." He crooked a finger at her and she moved closer until she was standing between his open thighs. He reached around and grasped hold of her ass. "You nervous?"

She let out a small laugh. "You could say that."

"Scared?"

"A little."

He nodded. "Only expected. You know I'd never harm you, right? This is the sort of dynamic I need. With me setting the rules and enforcing them. I realize that now more than ever. I love being an indulgent Daddy. But I also need to be a stern one too. Because if I let you get away with things all the time, then I'm not fulfilling one of my primary jobs. To keep you safe. To make you feel secure."

"I get it," she whispered.

"But in saying that, there is never a circumstance where you can't use your safeword, got me? I'll stop immediately. You trust me?"

A sense of calm came over her. She knew he would stop if she used her safeword. And he would never harm her. She knew the rules. She'd broken them. And after hearing about his family, she knew he was always going to be overprotective; she'd never had that before and she craved it. Needed it. He just sat there silently, massaging her ass as she thought this through.

"I understand. I know I broke the rules. I deserve a spanking."

"Won't just be my hand," he warned her. "It was gonna be when it was only about our conversation in my office, but when you raced at that guy without a thought to your safety. . .well, I need to make sure you don't do that again, Sunny."

"What does that mean?"

"It means, you're getting twenty with my hand. Ten for calling yourself names. Ten for the little tantrum, cute as it was."

She had to bite her lip at that.

"Then you're getting fifteen with the hairbrush for rushing that guy."

"Fifteen!" She gaped at him.

"Yes, and it would be more if this wasn't your first serious spanking."

More. Jesus. Christ.

He sat and patted his lap. "All right, little rebel. Lay yourself over my knee."

"O-okay." Anticipation and nerves warred inside her as she took hold of his hand and let him help her lie across his lap. He adjusted her so her feet hung in the air, her hands able to touch the floor.

"Do you need me to hold your hands for you?"

"No."

"No, Daddy."

"No, Daddy."

"That's my girl," he said warmly, soothing some of those nerves. Then he grabbed hold of her pajama bottoms, pulling them and her panties down over her ass in one push, baring her completely. She yelped, not expecting that. She thought he might spank her over her panties again.

Without a moment's hesitation, he laid his hand firmly on her lower back and started to pelt her ass with stinging smacks of his hand. Ouch! This was far harder than the other spanking he'd given her.

Her ass was starting to burn as he paused and rubbed the heat in with his hand.

"How are you doing, little rebel?"

Well, she was starting to wonder how the hell she was going to take another ten from his paddle of a hand then fifteen with the hairbrush but other than that, awesome.

"I'm okay."

"You need to use your safeword?"

"No, Daddy."

"Here's the rest, little rebel. You're doing well." Those three words were what she needed to hear. Especially as his hand laid smack after smack on her already warm cheeks. The sting moved to a deeper burn, her ass throbbing as she started to sob, tears dripping down her cheeks.

When he paused this time, he rubbed her lower back instead of her bottom.

"Baby girl, I don't ever want to hear you calling yourself an idiot or a fuckup again, understand me? None of it is true and it hurts me that you are so hard on yourself. You need to learn that it's all right to mess up."

"I. . .I know. I'll try," she sobbed.

"Good girl. Now, I know this next bit is going to be hard for you. I'm sorry I have to give you such a hard spanking. But I want you to know how important it is to me that you're safe. If something had happened to you. . .if he'd stabbed you. . ."

She tried to turn to look at him but couldn't manage it in her current position. He sounded almost broken.

"I promise I'll be more careful. I didn't think. I promise."

"Good. Hopefully this will help remind you."

He reached over, to grab the hairbrush. She sucked in a breath then let out a squeal as it landed with a thump.

Oh. Sugar. Sugar. Sugar.

Her breath sobbed out as another smack landed.

Shoot. Darn. Shiiiit!

Two more landed. She sobbed. Tears raced down her face as she wiggled, trying desperately to free herself of his hold. She couldn't stand it. She couldn't take it.

Smack! Smack! Her ass was burning. A deep, fiery pain.

Another two. She grasped hold of his leg, using him as an anchor.

Smack! Smack! Smack!

Her sobs grew louder. Her legs kicked back and forth. No. No. No.

The last smacks landed quickly and sharply as though he was trying to get them over with as quickly as possible. She could barely take in the breath to scream. When the last one landed, she let out a huge screech.

Sobs had her heaving for breath as he pulled her up. He lay on his back on the sofa, arranging her on top of him, her ass still bare. It was so hot and painful she knew she couldn't stand to have anything touch it.

He just held her, murmuring to her quietly as he ran his hand up and down her back.

"Good girl. You're such a good girl. Let it all out. That's my girl. That's it. I have you. I have you, baby girl."

He just held her as her tears soaked his T-shirt.

"Shh. Now. You'll make yourself sick. Shh. You're safe. I have you."

Her tears slowed and she sniffed then moved her head up to look around. "Tissue?"

He brushed her hair back from her face and laid a kiss on her sweaty forehead. She grimaced. Hadn't been much point in showering before her spanking, it seemed.

He laid her back on her side then got up, leaving the room. He returned a minute later with some tissues and a wet cloth in his hand. She reached for them, but he drew them back.

"Let me," he said gruffly. He held the tissue to her nose. "Blow."

"Jeez," she muttered. "I can blow my own nose."

"Sunshine River, stop grumbling and let me take care of you."

"Yes, Daddy," she replied. She blew her nose, letting him wipe it. Gross. Then he washed her face with the cloth and that felt really nice.

"Want your pajama bottoms pulled up?"

Huh? She looked down at herself then went bright red as she saw her pajama bottoms were still down around her thighs and her top wasn't long enough to cover her pussy.

"Eek!" She pulled the bottoms up, wincing.

"Why don't you leave them off?" he suggested. "I'll give you one of my T-shirts to wear."

She nodded gratefully and he left, returning with a large T-shirt. She quickly put it on over her own T-shirt. When she was done, he drew her against his chest and kissed the top of her head.

"I'm really proud of you."

"For getting spanked?"

He smiled. "No. For being brave enough to acknowledge what you need. You trust me. It's not something I will ever betray."

It was funny, she'd just been spanked until she'd sobbed and she knew she wouldn't sit comfortable tomorrow. And yet she felt lighter, freer, happier than she had in a long, long time.

"Ouch, Daddy. Can't we stand while you do this?" she complained, sitting between his legs as he brushed her hair. After that spanking, sitting on her bottom was not pleasant. She rubbed at her eyes. Shoot. Her early morning wake-up was going to make today hard.

"Part of being punished is having to sit on your sore bottom. Helps remind you to behave."

Well, that just sounded like a stupid rule to her. She shifted around on her bottom. Even the cushion he'd put on the floor for her to sit on wasn't helping.

"Sit still, little rebel. I'm trying to get these pigtails straight."

She heaved a sigh and tried to sit as still as possible as he finished doing her hair. She jumped to her feet as soon as he declared he was done. But before she could move away, he wrapped his hands around her hips.

"Let's have a look at how bad this bottom is."

Uh-oh. She hadn't expected that.

"It's fine," she said hastily.

"Really? All that complaining and now it's fine?" he drawled.

She didn't do that much complaining, had she? Sugar. Maybe she had.

"It's all good now that I'm standing."

"Let me see it, Sunny. I need to know that I didn't go too hard on you." His voice was serious and she turned her head to look down at him.

"It's fine, Daddy. I promise."

He shook his head. "T-shirt up, panties down and bend over."

Her mouth dropped open in shock. He couldn't be serious! "I can't do that!"

He gave her a firm look. "Now, Sunshine River."

Damn it. She hated when he used her full name. With a pout, she turned back around and pulled up her T-shirt.

"Panties too."

She groaned, but wiggled her panties down.

"Now bend over."

"Daddy," she whined.

"There's nothing for you to be ashamed of, baby girl. All of you is beautiful. And there isn't anything you should keep from me. I want to know all of you, inside and outside."

She sucked in a deep breath. Fine. But if he was disappointed in any part of her, he better not come complaining.

She bent over. This was so embarrassing.

"Still a little red, but not so bad." He ran his fingers lightly over her bottom. "Gonna be a little sore to sit on today, but that's a good reminder."

Wow, he was all heart.

"It is missing something, though," he mused.

"What?" She stood up and turned her head to look at him.

"Bend back down, little one. You can just stay in that position and think about why you were punished this morning." He left the room.

Crap. Sugar. Shoot.

This was worse than standing in the corner and that was bad enough.

"Right, kick off your panties then turn and place your hands on the seat of the sofa for balance and spread your legs wide."

What was he doing? What the hell was going on? She turned to look at him, her eyes widening in shock as she took in what he now held.

Was that a butt plug?

"Um, Daddy?"

"You said you were open to anal play, has that limit changed?" he asked.

She shook her head.

"Words, little one."

"No, Daddy."

"Then do as you were told," he said sternly. "You're going to wear this plug while watching cartoons this morning as a little reminder. Not that I should be letting you watch cartoons."

Her jaw dropped. "No cartoons! You can't do that."

"Keep protesting and see what happens."

Jeez, he'd woken up a real grumpy pants this morning. She mumbled under her breath as she turned and got into position.

"Spread your bottom cheeks for me, I want to see that naughty bottom hole."

Oh, he was kidding, right?

"Little rebel," he warned.

Sugar. Crap.

She let out a deep breath, dying of embarrassment as she reached back and parted her bottom cheeks.

"Good girl. That's very pretty. I need to get you into this position more often." He ran a cool, wet finger down over her asshole. He'd obviously put lube on his finger. He started to probe her back hole with his finger and she groaned. Fuck. Her clit throbbed. Who knew this would be such a turn on?

Then his finger pressed inside her.

Oh. Oh!

He moved his finger back and forth. "Such a good girl, taking my finger in your bottom. That's a good girl. Just relax. Well done, you're doing so well."

She loved when he called her a good girl. Better yet when he called her his girl.

She was his. He was hers.

It hit her sometimes, just how much her life had changed in a few short weeks. But like Jewel said, she could decide to embrace it or fight it.

She was going to embrace it.

His finger slid free of her bottom.

"Take in a nice, deep breath. That's it, little one. Now breathe out as I push the plug inside." She let her breath out as something firm and cool pushed against her back hole. "You can let go of your bottom now."

She moved her hands back to the cushions of the sofa, grateful for the added support as he slowly and carefully pushed the plug inside her.

"My good girl. Doing just what Daddy requires from her. There it is, sitting nice and deep in your bottom. This one is slim; we'll work you up to bigger ones."

Holy shit.

He slipped an arm around her waist. "You can stand up now, baby girl."

She stood and he pulled her back so she was leaning against him. Her head spun a little and she was grateful for the added support.

Duke kissed her neck. "That's my brave girl. Well done. You took that beautifully."

"I. . .I need to put my panties back on. How long do I have to wear it for?"

"Until I say otherwise and there's no panties while you have the plug in."

"What? Why?"

"Because I want to be able to raise my T-shirt up over your ass and inspect you whenever I like. Panties will just get in my way."

Oh. Dear. Lord.

~

TWO HOURS LATER, the plug had been taken from her ass. A process that turned her on as much as it had when it was placed inside her. He'd also made her sit and write out everything that she did well. That had taken her longer than she liked to admit. Now she was dressed and searching for her phone.

"What you looking for, little rebel?" Duke asked, watching her search through the living room.

"My phone. I can't find it."

"You don't need it."

"I do. Jewel was going to text me about going shopping this weekend."

"You're not going."

She froze then turned to look at him. "Excuse me?" He hadn't just said that, had he?

"You're not going."

"Yes. I am."

He turned his head from the T.V. to give her a firm look. "No. You. Are. Not."

She tapped her foot against the floor. "Listen here, buster—"

He grinned. "Buster? Really?"

"Duke! You cannot stop me from going shopping with Jewel! It's not unsafe. I'm going."

"No."

"Yes! And stop being a. . .a. . .big old jerkface!"

His eyes widened and she suddenly realized what she was doing. Why was she arguing with him? What if he got annoyed with her and didn't want her anymore? So what if he didn't want her going out? It wasn't like staying with him was a hardship.

"I. . .I'm sorry," she said suddenly. "I won't go out if you don't want me to."

He frowned, studying her.

"Do you want me to do anything while I'm here? Housework? I could make us some dinner to take to work."

"Okay. Rewind."

"What?" She stared at him in confusion.

"We were having an argument and suddenly you turned into some timid, stepford wife. Let's go back to that argument."

"You want me to argue with you?" What was happening

right now?

"No. Cute as you are when you try to insult me, I don't like arguing with you."

"Then what are you trying to say?" Because she was confused as hell.

"I don't want to argue with you, little rebel. But I do want you to know that you can argue with me."

She rubbed her head. "I'm sure that makes sense in your mind."

"Why'd you stop the argument, Sunny?"

"Um, because I don't like arguing?"

"I'm sure that's true but that wasn't the reason you stopped." He came closer and grabbed her hips, tugging her towards him. "Why, Sunny? Tell me."

"I don't want to," she whispered.

"Why not?"

Her head was starting to really pound. "I don't want to tell you what I was thinking."

"But you're going to. Why did you stop, Sunny?" He ran his finger down the side of her face.

"Because I had the thought that if I argued with you then you might get sick of me. You might decide you didn't want me anymore," she blurted out.

His eyes grew dark. "I'm not Greg. I'm not going to get sick of you just because you call me out on my bullshit."

Her eyes widened. "You knew you were being unreasonable?"

He blew out a breath. "Newsflash, little rebel. I'm not perfect either."

"I know that," she muttered then covered her face with her hands as he chuckled. "Sorry, can't believe I just blurted that out."

"I like when you blurt things out, gives me an insight into what's going on in here." He tapped her head. "Need it so I'm not blundering around in the dark."

She'd always thought of herself as an open person, but then hadn't she always had secrets? About her homelife? About her real feelings and desires? Things she'd shut away from other people.

"I was being an asshole," he told her honestly. "And you had every right to call me out for it. I don't want you to be scared to argue with me, Sunny. If I'm being a dick, you can't let me bulldoze over you."

"So. . .why?"

He blew out a breath. "Why don't I want you to go out?"

"Yeah."

"Couple of reasons." He took hold of her hand and led her over to the recliner. He sat and pulled her onto his lap.

She loved being held like this. She felt so safe. He rubbed his hand up and down her back. "I'm feeling very protective of you today. More so than I usually do."

"Because of yesterday?"

"Yeah. You scared the shit out of me, Sunny. Then, with that nightmare this morning. . ." He let out a deep breath. "Knowing I wasn't there to help you. . .it fucking grates at me. I can't bear the thought of anything happening to you. You're fucking part of me. Get me?"

She nodded. She understood what he was saying because she felt the same. A knot of tension unraveled in her stomach that she hadn't even realized was there.

"I'm angry about yesterday, worried about you. Being around you helps me regain equilibrium. The more control I have the better. When you're in Little mode, I don't know how to explain it exactly. . .but when I'm looking after you, it relaxes me."

She'd never heard him talk like this. He was always just Duke. Indestructible, almost. Stoic. Calm. Smart. Nothing seemed to faze him.

But right at this moment, he seemed almost vulnerable.

He needs me.

She'd known it on some level. But this might be the first time she really got that he might just need her as much as she needed him.

"So what you're really saying is that spanking me is relaxing?" she teased.

"Yep," he replied with a wink.

"That doesn't bode well for my ability to sit down in the future," she muttered, shifting around on her still tender bottom. But something had shifted inside her. "I'll be here for you whenever you need me."

He tilted her chin up and kissed her lightly. "I know you will be. But you need a life beyond me. I guess."

She rolled her eyes then bit at her lip. "This is all very different for me too. I've never been in a relationship like this. But I've also never had a friend. I want to go out with her, Duke."

"And that's exactly what you'll do. Like I said, I was being a selfish ass. But. . ." he trailed off.

"There's something else, isn't there?"

Duke wasn't a jerk like Greg. Oh, he could be abrupt and grumpy and she was certain he could be selfish too. But this had been unusual for him. Even taking yesterday into account.

"Yeah. There is." He ran his hand up and down her hand lightly. "What I'm about to tell you only a few people know. Me, Reyes, Spike, Ink, Razor, and Jason. Basically, the inner circle at Iron Shadows. Those guys I trust with my life and more importantly, I'd trust them with yours."

He was lucky to have people in his life like that. She wished she could say the same.

"If anything ever happens to me, you go to them. They'll take care of you."

She twisted back away from him so she could see his face. "Why would anything happen to you? Duke, what's going on?"

He blew out a breath. "Didn't want to tell you this. But there's things in my life I'm not proud of. Many things I wouldn't want to ever touch you. That something I've done could hurt you makes me feel fucking furious and ill. I also guess, well, I like when you look at me like I can do anything. Like you think I'm everything."

"You can and you are," she whispered. "Whatever you have to tell me won't change that."

He tucked some hair behind her ear. "Baby girl, I definitely don't deserve you."

"That's where you're wrong. You are not a bad person, Duke. The way you look after me so thoroughly and ferociously is proof of that. You're loyal. Smart. Sometimes even kind."

"Don't go spreading that around," he grumbled but she saw the twinkle in his eyes.

"Just tell me. I promise it won't change how I look at you."

He let out a breath then nodded. "Our old club President, Smiley, was a real asshole. He got us messed up in all sorts of shady shit. And he had enough supporters to make life difficult for those of us who didn't want to get mixed up in drugs and protection." He grimaced. "Wasn't always able to get out of whatever shit he'd gotten the club messed up in and I did things I've tried to forget."

"It's okay, I get it."

"I did it because I had family in the club. I couldn't leave them and Smiley didn't let anyone leave." He looked slightly ill. She took his hand in hers.

"What happened?"

"Reyes joined our club, didn't like what he saw and started to rally those of us who were tired of Smiley around him."

"A coup?"

"Yeah. A bloody, messy one. But one Reyes won. However, Smiley left us with some of his fuck-ups. He got us mixed up with the Bartolli family, you heard of them?"

She shook her head.

"They're a crime family in Seattle with ties to Chicago. The head of the family, Fergus Bartolli had us doing some blackmail job for them. Turns out they'd been laundering some money through the club and they threatened Reyes to get us to do their dirty work. The blackmail was to do with a US Senator. Bartolli had photos of him with a very young girl. She was tied up, naked on his bed and she looked out of it, drugged."

"Oh God. You don't think she was there of her own free will?"

"It didn't look that way," he told her grimly. "And even if she was, she looked underage. This senator is married. He obviously didn't want these photos getting out and he paid the blackmail. To cut a story short, Bartolli is now dead and his hold on us is now gone."

"How did he die?" she asked worriedly.

"Not by my hand."

Relief filled her. Not that it would have changed how she felt about him and it sounded like Bartolli was a rotten man, but she didn't want that for him.

"But that still left us with the senator. If the girl in that photo was young, if she was there unwillingly. . ."

"Then you couldn't just leave it at that. I'm guessing you didn't go to the cops."

He smiled at her. "No, babe. Cops aren't someone we want sniffing around us."

She nodded. "So what have you been doing?"

"Watching the senator as much as we can. Trying to figure out who the girl is, if there's any more."

"And have you found out anything?" She thought it said a lot about them that they hadn't just wiped their hands clean of this.

"The girl in the photo turned up dead last weekend," he explained. "She was seventeen. A runaway."

"Oh God."

"We also caught one of his personal bodyguards meeting with

a pimp. Could be the guy who supplied the girl. Could be he's done it in the past too."

She felt queasy just thinking about it.

"Thing is, there's something else. We can't be certain that it's related to the senator, but it seems the most likely explanation."

"What else?"

"Remember the day I came home to find you mowing my grass?"

"Yeah, vaguely," she teased.

"Brat," he muttered. "Right, well, that day you remember getting my mail and accidentally ripping one of the envelopes?"

"Yeah, and you got all grouchy and accused me of opening it."

"Well, inside were some photos. Of me and the guys on surveillance of the senator."

She frowned. "Why would someone take photos of you watching the senator? And why send them to you?"

"That's what we want to know, baby girl."

"And you don't know who sent them?"

"That's where it gets a bit trickier. There was no note or anything, but on the back of one photo there was an image of a fox's head."

"What does that mean?"

"Well, there's been stories or rumors, whatever you want to call them, of an assassin who calls himself the Fox."

Her heart raced so fast she felt ill. "An assassin? That can't be true, right? Why would he send them to you? Why would he be involved?"

"That's what we don't know. It's got to be a warning to stay away from the senator."

"But you didn't?"

"No, we weren't willing to do that. We've tried to be more careful. To go in pairs. To keep well hidden."

"Has he sent any more warnings?" she asked.

"Yeah. That same image of a fox's head was spray-painted onto a wall at the compound. That was a few weeks ago and he's been silent since. He could have done what he was here to do and gone or he could be still around, waiting for something."

She swallowed heavily. "He knows where you live. He could come after you, hurt you."

"So far, he hasn't been violent. He hasn't done anything but try to warn us off. And we haven't had any warnings in a couple weeks. However, if he decides to act, I don't want you caught in the crossfire. And yesterday taught me that I can't watch you every second, much as I'm going to try."

She frowned. "But yesterday can't have been anything to do with the Fox. It was too random, right? He had no idea I would come out then. And that guy didn't strike me as a deadly assassin."

"I don't think that has anything to do with the senator or the Fox. But my protective instincts have gone into overdrive. I've also told Reyes I can't be on senator watch anymore."

She heaved a sigh of relief. "Good. Although I'm still worried about the other guys." She bit her lip. "But someone has to help those girls. Shoot. I don't want you to stop just because you're worried about me. I'll be much more careful, I promise. I won't go shopping with Jewel."

He ran a hand through her hair. "No, that's not fair. Not when I'm probably just being paranoid. But I'd feel better that if you want to go anywhere in the near future that you have either me or one of the guys with you. Madden would do as well. Not Rory."

No. Not Rory.

"I'm probably being overly cautious, but just let me stick someone on you when I'm not around. I need that after yesterday."

"Yes. Of course."

"Call Jewel. Arrange to go shopping tomorrow. I'll get someone to go with you. Jason would love to go shopping, I'm sure."

She rolled her eyes at that.

"Thank you, baby girl."

"What for?" she asked in surprise.

"For giving me peace of mind. For not telling me I'm a paranoid bastard."

"I'll just think it instead," she teases.

~

She was so tired that she could barely see straight. She poured herself another cup of coffee, knowing she was going to need it to get through the afternoon.

"Hey, babe, pour me one too, will you?"

She glanced over at Duke, noticing he looked tired as well. Guilt filled her. "I'm sorry I woke you up so early this morning."

She brought him his coffee and he took both cups from her, putting them on the small table in the break room. "I'm not. I'm glad you were in my bed and not alone." He tugged her close, hugging her. She leaned into him, taking in his scent.

"Me too."

A throat clearing had her trying to pull back. But Duke held her close.

"Rory. You're late."

"Doesn't look like you're all doing much work anyway," Rory sneered. He slammed his locker door shut and left.

Duke sighed. "That asshole is on his last legs."

She didn't say anything, just drew away and picked up her coffee.

"I've got a client coming in soon," he told her. "Don't drink too much coffee."

She snorted after he left. Right now it felt like caffeine was the only thing keeping her upright.

18

Sunny groaned silently, rubbing her sore stomach as she yawned. She was tempted to have another coffee, but it felt like the caffeine was eating her stomach lining. Her hand shook as she filled up a glass of water. She should probably eat but she felt slightly nauseous.

Duke had been with his last client for the past two hours. This client had been in each week for the last three weeks. Today they were finishing off a large tattoo on his back. Today was pretty quiet, a few regular clients with longer bookings so there wasn't much for her to do.

She yawned again, her eyes watering. Crap. She needed more coffee. Her stomach would just have to cope. She poured a cup and then sat at the table with a slump. Her hand shook as she took a sip.

Sugar. She couldn't wait for bed tonight.

"Hey, little rebel," a deep voice said and she sat up with a smile. Whoops. Even though he was her boyfriend, he was still her boss and seeing her sitting around looking half-dead probably wasn't a great look.

"Finished with your client? I'll go rebook them. Sorry, was just having a short break."

He waved his hand. "It's okay. All dealt with."

"I'm sorry. I thought you'd be with them a bit longer." Now she really felt like shit.

"Sunny, it's fine," he said firmly with a frown. "I'm more worried about you. You feeling well? You look pale."

He came closer and placed the back of his hand on her forehead. She had to resist the urge to lean into him and close her eyes.

"I'm fine. Nothing another cup of coffee won't fix." She forced a bright smile on her face. He didn't look fooled. He watched as she reached out a shaky hand for the cup.

He plucked it from her hand before she could take a sip. "Just how many coffees have you had today?"

"I don't know. Seven? Eight?"

"Okay, little rebel. You can consider yourself cut off."

What? They were open for another two hours! She wouldn't get by without coffee.

"Hey, you can't do that!" she protested, getting to her feet as he poured the coffee down the sink.

"Just did."

"Duke!" She scowled up at him.

"Babe, you're shaking because you're on caffeine overload. You're pale as hell and you've got dark smudges under your eyes. You've barely eaten today so I'm guessing your tummy doesn't feel great, huh?"

"I'm fine." She reached around to grab for the coffee pot once more.

He gave her a sharp smack on the ass. She gasped and looked around. "Duke!"

Grasping hold of her hand, he led her towards his office.

"What are you doing? I need to get back out front. I have work to do."

"Today is quiet. All our clients are regulars. We can handle any walk-ins." He led her into the office and shut the door behind him.

He pointed at the sofa. "Sit down. I'm going to go get you some water and something to eat. Then you're going to take a nap."

"I'm working."

He rested his hand on her hips. "And I'm the boss."

"You can't pay me to sleep!"

"I can do what I like, baby girl. And frankly, I'm far more worried about your health than what it is I'm paying you to do. So either you get something healthy in your belly and have a sleep or I'm going to reschedule my next client then take you home and put you to bed for the rest of the day."

He'd do it too. She could see the determination on his face. She huffed out a breath. "Okay, fine."

"Seems someone gets a bit grouchy when she doesn't get enough sleep, huh?" He turned and left before she could snap back at him.

With a groan, she sat. Who was she kidding? He was right. She needed plenty of sleep, it was just the way she was. And her head was thumping, her tummy bubbling with nausea which was a combination of fatigue, caffeine-overload and lack of food.

"I'm sorry," she said as soon as he came back.

He gave her a surprised look. "For what, baby girl?"

"You're just trying to take care of me and I'm being ungrateful and grouchy."

He sat next to her on the sofa and handed her a bottle of water and an egg salad sandwich he must have popped next door to get.

She attempted to unwrap the sandwich, her hands fumbling. He grabbed it from her and took off the wrapping but instead of handing it back to her, he held it up to her mouth.

"It's okay, baby girl," he told her. "I can tell you're not feeling so great. You're tired and out of sorts."

She swallowed her mouthful and took a drink of water. "I've always needed at least nine hours of sleep at night to function."

He held up the sandwich and she took another bite. It was starting to settle her stomach, but her headache was getting worse.

"Which means that you really do need a nap."

She rubbed her forehead. "I think if I take some painkillers, I'll be good."

"No, little rebel. You're having that nap. This is nonnegotiable. Daddy's putting his foot down."

"His foot?" She stared at him in surprise. He fed her another bite.

"Yep."

"Is this like your counting?"

"The foot is much more serious. The foot must be obeyed or there are dire consequences."

"Sounds ominous." She smiled.

"Oh, it is. Disobeying the foot means that you end up standing in the corner with a very sore, red bottom on display. Now, finish eating that while I get you some painkillers for that headache. Do you need to go to the toilet?"

She nodded and finished off the sandwich before using the bathroom. When she came back, he held out two painkillers and the water for her. Then he led her to the couch. He'd placed a pillow and blanket on the sofa. He helped settle her then gently massaged the back of her neck as she yawned and closed her eyes.

He moved his hand lower to pat her bottom. "Sleep, baby girl. I don't want you moving from here until I come back, understand me?"

"Yes, Daddy."

"That's my good girl."

~

DUKE WALKED into the office and stared down at a sleeping Sunny. She looked so peaceful. He was glad she was managing to sleep without nightmares. When she'd woken him up screaming this morning, he'd nearly gone for his gun, thinking she was being attacked.

He fucking hated that she was having nightmares because of what happened yesterday. He breathed in deep and let it out slowly, trying to ease the knot in his gut.

She mumbled as she moved onto her back, wincing slightly. Damn. Maybe he shouldn't have spanked her this morning after she'd just had a bad dream. He ran his fingers though his hair as he moved to the sofa and gently lifted her shoulders up then turned himself so her back was resting against his chest, his arm secure around her.

He picked up the water bottle she'd barely sipped from. He needed to take better care of her. She'd drunk far too much caffeine today and not eaten enough. She was exhausted.

He loved being both her man and her Daddy. He fucking loved. . .her. He loved Sunny. Couldn't imagine his life without her. Leaning in, he kissed the top of her head. It was nearly time to go home and he hated having to wake her up but she'd rest better at home.

Time to step up and really take care of her. He lifted the bottle of water to her lips.

"Have a drink, baby girl," he whispered quietly. He pulled the blanket up around her. Then gently pushed the tip of the bottle into her mouth. She opened her mouth and started to suck.

"That's a good girl. I want you to drink all of this."

He enjoyed holding her like this when she was all sleepy. She sucked on the water for a while then he felt her stiffen and knew she was waking up. She tried to move her mouth away but he held her tight.

"Uh-uh, you're not getting up until all this water is gone, baby girl. Settle back. You're all right. I've got you."

And if he had his way, he'd never let her go.

She laid back and drank it all. He put it down and then drew her up so she was sitting on his lap.

"How you feeling, baby girl?" he asked, brushing her hair back.

"Better." She ran a hand over her face. "How long have I been asleep? What time is it?"

"Five-thirty."

"I slept for two hours?" She gaped up at him and tried to scramble off his lap but he held her still. "Why didn't you wake me?"

"Because you needed some sleep. You're exhausted."

"Shoot. I need to get back to work."

"Nope."

"Nope?"

"We're leaving a little early. Madden is going to close up. I just came to wake you up." He set her on her feet and stood, holding her until he was certain she was steady. "Go to the toilet while I get our stuff."

"I don't need to go."

He snorted. "And as soon as we start home you'll have to pee."

She blushed slightly but just nodded. He raised her chin up to lightly kiss her lips. Then he turned her and gave her a smack to the ass. She yelped and rubbed her bottom, glaring at him over her shoulder.

He just grinned. "Go."

He lifted her up into the truck, and she scooted along into the middle seat. He climbed in and shook his head at her. "Back in the other seat, little rebel."

She pouted. "But I want to sit next to you."

He tapped her nose. "And I want you to be safe. The middle seat is just a lap belt. Not safe enough. Scoot over. Now. Or you're gonna see a good use for a bench seat."

"Sex?"

He let out a surprised bark of laughter. "No, baby girl, our first time is not going to be on the bench seat of Spike's truck."

"This is Spike's truck?" She looked around, slightly surprised. She'd expected something all black and chrome from the surly man.

"Yeah. It's his baby. Don't think he'd appreciate us breaking it in like that. He'd have no objections to me putting you over my lap for not listening, though."

"You wouldn't!"

He just stared at her. Oh. He totally would. She slid back into the seat. He reached over and fastened the seat belt. She was feeling pretty good after her nap.

"Can we watch a movie tonight?"

"Figured I'd make us some dinner, you can get in your pajamas then go to bed straight after, little rebel."

Her jaw dropped open. "But that's so early!"

"You need to catch up on missed sleep."

"I had a two-hour nap!"

"Which is a good start. But you're still a little too pale for my liking. I want you in bed early."

"I'm fine, Daddy. I promise," she said softly.

"You're still going to bed early."

She sighed, knowing she wasn't going to win.

"What are we having for dinner?" she asked as they pulled into his driveway.

"I'll fix something for you. I want you to relax on the sofa."

He came around and opened her door, undoing the seat belt and lifting her out. But instead of setting her on her feet, he held her against him, his arm under her ass. She wrapped her legs around his waist.

"Daddy!" she squealed. A giggle escaped her as he shut the door. She turned her head, resting her face on his shoulder as he walked towards the house.

"Hello! Duke!"

Sunny stared over at where Paisley stood by Duke's mailbox. She was dressed in her usual work-out gear.

Duke half-turned. "Yeah? What do you want?"

"Duke," Sunny scolded.

"Oh, well, I just wanted to see if you wanted to come over for dinner tomorrow night. I'm making smoked salmon potato cakes over a crème fraiche mash."

Seriously? She was actually inviting him over to her place while he had Sunny in his arms?

"He's busy," Sunny told her.

"Well, I'm sure he'd like to decide that for himself," Paisley said in a snotty voice. "Duke, darling?"

Sunny rolled her eyes at the simpering tone.

Duke just turned and walked away.

"Duke? Aren't you going to reply?" Paisley called out.

"Sunny already gave you my answer," Duke called back. "I'm busy."

"A different night then?"

"He's busy every night," Sunny said with a grin. Not very nice of her, but then how many ridiculous fines had that woman given her?

Duke unlocked the door and then set her down to deal with the alarm before he drew her back into his arms. "Thank you, little rebel."

"For what?"

"For saving me. That woman has been trying to get at me ever since I moved in here." He gave an exaggerated shudder. "Could you imagine what she'd do to me if she got me in a room alone?"

She had to giggle. "I think you could defend yourself."

"I'm glad I never have to find out. Because I am most definitely busy every night." He cupped her face and kissed her sweetly. "And so are you."

Her heart raced as her insides danced.

"Now, let's get my little rebel into her pajamas so she can relax on the sofa while I make her dinner." He took hold of her hand and led her down to the bedroom.

He pulled a pair out that had a picture of a grouchy looking crab on them and the words, *Crabby in the morning.*

He silently helped her into her pajamas. Then he picked her up and walked into the living room, setting her on the couch. He turned the T.V. on to one of the shows she liked.

"Stay here on the couch." He tapped her nose and she wrinkled it at him, but settled in. Truthfully, she was still a little drained. She was watching one of her favorite shows when she became aware of the scent of smoke. She sniffed. What was that? Was something on fire?

The smoke alarm started blaring and she heard Duke swearing loudly from the kitchen. She jumped to her feet and raced into the kitchen, in time to see him open a window and throw a smoking pot out of it.

"What happened?" she yelled over the blaring smoke alarm. She rushed over to open other windows as he reached up to unscrew the alarm. The silence was a huge relief.

He grimaced. "Burnt the playdough."

"What?"

"I was trying to make playdough for you and I burned it. I don't have anything for your Little here and I found a recipe and it seemed so simple. Turns out, I'm—oomph!"

He wrapped his arms around her, managing to keep his balance as she slammed into him, wrapping her arms around her middle.

"Baby girl? You okay?"

"Yeah. . .I just. You were really making me playdough?"

"Yeah. Fucking failure that was."

"I don't care."

"Babe, that stuff is burnt to shit. You're not touching it."

"No, I mean, I don't care that I can't play with it. It's just. . .that was really sweet." She gazed up to him. "Thank you, Daddy."

"You're welcome, baby girl. Just do me a favor."

"What?"

"Do not tell anybody that just happened. Ink would never shut up about it."

She giggled. "Your secret's safe with me."

He sighed and shook his head. "Come on, let's get you back on the sofa."

"Can I stay here with you, Daddy? Please? I can help you cook dinner."

He nodded. "All right, but if I burn another fucking pot, we're ordering pizza." He set her down at the kitchen counter then picked up another bottle of water, putting it in front of her with a raised eyebrow.

"Yum, pizza. A vegetarian, tofu, no-cheese one?"

He just gaped at her. "You kidding me?"

She giggled. "Yep."

"Little brat." He grabbed a carrot from the fridge and started chopping it.

"Can I help? I can do that."

"You cannot. This knife is far too sharp for you." He placed some bits of carrot in front of her. "Nibble on those while I cook our feast of. . ." he drew out a box from the pantry. . . "Mac n' cheese. Can't fuck that up, can I?"

"Hmm, I'm really not sure about that, Daddy."

He pointed a finger at her. "Enough sass out of you, little one, or I'll get out my wooden spoon."

She just giggled.

19

Jason pulled up outside Duke's place.

"Pull into my driveway," she suggested, seeing all the vehicles already parked on the road. "I'm going to put this stuff away."

Duke had mentioned the guys were coming over while Jason took her and Jewel out shopping. She wasn't sure why Duke didn't come. She guessed he wanted to give her some space with her friend or something like that. They'd spent most of the day shopping. Her feet hurt. She was hungry, thirsty and she desperately had to pee.

"I'll get the bags," Jason rumbled. She guessed that he'd pulled the short straw having to come out with her today, but he hadn't moaned about it once. Today had been pretty awesome, even if she was exhausted. She searched for her keys in her bag. It was a pain not being able to keep them under one of her flower pots anymore.

Her bladder grew more insistent. There they were. She unlocked the door and sped through. "Make yourself at home! Bathroom break!"

When she came out of the bathroom, Jewel was searching through her kitchen cabinets while Jason stood by awkwardly.

"You got any booze in this place?" Jewel asked.

"No, sorry, I don't drink much."

"Seriously? Not even vodka? I mean, that's barely considered alcohol."

"It isn't?" she asked.

Jewel shrugged. "Sure. If you're Russian."

"You're Russian?"

"Nope." The other woman grinned then grasped hold of her arm. "Come on, let's get you ready. Jason left your packages in your room."

Sunny turned to him. "Thanks for coming today. Go over and grab a beer with the guys, you've earned it."

He shook his head. "I'll wait for you."

"Well, thanks." She followed Jewel into her bedroom. "He's a really nice guy, huh?"

Jewel grinned. "Nice, sure."

"You don't think he's nice?" She raised her eyebrows.

"Uh-huh, I think he's really nice."

"How come he doesn't have a nickname like the others? I didn't want to ask in case it was a sore point."

Jewel started laughing. "Jason is his nickname."

"That's a weird nickname." As they talked, she put her new clothes away and Jewel set out her new make-up. She couldn't believe she'd spent so much money. But everything Jewel had suggested seemed perfect and she'd been unable to resist. She had to go see Ronny tomorrow. She wasn't looking forward to it but he owed her that money.

"His real name is Pike."

"Pike? Seriously?"

"Yep."

Jewel drew out a denim skirt and this cute, pastel blue top that tied at the back with a bow and placed them on the bed. "I think you should wear these."

She nodded and pulled them on. She'd learned early into their shopping trip that Jewel didn't have any hang-ups about getting naked in front of her. Not that she should. The woman was built with curves in all the right places.

She dressed then sat while Jewel played with her make-up. "Just going to go light since you don't need much. Your skin is beautiful."

She blushed. Jewel wasn't afraid to hand out praise, but she did it in such a way that Sunny knew she spoke the truth.

"Perfect," Jewel proclaimed, stepping back to examine her. "You've got the lingerie ready?"

"Yep. Oh hell. What if I can't do it?"

"You can. Believe me, Duke already wants you. The lingerie is just like window dressing. It will give him the push he needs to get over this idea of taking it slow. Remember, blow jobs are king."

She had to duck her head. She wished she had a tenth of Jewel's confidence. She stood and took a look at herself in her full-length mirror, barely recognizing the woman who stared back. Jewel had convinced her to get a haircut, nothing major, the hair stylist had lightened it and put in layers so it felt lighter but it had more of a curl to it with the weight out and the highlights mixed in well with her own dark-blonde tones.

The make-up was subtle, but it made her eyes look bigger, her cheeks higher. The clothes were something she'd never dare wear before. The skirt was short and the top tight, yet it was totally her.

"I feel beautiful."

Jewel stepped up behind her. "You were always gorgeous, Sunny."

She nodded. "But now, I feel like me. Rather than trying to be someone that someone else wanted me to be. And I look. . .I look happy."

And that had nothing to do with her clothes.

Jewel winked. "You're gonna look even happier after you get yourself some."

"I hope so."

"You'll knock him dead, babe. Call me tomorrow and give me all the nasty details."

She blushed then turned to her friend. "You're going now?"

Jewel nodded. "Got a shift at the club."

"Thank you!" Sunny moved on instinct and wrapped her arms around her new friend. "I couldn't have done it without you."

Jewel was stiff for a moment then she wrapped her arms around Sunny, holding her tight. "Pleasure was all mine, babe."

~

INK LET OUT A LOW WHISTLE. "Damn, looking good, Sunny-girl."

Duke turned and felt his mouth drop open slightly. He placed his bottle of beer down, barely aware of it tipping over and Spike righting it.

Sunny walked up onto the deck, Jason behind her. She was dressed in a short skirt and tight top and her hair was flowing down her back. It looked lighter, curlier and her eyes seemed brighter.

The top stretched across her breasts and accentuated her small waist and those legs of hers. . .hell she wasn't that tall and yet they looked like they went on forever. He walked towards her, drawing her close, dipping his mouth to kiss her. His tongue slid inside her mouth and she wrapped her arms around his neck.

He heard a low whistle then remembered the boys. Not that he cared. In fact, it might be good if they all fucked off.

"Hey, baby."

"Hi," she said breathlessly, staring up at him with dazed eyes.

He drew back to look her over. "Looking fucking good, babe. But you always did."

She gave him a happy look. "I never liked my old clothes. They were old and too big for me. But I like these new outfits. I feel sexy."

"You look damn sexy, too, Sunny-girl," Ink commented.

Duke turned to glare at him as Sunny blushed.

"Isn't it time you assholes hit the road?" Duke told them all.

Ink grinned and leaned back in his chair. "I thought I'd have a drink and shoot the shit with Sunny."

Spike gave the other man a whack on the head. "Hey!" Ink rubbed at the spot.

"You thought wrong," Duke growled. "Go."

Ink sighed, but she saw the humor in his eyes as he stood and finished his beer. They all left quickly, calling out goodbye.

"I didn't mean to ruin your party."

"Wasn't a party, babe. Just a few drinks with the boys. And I'd rather be with you. You had a good time?"

"I really did. Although, I didn't realize how fit you needed to be to go shopping. My feet hurt."

"Come inside. I'll order in some dinner and rub your feet."

"Rub my feet? Are you serious?"

"Yep."

"How has no woman ever snapped you up?"

He smiled and kissed her. "Guess I was just waiting for you."

~

He gave foot massages.

She already knew she'd hit the lottery but that was just icing on the cake. She groaned as he rubbed a particularly sore spot. They'd ordered in some Chinese and while they were waiting, he massaged her feet.

Pure bliss.

"You got any plans for tomorrow?" Duke asked her, putting her feet down.

"Ah, yeah, unfortunately I've got to go and see my old boss."

"Why? You want your old job back?"

She was surprised by the question. "No, of course not. If I never saw Ronny again, I'd be happy."

He frowned. "Then why?"

"He hasn't paid me the hours he owes me and I need the money."

"That shithead hasn't paid you? Why didn't you say anything?"

She blinked. "Say something?"

He gave her a light shake. "Yeah, babe. Why didn't you say anything to me? Your boyfriend."

Her boyfriend. She smiled wide.

"What's with the Cheshire grin?"

"Did you just make an *Alice in Wonderland* reference?" she asked.

"Yeah. . .well. . .seems my girl has a thing for tea parties and white rabbits," he muttered.

"Did you read it?" she asked, delighted.

"It's not such a big deal, but. . .ahh hell wasn't going to show you this until tomorrow. Come on." He grasped hold of her hand and pulled her towards the spare bedroom. He opened the door and switched on the light. She gasped.

"Oh my God, when did you do this?" She stepped into the room and turned around, taking it all in.

He shrugged, looking slightly embarrassed. "Might have done it while you were out with Jewel today. The boys came to help me."

She paused at that and he walked forward to wrap his arm around her waist. "Don't worry, they'd never tease you about this. Razor's wife was a Little. Both Reyes and Ink are Daddy Doms. Spike is, well, Spike. He doesn't like labels."

She snorted out a laugh. "Spike doesn't like anything."

"So, you like it?"

"Like it? I love it." The walls were no longer white they'd been painted a pale green. There was a large white, fluffy rug that covered most of the plain brown carpet. The baseboards had been painted white. And covering all of one wall and half of the next wall was a scene from *Alice in Wonderland*. Alice was there. The rabbit, the Cheshire cat and the Mad Hatter were all there too. As she stared at it more, she could see more and more details. It was beautiful.

On another wall was a quote from the book,

Every adventure requires a first step.

The mustard-colored lamp shade had been replaced with a chandelier. There was also some white furniture. A gorgeous armoire and a desk and padded stool.

"This is truly amazing, but you can't have organized all of this," she stated.

His cheeks went slightly ruddy. Was he embarrassed?

"You need a playroom. This room was empty. You told me that *Alice in Wonderland* is your favorite story. So I ordered some things online and stored them until I got a chance to do all this."

Tears dripped down her face. Then she turned and flung herself into his arms. "This is the nicest thing anyone has ever done for me. I never had more than some free posters I got from the library to stick on my walls when I was growing up. This is. . .it's amazing. Thank you!"

He held her tight, lifting her up into his arms. "This isn't everything."

"What more could there be?" She pulled back to look up at him.

"Baby girl, you can't have a playroom without any toys."

"Toys?"

"Yes, baby, toys. I'm going to take you shopping tomorrow."

"You're taking me toy shopping?"

He raised an eyebrow. "You're saying you don't want toys to fill your playroom?"

"No, I do. I do. I just. . .we're going toy shopping." She smiled widely.

He snorted out a laugh. "I can see that makes you happy."

She hugged him tight. It did. Although she really did need that last paycheck from Ronny now. Toys didn't come cheap.

"I can hear you thinking from here." He carried her out into the hallway and down towards the living room. The doorbell rang and he left her there to get the Chinese. She picked up some forks and met him in the living room.

"I still need to see Ronny," she told him as she swallowed a mouthful of vegetarian chow mein.

"Nope."

"Duke, be reasonable. I need that money."

"Not saying you don't. But you're not going to see that asshole. Don't worry, I'll get it for you."

"It's my problem." She worried at her lower lip.

"You're not on your own anymore, baby girl. You've got someone in your corner. Someone who doesn't want you around assholes like that. Someone who can take some of that load off your shoulders."

"I just don't want to weigh you down."

"In case you haven't noticed, I've got big shoulders. I can take it."

She rolled her eyes. Although they were very, very nice shoulders. She reached over and grabbed the beer she'd asked him to get her. He'd given her a surprised look but hadn't said anything. She was trying for a bit of Dutch courage. Her new lingerie was stuffed in her handbag and she wasn't sure she was ready to get it out.

"I'm going to go have a shower," she said when they were finished eating. She left before he could say anything.

You can do this. You can do this.

She picked up her handbag and carried it into the bedroom, pulling out the teddy and locking herself in the bathroom. After her shower, she pulled on the deep blue silk teddy that had lace over her bottom and pussy with a slit over her lower lips.

It was the sexiest thing she'd ever owned in her life and she would never have had the courage to even buy it let alone wear it without Jewel's help.

She pulled it on and stepped out into the bedroom, immediately feeling self-conscious. She drew out one of Duke's T-shirts and slipped it over her head, covering up the teddy. Then she walked out into the living room.

Duke was sitting back on the corner of the sofa, watching T.V. She walked in front of him, watching his eyes move to her. He smiled. "Love the cute PJs, babe, but love you in my shirt more."

"And what do you think of this?" She tried for sultry, but she thought her voice sounded more timid than anything else. She drew off his T-shirt, revealing the teddy underneath and stood there, just watching him.

Nerves filled her when he just sat there, frozen. Then she dropped to her knees, wincing at the impact.

That could have been more graceful.

"Little rebel?" he asked.

"I don't want to go slow anymore, Duke. I want you." She pushed her hand up under his T-shirt, circling his nipple. She heard his breath catch as she ran her finger over the ridges of his abdomen. Then she moved her hand lower to place it over the button of his jeans. "Can I?"

His eyes had grown darker, his breathing coming quicker. "You sure?"

"I'm sure. I want this."

"Fuck yes." He sat forward and pulled off his shirt then patted his lap. "Get up here, babe. Let me see you."

"Actually, I wanted to taste you." She undid the button of his jeans then pulled down the zipper. "Please?"

"Take a stronger man than me to say no to feeling your lips around my cock." He raised his hips then shoved his jeans and boxers down, freeing his cock. He shoved them further down his legs, pulling them off until he was completely naked. But she barely noticed, she was too busy staring at his dick.

"Babe? You all right?"

"Greg had a tiny dick. Yours is like a bratwurst and his was a cocktail sausage."

Duke burst into laughter. "Can't say I've ever had my dick compared to a bratwurst before."

She went bright red. "Sorry, I'm not very good at this." She attempted to pull back, to slide away from him but he reached out and wrapped his hand in her hair.

"Uh-uh, babe. Wasn't laughing at you. I don't care what you compare my dick to, but maybe we should refrain from talking about Greg's package, huh?"

"Okay," she replied breathlessly as he reached out and lightly plucked her nipple.

"Damn, your tits are gorgeous. I have dreamed of sucking on these nipples."

"You have?"

"Oh, fuck yes. There isn't much I haven't dreamed of when it comes to you and then I would wake up with my dick hard and fucking aching. And believe me, my hand just isn't satisfying."

She rubbed her thighs together at the idea of him taking his cock in hand.

"You want to watch that?" he asked, cocking an eyebrow.

She nodded. "Is that weird?"

He huffed out a laugh. "Weirder than having my cock

compared to a bratwurst?" His eyes twinkled, taking any sting out of his words.

She groaned. "You'll never let me forget that, will you?"

He just smiled then he wrapped his hand around his dick and started to rub it up and down the length. Her entire body went still, her eyes riveted on the sight of him playing with his dick.

"Oh wow," she murmured.

"You like watching?" he asked.

"I've never. . .I've never seen anyone do that. . ." she trailed off awkwardly.

"Masturbate? Jack off? Beat the monkey?"

"Beat the monkey?" she grinned, knowing that was his intention. "That sounds sore. This looks. . .hot."

He let his cock go, and she let out a murmur of protest. He reached out and wrapped his hand around the back of her neck, drawing her up onto her knees so he could kiss her. "I promise, another night you can watch. But right now, I want to do other things."

So did she. She licked her lips. "I'm not very good at this, will you tell me what you like?"

"Fuck, babe. You have no idea what you do to me. Yeah, I'll fucking tell you. But basics are not to use your teeth and be careful with my balls."

She knew that much. She leaned down and wrapped her hand around the base of his shaft.

"Harder," he told her. "Nice and firm. That's it. Now take the head into your mouth."

A few weeks ago, she'd never have thought she would be kneeling between her next-door neighbor's legs, sucking his thick, gorgeous cock. She sighed happily then licked her tongue across the head of his dick before taking him inside her mouth.

"Oh hell. Fuck. Baby girl, you are killing me, suck on me. That's it. Now pull back. Hell yes." He wrapped his hand in her hair again, guiding her movements gently. "Good girl. Take me deep. Shit. Shit. Shit."

She looked up to see his jaw was clenched tight, his breath coming quick. Courage filled her and she reached up with her hand to lightly cup his balls. He groaned and she froze. Then she slid her mouth free of his dick. "Did I hurt you?"

"No, baby. Hell no. Don't stop."

She smiled as she returned to sucking him, very carefully playing with his balls. She loved the sounds that came from him, from knowing that she was giving him pleasure. It made her feel powerful.

"Babe, I'm going to come now. If you don't want to swallow, you need to pull back."

Hell no. She took him deep, loving the sound of him groaning. She swallowed him down. She licked her way up his still semi-hard shaft and placed a small kiss on the head of his dick. Then she sat back with a smile. "Did I do okay?"

He opened his eyes and stared down at her. "Any better and you'd kill me."

Her grin widened. "Thank you."

He raised his eyebrow. "Pretty sure it's meant to be me thanking you. Come here." He leaned down and picked her up, pulling her onto his lap so she was straddling him. He ran a finger over her breasts which were spilling over the top of her teddy.

"You buy any more of these?" he asked.

"No."

"We'll get you some more tomorrow."

"You like it then?"

His gaze narrowed. "You could say that."

"You haven't seen the best part, though."

"No?"

She grasped hold of his hand and guided it between her legs. His eyes flared open. "It's crotchless?"

She nodded.

"Fuck. Yes."

Suddenly, she found herself sitting on the sofa and Duke was on his knees on the floor between her spread legs. He pulled the material of the teddy away from her pussy.

"Now that is a fucking delicious sight." He glanced up at her. "Bare your breasts."

Her heart raced as she reached for the straps of the teddy, prepared to pull it down.

He shook his head. "No."

"No?"

"Pull them up over the top."

Oh. Hell. That was so much hotter. She reached in and pulled one globe out then the other.

"Offer one to me."

Offer it? She cupped a breast and held it up, hoping this was what he meant. His gaze was caught on her nipple. "Ask me to suckle."

Sugar.

She licked her dry lips. "Will you suckle?"

He shook his head. Had she done it wrong?

"Please, will you suck on my tit?"

Oh, dear Lord. She had to clear her throat, and still when she spoke it was little more than a whisper.

"Please, will you suck on my tit?"

A wicked glint entered his eyes and he leaned forward to lick her left nipple before breathing over it. Then he did the same to the right nipple. "I thought you'd never ask."

He circled her nipple with his mouth and sucked. Hard. Her eyes bugged open. Holy shit. It almost felt like he was sucking directly on her clit. She moaned. It was hot. Decadent. And she wanted more.

He ran his finger up and down her slit, circling her clit as he moved his mouth to her other nipple and latched on.

"Please, yes. Please!"

He left her nipples, kissing his way down her stomach and she had to hold onto the cushions beneath her so she didn't grab onto his head and pull his mouth back to her breasts. Then he sat back and grasped hold of her hips, tugging them to the edge of the sofa. Her head fell back against the sofa.

"Put your hands behind your head and keep them there. You move them and I stop, understand?"

"Yes."

"That's my girl. If you're a good girl you'll be rewarded. Eventually."

Hell. What did that even mean?

"Ohhh," she groaned as he kissed his way down to her pussy and spread her lips, circling her clit gently with his tongue.

"Move your hands into place," he warned and she hastily shoved her hands behind her head.

"Have you ever had to hold off an orgasm, Sunny?" he asked.

"I've never had an orgasm I didn't give myself."

"Mother fuckers," he muttered.

She stared down at him.

"Change of plan. Tonight, you can come as many times as you desire."

Did that mean other nights she wasn't going to be allowed to come? She didn't like the sound of that. Then again, she didn't think she could come more than once anyway.

"But you have to stay very, very still, understand me? You move and I will have to punish you." His voice was deep, dark, and a shiver raced over her. He grinned up at her. "You might like that, though."

What was happening to her?

"And to think I always thought you were just the girl next door.

How did I miss this dark fire lurking underneath that shy exterior?"

"Maybe it's because you're the only one who has brought it out."

"I like that." He ran a finger down her slit then pressed it deep inside her. "We're going to do some other toy shopping for you as well tomorrow," he told her as he pushed his finger in and out of her passage.

"What?" Why did he want to talk about shopping right now? She had to bite her lip against the urge to move her hips. While the idea of punishment might intrigue her, she didn't want him to stop. She was so close to orgasm; she could taste it.

"I'm thinking some more butt plugs. A vibrator. A glass dildo. Restraints. How sexy would you look wearing this, with your wrists attached to your ankles? I could just sit you on the sofa and watch the game and play with you to my heart's content."

He chose that moment to drop his mouth to her clit, sucking on the tight bundle of nerves before he flicked it firmly with his tongue. It shot her up and over the edge and she screamed with her release.

Oh God. Sooo good. So good. Like nothing she'd experienced before. Her mind whirled, she didn't even know if she was breathing. If he was talking, she couldn't hear him. She was lost to the pleasure, floating on a wave.

And when she came to, she found herself in his arms. He was carrying her towards the bedroom. He laid her down on the covers then straddled her on his hands and knees.

"Now that's the smile of a woman who has just experienced a fucking good orgasm."

"Oh, it was better than fucking good. It was spectacular."

He snorted out a laugh. "I think I'm corrupting you. Then again, since you're the one who bought crotchless lingerie, maybe you're corrupting me."

She had to laugh at the idea of her corrupting Duke. Then he dropped his mouth to her nipple again and she groaned. Felt so good.

"These breasts are fucking amazing. Christ. I don't think I could ever get enough. You're going to keep them bare in bed. In fact, from now on, you're sleeping naked unless you're ill."

She hitched a breath as he moved to her other nipple. His hands seized hold of her wrists, placing them above her head.

"What if I get cold?"

He raised his head, grinning down at her. "Baby, I will make it my job to ensure you don't get cold."

"Okay," she squeaked out.

"I want to be able to roll over in the night and latch on and taste you. To slide my dick inside you. Sometimes I'll let you come. If you've been naughty, though, I won't."

She pouted. "That doesn't sound very nice."

"Sometimes, I'm not very nice."

"That's not true. You're always nice to me."

"Fuck, you're going to kill my reputation as an asshole."

She grinned. "Does it help that I thought you were a complete asshole that day I tried to mow your lawn for you?"

He groaned. "No. Because I was a dick to you and I'm not proud of it."

"I promise, your secret is safe with me."

He kissed her. Hard. Fast. "I don't open up with many people, Sunny. Most people I interact with will probably tell you I'm a dick. But I'm always going to be sweet to you, because you mean everything to me. You're my whole world and I love you." He froze then met her gaze with his.

"I love you too," she told him.

Then his shoulders relaxed and he gave her a smile. "I didn't mean to tell you in quite that way."

"I don't know. I think that was kind of perfect."

He moved his mouth to her neck, kissing down it. "In the bedroom sometimes I'll make love to you. Other times I'm going to fuck you. Most of the time you won't be allowed to come until I give permission. And if you're being punished you might not be allowed to come at all. Think you can handle that?"

Could she handle it? How could she not? She loved him and this was part of what he needed.

"If it's what you need, I can handle anything."

He kissed her gently. "Fucking made for me."

Yeah. She really was.

"Still okay with me taking you bare?"

"Yes. God, yes." They'd already had this conversation. Greg always used condoms, even though she was on the pill to keep her periods regular. And Duke hadn't gone bareback since he was a teenager. Plus, he'd recently been tested. She knew he wouldn't risk harming her in any way.

He lowered his cock to her passage and pressed the head inside her. "Fuck. So tight. Christ, baby. Tell me if I hurt you."

"You won't hurt me."

"You remember, you always have your safeword. No matter what."

She trusted him. She loved him.

"Wrap your hands around the headboard. Don't let go."

She'd had no idea he could actually get bossier, but it seemed he could. He pressed his dick deep inside her and she threw her head back with a cry as he filled her.

So good.

"That's it, baby. Open for me. Let me inside you. Damn, you feel so fucking good wrapped around me. How the hell am I ever going to leave this when you feel like fucking heaven?"

She had no idea. Because she felt the same. He moved up his pace, thrusting deep inside her. Suddenly, he slid over a spot inside her and she cried out, clamping down around him.

"Fuck yes, baby."

"Please, more. More." She'd never felt this before.

"Don't you let go of that headboard," he warned. "I do not want to stop to fucking spank your ass."

She didn't want that either. Well, maybe another time that might be hot but not right now. His hips drove against her, his dick thick and hard inside her. His face was filled with heat then he lowered his mouth to hers, nipping on her lower lip.

Suddenly, he drew out of her.

"Noo," she cried.

"Let go."

She let go and he grasped hold of her hips flipping her. Then he smacked her ass. "On your knees, grab hold of the headboard again."

Oh God. This was so freaking hot. He grasped hold of her hips once more, settling in behind her as he drove in deep. She threw her head back with a cry and he wrapped her hair around his fist.

"Yes, baby. That's so damn good. Fuck. I'm gonna come. Touch yourself."

"What?"

"Touch your clit. You're coming with me."

"I can't!"

He froze. "I'm not moving until you touch your clit."

Her breath came in hard pants. No! "I won't be able to come again. I can't!"

"Trust me. Touch yourself." She slid her finger down to her clit and circled it gently. He started moving again, finding that spot inside her and it wasn't long until the orgasm roared through her, sending her floating with a cry as she pulsed around him. He continued to thrust inside her until with a yell he came.

She collapsed onto the bed with a sigh of satisfaction. He rolled to her side and reached up to disengage her hand from the headboard. Then he lay down on his back. "Come here, baby girl."

He pulled her onto his chest, so she was lying on top of him. He grabbed hold of her ass, massaging her bottom cheeks as they both caught their breath.

"You know that you were already mine, but that just cemented it. You're not leaving me. I'm not leaving you. I don't care what you need to make that real in your mind. A wedding ring, some sort of commitment, whatever you want, I'll do it. But as of right now, Sunshine River Bright, you are totally and utterly mine."

It was a totally Neanderthal statement and maybe if she'd had more energy, she would have told him that he better not think that that was in any way an acceptable wedding proposal, but she was still having trouble breathing. And her pussy kept contracting, sending little waves of pleasure though her blood.

"Mine, Sunshine. Forever."

Yeah. And maybe she didn't want to argue, because no matter what, she was most definitely his.

20

"We don't have to do this," she said as they walked into the huge toy department. He grabbed a cart. "And I don't think we need a cart."

Although since it was a Monday morning, the place was mostly empty. At least the adult toy shop had been closed and Duke had decided they'd buy them online. That might have pushed her over the edge.

"Yes, we do. Can't have a playroom without toys."

Well, he was right. And as she looked around, her excitement grew. How often did she get to go shopping for toys for herself with a hot man that had not only given her two orgasms last night but had woken her up this morning with his mouth between her legs and given her three more before taking her again?

She might be walking slightly funny this morning, but oh, it had been worth it.

Still, she didn't want him spending too much money on her.

"I want to pay for anything we get, though."

He came to a stop then looked down at her. Without even

looking around to see if anyone was near, he gave her a stern look. "Little girls don't pay for their toys."

"But. . ." she nibbled on her lip. "That doesn't seem very fair."

He drew her close and leaned in to whisper in her ear. "Everything doesn't need to be equal. There are so many things you do for me. You give me your submission, your trust, you cajole me out of my bad moods, you've made me smile more in these past few weeks than I have in all the years before. So if I want to take my little girl shopping and spoil her then I damn well will. Daddy's prerogative."

She grinned. "That's a rule, is it?"

"It is." He gave her a firm nod. "From now on, you have to let me spoil you without argument or trying to keep things damn well even, for fuck's sake, or your ass is toast."

Well, if he wanted to spoil her then who was she to argue?

"Okay, Daddy."

"Good girl."

For the next hour, they wandered through the toy aisles. She'd pick out a Barbie and he'd add two more. She chose the smallest doll's house and he swapped it for the biggest one in the shop, which was absolutely beautiful and also cost a freaking fortune.

"Ooh, Daddy, what about this?" She picked up a stuffed unicorn that was almost as big as her. She hugged it tight.

Duke raised his eyebrow. "Not sure that thing will fit in the truck."

"It will. Or we can have it delivered."

"Oh, we can, can we?" He reached out and tweaked her nose. "That thing is bigger than you are."

"He's so cute. I think I'll call him Sparkle Pony."

Duke rolled his eyes, his lips twitching. "All right, but we're taking a photo of that thing riding in his truck to send to Spike."

She giggled at that. Somehow, Duke stuffed the giant unicorn on top of the rest of her toys. She had coloring books, crayons, playdough, Barbies, Legos and now a giant unicorn. She sighed happily. "Ooh, tea set."

She took off in that direction. Duke pushed the cart behind her. "Don't go too far from me," he warned. She ignored him, rushing around the corner as she searched for a tea set. This was so much fun.

She found the tea sets and bent over to look at them. A sharp smack to her ass had her standing with a small yelp. She rubbed her ass.

"Daddy!"

She glanced around but there was no one in this aisle.

"Did I not just tell you to stay close by?" he drawled in a low voice. "And what did you immediately do?"

She stared up at him, biting her lower lip. Uh-oh.

"Sorry, Daddy. I'll be good and stay close to you."

He raised his eyebrow. "You better. I'd hate to have to take you out to the truck, pull you over my lap, draw down your pants and spank your bottom."

He wouldn't. Would he? She was fairly certain he wouldn't.

But not enough to push him.

"From now on, you hold my hand or the shopping cart, understand?"

"Yes, Daddy. Sorry."

He leaned over and kissed her gently. "Good girl. Now get that tea set."

She smiled and picked up the tea set, handing it to him. By the time they were finished, the cart was overflowing. She didn't even want to know what the total was, so she didn't look as the woman rung it up.

"Some little girl is going to be very spoiled," the woman said as she handed Duke the receipt.

"She deserves it," he rumbled, sending Sunny a wink.

She smiled back at him. She held onto the side of the cart as they moved out into the parking lot, towards Spike's borrowed truck. Duke took a photo of the unicorn sitting in the back seat with its head out the window.

Duke lifted her into the truck and did up her seat belt. But instead of driving her straight home, he drove a few blocks over and pulled into a garden center.

"What are we doing here?" she asked.

"Well, you did offer to plant some flowers for me."

"You. . .you want me to plant you a garden?"

"Yeah. Like I said, never been able to keep much alive. But figure that's your job now."

She smiled at him. "I'm okay with that."

He undid her belt and pulled her across the bench seat. "Means you're gonna have to stick around. For a long, long time. After all you can't let the poor plants die."

"No, got to think of the plants," she said solemnly.

He snorted then kissed her lightly. "Move in with me, Sunny." He watched her carefully, almost as though he was worried about her reply.

He needn't have. "Yes."

He kissed her. His mouth hard. Possessive. When he pulled back. "Thank God for that."

"You were really worried I'd say no?"

"Course not," he replied arrogantly. "How could you say no to the man who buys you toys and flowers?"

"You're forgetting the spectacular orgasms," she noted.

He grinned. "Believe me, I could never forget those." He cupped her face between his hands. "Love you, Sunshine River Bright."

"I love you too. So much."

"Good. Now let's go get some fucking plants and go home."

"Hello, Sunny-girl, what you playing there?"

Sunny started then stared up at Ink, her eyes wide. What was he doing here? She looked down at the picnic blanket Duke had spread out on the floor. She had her toys, including Sparkle Pony, gathered around the blanket and was pouring out tea into the small delicate cups of the tea set Duke had bought her that morning.

Duke had popped out of the playroom after his phone rang, telling her to stay there. She hadn't really thought much about it, continuing to play happily.

"Oh, um, Ink." She knew her face had to be scarlet. What should she say? Do? Ink knew she was a Little. He'd helped get this room ready, but having him see her like this was different than him just knowing that about her.

"Can I have a cup of tea?"

She blinked at him. He just smiled. Then the heavily-tattooed man with the shock of blond hair and the party-guy, surfer vibe sat crossed legged across from her. She still didn't know what to say. Did Duke know he was here?

"Duke is. . .he's. . ."

"He's talking to Spike. He doesn't know I'm here. I had to go to the toilet and the door was open so I peeked in to check out your room. You like it?"

"I love it," she whispered.

He studied her. "I can leave if you like, Sunny-girl. I don't want to make you feel self-conscious. It's just been a long time since I was at a tea party."

"Have you had a Little?"

"Yep. While ago. I miss it. Taking care of someone that way, having their total trust, it just fucking does it for me."

There was a hint of sadness in his voice that tugged at her. He went to rise and she reached out and took hold of his hand. "You can stay."

"You sure?"

"I'm sure."

He sat and picked up a tea cup holding it slightly awkwardly with his thumb and forefinger. She poured him a cup of tea. "Here you go."

"Why thank you, princess," he said seriously.

She had to drop her head to hide her smile at the big tattooed biker sipping tea from the tiny, delicate cup.

"Would you like a cupcake?" she offered a plate of plastic cupcakes.

"Hmm, who baked them? The unicorn?" He nodded at the big stuffed toy.

She giggled. "'Course not, Sparkle Pony can't bake."

"Sparkle Pony, huh? Hope he is a she."

She grinned wide. "Nope."

"Poor bastard is gonna get it on the playground." Ink shook his head as she giggled. He stayed for a few minutes, making her laugh with his silliness.

Then he got to his feet.

"You going, Ink?"

"Yeah, Sunny-girl, best go before your Daddy catches me in here and kicks my ass." He winked at her. He squeezed her shoulder gently. "Thanks for making him happy, baby girl. Last time I saw him this happy was before his parents and sister died."

Her breath caught and she glanced up at him. "You were his friend? The one he was staying with? It was your family that took him in?"

"Yeah, Sunny-girl. That was me. I've always considered Duke my brother. My parents think of him as another son. But it's not the same for Duke as having his own family. I love him. Would do anything for him. But I've never been able to give him his family back. What you've given him, it's what he needed to make him see it's worth living even after a shitty tragedy like that."

Without another word, he walked out.

DUKE LEANED back against the passage, waiting for Ink to walk out. "Good tea party?"

"Been out here a while have you?" Ink asked as red filled his cheeks.

"Yep."

"Spike tell you that Grady came through and the meeting with Frankie is set for Thursday night?" Ink asked, clearly trying to steer the conversation away from what he'd just been doing.

"Yep."

"You pissed at me?"

Duke reached out and grabbed him around the back of his neck and pulled him close, thumping him on the back. "I have a number of men I consider brothers. But only one I consider blood."

He let the other man go. Ink grinned at him.

"But don't go embarrassing Sunny again, you bastard, or I'll put you on your back."

"Aww, love you too." Ink took off with a laugh.

Cocky bastard. Duke just shook his head and went back to join Sunny for a tea party.

"Hey, baby girl," he said to her as he sat down across from her, in the same spot Ink had been in. "How's the tea party going?"

"Sparkle Pony has some atrocious table manners," she said with a cute shake of her head. "Moody is very disappointed in him." She picked up her monkey and turned him upside down so he was frowning.

Duke shook his head. "Hard to find a unicorn with good table manners nowadays."

"It sure is, Daddy," she agreed. "Tea?"

"Yes, please." He picked up a cup and held it up. She poked her tongue out as she carefully poured some tea for him.

"Everything okay, Daddy?" she asked, studying him.

"Of course it is, baby girl." And if it wasn't, he still probably wouldn't worry her. At least not while she was in Little mode. She deserved some carefree time to play.

They drank tea then played with the Barbies until it was time for him to cook dinner. He picked up a coloring book and some crayons, carrying them out to the kitchen while Sunny skipped behind him, holding Moody's hand and swinging him back and forth.

"Here you go, baby girl. You sit up here and color while I make some dinner." He lifted her onto a stool at the kitchen counter.

"Okie-dokie," she said in a cheerful voice, swinging her legs back and forth and looking so carefree his chest actually ached. He loved that he could give her this.

She tapped at her chin, giving him a mischievous look. "I'd rather play with some playdough, though. Think you could make me some?"

"That would be a no," he growled. "And I seem to recall buying you playdough in every possible color."

"But it's so much more special when you make it for me, Daddy," she wheedled.

He snatched up a wooden spoon and waved it at her. "Do I need to bring this over here and spank the sass out of you, little rebel?"

Her eyes widened and she gave him an innocent look. "Daddy, I was just talking to you about playdough, no need to get so grouchy."

She attempted to keep a smile from her face but failed.

"Do your coloring, brat."

She picked up a crayon as he started on dinner. He glanced over at her picture as he finished plating up their food. He had to smile as he saw the giant mess she'd made. She had drawn out of the lines; everything was the wrong color and it made him absurdly happy.

She grinned up at him. "What do you think, Daddy?"

"I think it's a masterpiece! Let's put it on the fridge where everyone can see it." He carefully ripped it from the book and secured it to the front of the fridge. She wrapped her arms around his waist, pressing her face to his chest.

"You really like it, Daddy?"

"Baby girl, you did a great job. Come on, dinner time."

He led her back to the counter and lifted her onto the stool. He should probably get a proper table and chairs.

She clapped her hands as she stared down at her plate. He'd bought it for her yesterday. It was an elephant with several sections so different foods didn't have to touch each other.

"Yay, veggies!" she said, spearing a piece of broccoli and chewing on it enthusiastically.

He shook his head. She was so weird.

But cute. Definitely cute.

He ate his chicken stir fry, watching her indulgently as she sat Moody up and pretended to feed him bits of food.

"Moody has had enough. Time for Sunny to eat some more." He pointed at her food with his fork. He still didn't think she ate enough. Her asshole ex had a lot to answer for.

"Okie-dokie, Daddy. Moody needs to have his face washed, though. He's a very messy eater."

He nodded solemnly. "Very true." And so could Sunny.

After they'd both finished eating, he stood and grabbed some wipes, cleaning her hands and face. "There we go, all clean."

"You take such good care of me, Daddy."

He kissed her gently. "And I always will."

21

"What are we doing here?" Sunny asked as Duke pulled up in front of the trailer that served as Ronny's office. All of the vehicles were gone from the yard, everyone was away on jobs for the day. That meant Ronny was likely alone and half-way through his morning porn show.

She shuddered at the thought.

"We're here to get your last paycheck."

She bit her lip. "I thought you didn't want me doing this?"

He turned to look at her. It was Tuesday and they were headed to work. They'd left earlier than usual because he'd told her he had an errand to run first. Little had she known that errand was talking to Ronny. Urgh, while she'd talked a good talk about confronting him, she wasn't sure she was prepared for this.

"I don't. I'll gladly do this for you. But I don't want to take this moment from you if you want to do it. This is your chance to tell him what a slime ball he was. But you keep the door open. He does any fucking thing you don't like then you yell out. I'm also only giving you five minutes before I come in after you. Understood?"

She looked from him to the trailer. She remembered the feel of Ronny grabbing her in the bar that night, of him firing her even though she'd been his best worker.

She nodded. "I'll do this. But if he's watching porn in there, I may need you to bleach my eyes."

"If he's watching porn, I'll fucking kill him." He climbed out of the truck then helped her down, leading her towards the trailer. He opened the door without knocking.

She couldn't hear any sounds of moaning or slapping so she guessed she was safe. Duke poked his head in. "He's not in there."

They heard the flush of a toilet and she grimaced.

"I can still go in with you," Duke offered.

She patted his chest. "I got this." She kissed his jaw and stepped inside, leaving the door open so he could still protect her while giving her this moment. She glanced around, grimacing at the smell of sweat and other bodily odors she really didn't want to think about.

Without thinking about it too hard, she pulled her phone out of her pocket and set it on record. She half tucked it into her back pocket just as Ronny stepped out, still zipping up his pants. He froze as he saw her.

"What are you doing here? Come to beg for your old job back? Not happening." A calculating look crossed his face. "Not unless you're willing to do a little something for me, that is."

"Oh yeah, what's that?" she asked.

"Suck the sausage and I might reconsider giving you your job back," he said slyly.

"Yeah? Isn't that what caused you to fire me in the first place? Because I didn't want you touching me?"

"All you had to do was give me a blowie," he whined as though she'd wronged him. "Then you could have kept your miserable job. You were fucking lucky to have it in the first place. My old man must have been going nuts to hire a fucking woman to do a man's job."

"So, I lost my job because I wouldn't suck your cock and because I'm a woman. You're a real class act, Ronny. Just for the record, there's no way I'd ever touch your disgusting dick."

She shuddered. Just the thought made her nauseous.

"What the fuck you doing here then?" Ronny demanded. "I got things to do."

"Sorry if I'm cutting into your porn time," she said dryly. "I've come to get my last paycheck. The one you were meant to deposit into my account."

"I don't owe you any more money."

"You do and you know it."

He sneered at her. "Well, you aren't seeing a dime of it. Now get the fuck out."

"You're not giving me what's owed to me?"

"You heard me right, bitch. Go. Before I make you."

"That's a shame. I guess my lawyer will be in touch."

"You're hiring a lawyer over a week's pay?" He barked out a laugh. "Fucking lawyer will cost more in billable hours, you twat."

"Oh, no, they'll be in touch because I'm suing for wrongful termination. I'll also be pressing sexual harassment charges."

"Like you can prove that," he scoffed.

She pulled out her phone. "Got it all on here."

He stood, looking shocked. "Hey! That's fucking illegal. You can't tape me and use it."

Fuck. He was right.

"Maybe not. But do you want to risk jail and a lawsuit over a week's pay?"

"Babe, let's wrap this up," Duke called out.

"Who's that?" Ronny demanded.

"Oh, that's my boyfriend. He may have been listening as well."

She clicked her fingers. "I think a witness statement is legal evidence, right?"

Ronny turned purple with rage. "Fine. I'll write you a fucking check, you bitch."

"You wanna watch how you talk to my girl," Duke rumbled as he walked into the trailer.

She knew the moment Ronny caught sight of him, he went completely pale and sat back in his chair. "Oh fuck. Oh shit. Uh, sorry. I'll just. . .I'll just write you a check." His hand shook as he wrote it out then he basically flung it at her. It landed on the floor.

Leaning down, she picked it up. "This is several hundred dollars more than you owe me."

"Just take it. For fuck's sake, take it and go. And don't come back."

She tucked it away and turned. Duke took her hand and led her towards the door. He stepped to the side so she could exit first.

"Ronny?" Duke called back.

"Yeah?"

"Better not hear of you harassing any other women, understand? I don't take kindly to that sort of behavior."

"Nope. I won't. You have my word."

Duke slammed the door shut then made a face at her. "Gross. I think he pissed himself."

She grinned and held up the check. "I did it!"

It wasn't the money that was filling her with joy, it was the fact she'd finally stood up to that jerk.

"You sure did, baby." He pulled her in and kissed her lightly. "Now let's go. I swear I need a shower just from breathing the same air as that disgusting pig."

22

"Sunny! Come help me with this fucking trash!" Rory called out as she passed the open door leading to the break room. She bit back a sigh. It was fifteen minutes until closing and she had stuff to do.

But then, she supposed she should help since it was meant to be her job. Duke made Rory do it because he didn't want her going out into the alley. He also made Rory do it because he didn't like him.

"What do you need help with?" she asked. The trash bag wasn't exactly heavy.

"Need you to hold the door open so it doesn't lock on me when I go out."

She didn't see why he couldn't use a chair to prop it open, but she just walked over. The door opened out into the alley and automatically locked when it shut. She pushed it open then stepped outside to hold it. Suddenly, she was grabbed from behind and pulled backwards. She let go of the door, kicking back at her assailant, clawing at the hand covering her mouth and nose, blocking off most of her air.

She was pulled further into the alley and the door shut, blocking off all the light from inside. Where was the security lighting Duke had installed? She struggled, trying to fight off her attacker as he dragged her out of the alleyway.

Where was Rory? Why wasn't he helping her? Oh God. She couldn't breathe! Duke! Duke!

The world around her started to fade as she felt herself being yanked inside a vehicle. A door slid shut and then everything went black.

"YEAH?" Duke said into his phone.

"Get over to the club," Reyes replied.

"What's going on? Did Frankie bail on the meeting?" He looked at the clock. The meeting between Spike and Frankie had been set for ten. It was nearly that now.

"Fucking bastard's been murdered. Looks like he was tortured for a while first. The Fox left his calling card."

Fuck. Shit.

"Jason thinks he's got a lead on the place where the senator might be taking the girls, though. One of the senator's bodyguards was left a cabin by his uncle. It's a few hours out of the city. We need to check it out."

"I'll get Sunny and be straight over." He ended the call then stood and moved out of his office. Why was the place so quiet?

"Sunny?" he called out. She should be getting her stuff and heading to his office by now. "Rory? Madden?"

"Hey, boss, I'm in here," Madden called out.

Duke walked into the break room. "Hey, you seen Sunny?" A feeling of foreboding filled him. She wouldn't go anywhere without him. Where was she?

Madden picked up the garbage bag. "Don't know. Rory's left

already. Asshole left the garbage here." He propped open the door with a chair and took the trash out.

Worry flooded Duke as he opened Sunny's locker. Her stuff was still here. He pulled out his phone and called her.

He heard her ringtone. Then Madden appeared in the doorway, his face pale, holding up Sunny's phone with its distinctive pink, glittery case.

Fuck. Fuck. He pinched the top of his nose.

"Light's aren't working out here," Madden told him.

Fuck. Shit.

He opened the contacts on his phone and called Ink.

"What's up?" Ink greeted him.

"Sunny's missing," he said quickly. "Need you to access the cameras around the shop."

"You got it," Ink replied. "Any idea how long? Have you tried pinging her phone?"

"Madden found it in the alleyway out back of the shop."

"Right. Stay close to your phone. Don't worry. We'll find her."

They better. He needed her. Fuck. Where was she? What the hell had happened?

He called Reyes quickly, filling him in. The other man said they'd all be there shortly. But there wasn't much they could do until he had some fucking idea of what happened to her. He paced back and forth across the break room.

Then his phone buzzed.

"My guys got it on camera. About eight minutes ago, she stepped into the alley and some bastard grabbed her from behind and pulled her into the back of a van. Couldn't see much of his face. But we got the number plate of the van. We're running it now. And Duke, Rory got into the driver's side of the van."

Anger roared through him. "That fucking mother-fucking bastard, I'm going to rip off his dick and feed it to him!"

"We have the direction the van is taking and we're tapping into traffic cams. Want to call the cops?"

"Fuck! Not yet. They'll just slow everything down."

"Send me Rory's phone number, my guy might be able to ping his location."

He ended the call just as he heard Reyes and the others enter the front of the shop. He sent Ink Rory's number.

He turned as his brothers walked into the room. "Sunny's been kidnapped by Rory and another guy."

Razor swore while Reyes' face grew even colder, but surprisingly it was Spike who spoke.

"Well, seems some fuckers are going to die tonight."

SHE SLAMMED into the something hard, groaning in pain.

What happened? Where was she?

"Easy on the corners, asshole!" someone yelled. "There's no fucking seat belts back here."

Back here? Where was here? She tried to look around, blinking to get her eyes to adjust to the dark. Was she in the back of a van? It was loud and smelled like diesel. Why would she be in a van? Where was Duke? Why wasn't she at work?

Another corner. She rolled, unable to find something to hold onto and banged into someone else. There was a whiff of body odor as the person shoved her away.

"Get off me, bitch!"

She froze. What was going on?

"Fucking hell, Rory, do you want the cops after us?"

Rory. Rory was here. Oh God. Someone had taken her as she'd helped Rory take the trash out. And Rory hadn't helped her. He was driving the van to take her. . .where?

"Who are you? Where are we going? Rory? What's going on?" she demanded.

"Shut the fuck up, bitch!" A hand reached out and slapped her.

She gasped in a breath, her eyes watering at the sharp sting.

"I want to make sure they can't catch up to us!" Rory said, his voice sounding panicked.

"They won't find us! Nobody saw us. We have plenty of time to have a little fun with this bitch before we kill her."

Oh God. What? "Why did you kidnap me? What's going on?"

"What's going on is that stupid MC club your boyfriend belongs to thinks they're too good for us," the man told her. "They think they get to reject Horse? To call me an idiot and that I'll let them get away with the insult?"

Wait. Horse. Rory's friend, Horse. Reyes had told Rory that he and Horse weren't allowed to become prospects. And they'd kidnapped her because. . .what? They were pissed off? What on Earth?

"Duke will kill you," she said loudly. "He's going to come for me and he'll kill you both. Sure you want to risk that, Rory?"

She appealed to Rory, because quite frankly Horse seemed to be missing a few brain cells. But then, Rory had to be as well because he had to know Duke was going to murder him.

"He won't find us," Rory stated, although she thought she heard a waver in his voice.

He took another corner too hard and she winced as her back slammed against the metal wall of the van. Her bladder took that moment to warn her that she needed to pee.

Awesome.

"He'll find you," she yelled. "He won't stop until he does. I hope getting a bit of revenge over some hurt feelings is worth the pain of what he'll do to you!"

"Shut up, bitch," Horse snarled. "They disrespected us. They have to pay. And Rory's been telling me how you got Duke pussy-whipped. You should have been nicer to my boy, then maybe we wouldn't have to cut you up. He did his best to get you fired. Messed up your work, but I guess when you're fucking the boss you got job security. I got the idea to take you after you interrupted me scratching up his truck. Going to have fun using my knife on you."

"C-cut me up? Rory!"

Wait. Horse had been the guy in the hoodie? Oh God. She felt nauseous.

"Shut up, bitch!" Rory yelled. "I'm trying to think!"

"I have to pee!"

"Nobody cares, cunt," Horse told her.

She was going to be sick. "And I'm going to vomit. You have to stop!"

"Horse?" Rory called back, sounding unsure.

"Let her fucking piss herself and vomit. Gonna be doing worse once my knife carves her up."

She pressed her lips together to hold in a whimper of fear. *Please, Duke. Find me.*

"She can't mess up the van," Rory whined. "It's my cousin's. He'll kill me."

They used a borrowed van to kidnap her? Were they fucking idiots? Suddenly, the van swung to the right and she went flying against the side, banging her shoulder.

Ouch. Ow.

Tears filled her eyes, a sob escaping.

No time to fall apart, Sunny. Duke will come for you. He'll find you.

The van rocked to a stop. "Get her out, she can pee in the bushes," Rory demanded. "There's no one around."

Horse grabbed her by the arm, holding her so tightly that she knew she was going to bruise. "Don't you even think about fucking screaming, bitch. You make a noise, you try to run, you even look at me funny and I'll carve you up right here and now."

She could barely breathe; her legs were shaking. The van door opened and Rory gestured at them. It was now fully dark and he'd pulled off into a parking lot by an old warehouse. She looked around in despair, but couldn't see anyone close by. Horse dragged her off towards the bushes while Rory brought up the rear.

"Keep fucking watch while she pisses," Horse ordered, yanking her a couple of feet away. He nodded at the ground. "Piss."

"Turn around," she demanded.

He just laughed. It wasn't a normal laugh and the sound of it chilled her to the bone.

"Not happening. You wanted to piss then piss. But I ain't taking my gaze off you."

She swallowed heavily. "I can't pee with you watching. I have a shy bladder."

He took a step towards her, slipping a large knife from the sheath attached to his thigh. He held it up. The shadows around them suddenly seemed more menacing.

"Maybe I ought to drain your bladder another way then."

She gulped. So maybe she could pee. Wasn't like he could see much in the near-darkness, right?

She reached for her jeans, fumbling. Then she crouched, silent tears tracking down her face as she emptied her bladder.

"Rory! Everything okay?" Horse called back, watching her intently. She couldn't see much of his face; the streetlamps didn't reach this far back. "Rory!"

She stood, pulling up her pants. Why wasn't Rory answering?

"What the fuck?" Horse was reaching for her arm, when he was suddenly pulled backwards. There was no noise, it was almost like he disappeared into the darkness. She let out a small cry. What just happened?

Who cares! Run, Sunny!

She turned, ready to race off when someone grabbed her from

behind. She didn't even have time to scream before she felt a prick in her neck.

Then everything went dark.

~

DUKE PUSHED THE BIKE FASTER, not caring that he was breaking the speed limit or that the last thing he needed was to attract the attention of the cops.

Ink's guy had managed to track Rory's phone. Duke was on Ink's bike since his was at home and the other man had stayed behind to co-ordinate. He sped towards the old, abandoned warehouse, pulling up a block away. Much as he wanted to get there quickly, the bikes weren't exactly quiet.

He turned the bike off then jumped off and started running towards the warehouse.

"Duke, wait the fuck up," Reyes called out to him. Duke ignored him. He raced into the parking lot, spotting a van over near the tree line. Fuck. Did they take her into the warehouse or the woods?

He turned and ran towards the van, aware of Reyes telling Jason and Razor to take the warehouse.

Please let her be there. Please let her be okay.

He gave the van a glance then headed towards the trees. Where was she? He tripped over something and nearly fell. Turning, he tensed as he saw it was a goddamn body.

"What the fuck?" He drew out his phone and used the light from the screen to check who the fuck was lying at his feet.

It was Rory.

And his throat was slit.

"I got a body over here," Spike called out. "Dead. Throat slit."

"Rory's here," Duke called back. No point being quiet if they were both dead. "Throat slit as well." He switched on the flashlight app on his phone.

There was a piece of paper under Rory's hand. He pulled it out.

"Fuck," Spike said appearing beside him. "Please don't tell me that's from the Fox."

"What? Why would you say that?" Duke asked, turning it over. Fuck. There it was on the back, the Fox's insignia.

"Frankie was tortured before his throat was slit," Spike told him grimly.

"Fuck. Shit." Panic filled Duke.

"There was barely any blood. He was cold. Been killed hours before and moved to the location of our meet."

"Someone knew Spike was meeting with him," Reyes said, moving up beside him. Duke turned as he heard people run towards him. Jason and Razor appeared.

"Warehouse is clear," Razor said, stepping up beside them. "Fuck. Is that Rory?"

"Yeah," Spike replied. "What does the note say?"

"Note?" Razor asked.

"A note was left under his hand," Reyes explained. "From the Fox."

"Fuck," Razor swore. "You're not saying that..."

"The Fox has Sunny," Duke said numbly, looking up from the note he'd just read. "And according to this note, we have until sun-up to find her."

23

"Wakie-wakie, sweet girl," a voice murmured.

She groaned. She was having the nicest dream. Duke had been holding her in his arms and rocking her back and forth. She didn't really want to wake up.

Something was pressed to her forehead. Something cold.

"No, don't!" She reached up and grabbed it, flinging the wet cloth away.

"Now, that was a bit naughty. Would your Daddy spank you for that, I wonder?"

That wasn't Duke's voice. Fear flooded her, making her heart race. She opened her eyes, and looked up into a stranger's face.

Hazel-colored eyes stared down at her from a tanned face. He looked to be in his late-thirties, there were few wrinkles on his face and no grays in his neatly-trimmed dark hair.

Who the hell was he?

Sunny sat up, noticing she was lying on a soft bed. She scrambled backward, away from the man studying her with interest.

"Who. . .who are you?"

"Why, sweet girl, I'm disappointed. Don't you recognize me?"

Sweet girl? She knew of one person who called her that. . .but that couldn't be right. Marv was homeless. He had long, straggly dark hair and blue-green eyes. He was far older than this man.

And yet. . .

"Marv?" she whispered.

He smiled at her. His teeth, rather than being yellowed, were a gleaming white. "Clever girl, Sunny. Far smarter than those biker friends of yours."

"Marv? What's going on? Where are we? Why did you bring me here?"

Had Marv rescued her? She'd just finished peeing when Horse had practically disappeared. Then someone grabbed her and there had been a prick. . .she raised her hand to her neck.

"Ahh, sorry about that, sweet girl. I had to drug you to keep you quiet."

"But why?"

He tilted his head. "Can't you guess?"

She shook her head. She didn't understand any of this. She thought he was homeless and yet here he was, looking so different she could have passed him on the street and not recognized him.

"The homeless thing was an act?" she whispered.

She took another look around the room. There were no windows. She was sitting on a four-poster bed in the corner of the room. Next to it sat a small bookshelf with what looked to be a collection of children's stories. In one corner of the room sat a white desk and chair. In the other corner there was a rug on the floor and a pile of stuffies along with a beanbag.

"Do you like your room?" Marv asked. "I had it done just for you. Thought it would make you feel more comfortable while you're waiting for Duke to rescue you."

"I don't understand," she whispered.

"Well, I admit I didn't understand at first, either," he admitted. "This whole Daddy/Little girl dynamic seemed rather odd to me. But as I did a little research, I came to realize that perhaps I'm a Daddy Dom. I rather like the idea of having a Little under my complete control. Maybe even two. Yes, I often work away so they could keep each other company. But then there's the whole discipline aspect. How would I care for them if I have to leave? Do you know if there are nannies you can hire for that sort of thing?"

She just gaped at him. "That. . .that's not the way it works. I'm not under Duke's complete control."

He frowned. "Hmm. . .but that doesn't mean it couldn't work that way. You see, I have such an issue with trusting others. Happens when you have so many enemies. But if I had someone who was completely dependent on me, well, they wouldn't be able to betray me, would they?"

What was happening here?

"You can't choose to be a Daddy Dom just so you can get someone to be completely dependent on you because you have trust issues."

"Well, why not?"

"Because that's just not right."

He surprised her by grinning. "Would it surprise you to hear I have a warped sense of what is right and wrong?"

"No. Not at all."

He chuckled. Then he clicked his fingers. "I have an idea. Why don't I just keep you? You're already broken in."

"Broken in? I'm not a dog!" She knew she should be scared of him. He was clearly batshit crazy. And yet, this was Marv. She'd never sensed any ill-will from him. Then or now.

Don't be foolish, Sunny. He drugged you. Kidnapped you. He's talking about keeping you.

"That was a joke." He winked.

Was it, though? She eyed him warily. He pulled the stool over from the writing desk and sat, facing her. He leaned his elbows on his legs. "All right, enough about the fun stuff, let's get onto serious business."

"What's going on? Why disguise yourself as a homeless person? Why bring me here? Where is here?"

"This is one of my safe houses."

"Safe houses? You're a cop?"

He threw his head back and laughed. She just stared at him until he reached for a tissue and wiped under his eyes. "A cop? Oh, Sunny I didn't realize you were so funny. Are you sure you won't stay? No? Shame. No, I'm not a cop."

"Then why do you need a safe house?"

"It's always a good idea to have a place to retreat to if things get a bit hot. This time, I sacrificed one of my houses for you. Did I do a good job of creating a room for you to be comfortable waiting in?"

Her mouth dropped open. "You created this room because you wanted me to be comfortable?"

"Yes." He frowned. "Did I not get it right? I think it needs more toys; however, it's late and little girls should be in bed. And I'm hoping those bikers combine their meagre brain cells and actually manage to find you by morning."

Her mind raced, trying to work all of this out. "I don't get it. If you expect Duke to find me then why take me in the first place?"

"Because you're my distraction, of course. I need them to focus on something else for a while so they're not in my way. So, I gave them a little treasure hunt. Laid out my clues that will lead them here. Quite clever really."

Yep. He was definitely deranged. And his ego was out of control.

"Distracted from what?"

"Oh, from the senator. I need to kill him tonight. While I'd normally just take out anyone in my way, I thought that might upset you."

Take out? What was he talking about?

Oh. Fuck.

"You. . .you mean you were going to murder Duke and his friends but you didn't because you thought I'd be upset?"

"Yes. Was I wrong? Sometimes I get these things wrong. Understanding others emotions isn't my strong suit. I find it hard to care about people. You're an exception."

Lucky her.

Actually, it *was* lucky her, she realized. Because if he didn't care about her then Duke and the others. . .

"You're the Fox," she whispered as it hit her.

"The one and only." He smiled gently.

"You were hired to kill the senator." She put her hand over her tummy, feeling ill.

"Ahh. . .yes. That upsets you?"

"That you're going to kill the senator? Well, yeah."

"Why?" He frowned. "He's a nasty piece of work. Buys underage girls, ties them up and rapes them. I recently discovered where it is that he takes them to play with them. I took out the pimp who has been supplying him with the girls and now all that's left is to take care of the senator and his bodyguards. They're both in on it, you see."

"You're an assassin."

"Well, yes. See, there's not many jobs where you can make good money when your moral compass is slightly warped."

Slightly warped.

"I mean, I guess I could murder for the fun of it. . .but no, I get a strange sense of satisfaction in taking out rapists and murderers. And this way, I get paid."

He didn't seem to count himself as a murderer.

"You only kill rapists and murderers?" she asked, trying to understand him. Although she had a feeling it would take someone far smarter than her to figure out the Fox.

"Ahh, well, I'm not saying I was always so picky about what jobs I took. But it's more of a hobby now, so I can pick and choose. The senator is dark and evil on the inside while pretending to be moral and upstanding on the outside. He hurts young girls. He doesn't deserve to live now, does he? I'm sure your Duke would agree with me. Along with his friends. It's strange, I couldn't work out their motivation for watching him in the beginning. That's why I became Marv. I needed to gather some information on them before I acted. Wasn't sure if they were trying for more blackmail material on him, or if they wanted a cut of the action. I was shocked to find out that they were trying to take him out. And for no financial gain." He shook his head.

"They're good guys."

"Oh, I'm not so sure about that." He studied her. "But you, Sunny. You are good. You saw me when I was just an old, homeless man. Most people walked straight past me. You tried to help. You cared. And in the end, that's what saved all of you. I'm sparing them for you, Sunny."

What did she even say to that? To say she was confused about the Fox was an understatement. On the one hand, he was an assassin for hire, his moral compass completely off and he seemed to have some psychopathic tendencies.

But on the other hand, he'd made this room to make her feel more comfortable. He'd rescued her from Horse and Rory. He was drawing the guys away from the senator to keep them safe. Even if by doing that, he'd kidnapped and scared the shit out of her.

"What. . .what happens now?"

"Well. I've got to go kill a senator. Not every day you get to say that. Although this isn't my first senator. Popped that cherry a while ago. There's a bathroom through there." He shook his head. "I couldn't believe it when those two idiots got to you before me." His face zeroed in on her face. "They paid for hurting you. I don't like anyone hurting you."

He reached out as though to touch her face.

"You're kind of scaring me a little," she whispered, hoping like hell she didn't piss him off.

Something strange crossed his face. Sadness? That couldn't be right. "Yes, I have that effect on people."

She swallowed heavily. "Who hired you to kill the senator?"

"Ahh, sweet girl, you know that's confidential. I have to go now." He stood and put the chair back. "Use the bathroom. Sleep. I wouldn't advise trying to escape. You'll just wear yourself out. There's a small fridge in the bathroom with water and food. If Duke doesn't find you by morning, I have arranged for you to be released by lunchtime. Goodbye, Sunny."

"Wait." She stood. "I. . .umm. . .how did you know about all this?" She waved her hand around. She hadn't been going to ask that, but she wasn't quite sure what she wanted to say to him. It would be weird to thank her kidnapper.

Right?

"I bugged the tattoo parlor. Some interesting things went on there."

He winked at her and she blushed. Holy. Shit.

"How did you manage that?"

"That wasn't so difficult. You see I always wanted to get a tattoo on my back."

On his back? "You were a client?"

"Your biker does do good work. I'll give him that."

He turned away.

"Marv. . .I mean, Fox, whatever your name is."

He turned back.

Oh, screw it. "This is weird and I don't know how I feel about you. But I do know that Horse and Rory would have killed me. So thank you."

"You're welcome, sweet girl." Then he opened the door and left. She attempted to open the door. Locked. She looked across at the other door and dashed over to use the bathroom. After going to the toilet and washing her hands, she studied herself in the mirror. She grimaced at the red mark on her cheekbone and her disheveled appearance.

Oh well, it wasn't every day you got kidnapped twice. A giggle escaped her and she slammed her hand over her mouth.

No point in getting hysterical. *You should try to escape.* She glanced around the small bathroom. No window. No way out.

She searched through the bathroom. For what, she had no idea. But all she found was some soap, some bubble bath and extra toilet paper.

All good things to have, she supposed. She moved into the bedroom and systematically searched her way through it. There was no secret hidden door or lock-picking kit. Not that the door even had a lock. It must have a deadbolt on the other side.

She didn't exactly know how to pick a lock anyway.

Exhaustion filled her as she made her way to the bed. She bent and studied the bookshelf, pulling out a copy of *Alice in Wonderland*. She looked it over. It was a beautiful version and it looked old. Opening it, she gasped as she saw it was a first edition.

Holy hell.

So, okay, the invasion of privacy was disturbing. He'd bugged the tattoo shop for goodness sake. She blushed as she thought of everything he might have heard.

And yet, he'd bought her this.

He's a killer, Sunny. He would have murdered Duke and the others just because they were in his way.

But he didn't. For her.

Disturbing and yet she couldn't quite bring herself to be as horrified as she thought she should be.

"Maybe I'm still in shock," she muttered as she moved to the bed and sat, opening the book. A card fluttered out. On the one side was the image of a Fox's head. On the other side was a phone number. And a small, handwritten note.

In case you ever need me.

Maybe she was the one with a few brain cells missing. But she found herself kind of liking the guy. She opened the book and started to read.

24

If she wasn't here, he was going to fucking lose it. He was holding on by a thread as it was. It was nearly sunrise.

If the Fox fucking hurt her...

"Easy, man. We need to do some recon first." Reyes placed his hand on Duke's shoulder. Squeezing.

"Easy? How can I be easy? He sent us on a fucking goose chase for hours. Five places. Each time another stupid fucking note from him with another fucking clue. Guy's a fucking nutcase. I'm going murder him. What if he's..."

Hurt her.

He swallowed heavily.

"Don't say it," Reyes told him. "Don't even think it. Sunny will be all right."

She better fucking be. He didn't know what the point of this fucking was. Taking her. Sending them chasing around the city, looking for her. First, they'd gone to a bar called the Fox and the Ferret, then a stripper joint called Foxies, then a popular nightclub called Fox's Hole. Fucking bastard thought he was hilarious.

At each place another of the Fox's fucking notes had been

given to him. Delivered by nameless, faceless little pricks who had brushed past and tucked them into his pocket. He'd managed to catch hold of the last messenger, but he was just a kid and he hadn't been able to give them any information. He'd been handed the job by a nondescript looking guy who'd paid cash and given them a description of Duke so they'd know who to give the note to.

The last set of directions had been different. A set of co-ordinates leading to what looked to be an abandoned cabin about an hour out of the city.

"I'm never fucking letting her out of my sight again."

The house was in the middle of nowhere. Surrounded by woods on three sides, it was quiet and ominous. Dawn was just streaking across the sky, making his gut tighten further.

They needed to find her.

A low whistle sounded giving them the all-clear. He jogged his way up to the front door, jiggling the door handle.

Locked.

Drawing back, he was about to ram it, when Reyes grasped hold of his arm. "Wait. Thing's made of steel. There's no getting in that way."

"I've checked all the windows. Bars on all of them," Razor called out.

Bars on the windows? A steel door? How the fuck would they get in? He looked around, noting the unusual number of potted flowers on the small porch.

"Check under the pots," he said urgently.

"What?" Razor asked.

"Under the flower pots. Sunny used to keep her keys to her house under a flower pot on her porch. The key to here might be under one."

"Here!" Jason held up a set of keys he'd found under a pot.

Fuck. It was disturbing to realize that the Fox had been

watching her that closely. How had Duke not noticed him? How had he failed so spectacularly to keep her safe?

Never again. If he had to tie her to him to keep her safe, he would.

Jason unlocked the door. Reyes and Spike grabbed Duke when he would have stormed inside. He growled at them both, trying to shove their hold off.

"Hold it together, Duke," Reyes said quietly. "Let Jason check the place first, make sure it's not a trap."

Jason was ex-military. It was probably a good call but it still chafed to stand back and wait.

Razor was behind them all, watching their backs.

"Clear," Jason called.

Spike and Reyes immediately let him go and he strode in. "Where is she? Is she not here?"

"There's another locked door back here. Steel again. There's a deadbolt on this side," Jason called out urgently.

He rushed over to him just as Jason unlocked the door, opening it. He stepped inside the dark room.

Duke pulled out his phone, turning on the flashlight. He ran it around the room. What was this fucking place? It looked like a kid's bedroom.

Or a Little's play space.

Finally, someone found the light switch. His gaze immediately settled on the bed. And the sight of a figure lying on top of it, her dark-blonde hair spilling out across the white coverlet.

"Sunny!" he yelled out. Oh God, she was so still. Had he killed her? Had they gotten there too late?

"Sunny!" he roared. He didn't hear what the others were yelling at him as he dove towards her.

He picked her up and held her close. "No! Sunny!"

"Duke? Duke, what's wrong? Oh God, what's happened? Did someone die? Duke?"

Arms wrapped around him cradling him against her chest.

"Duke man! She's alive. Stop it! She's fucking alive!"

The words penetrated. Along with the fact that she was holding onto him. That she was talking to him. He pulled back abruptly, taking hold of her shoulders.

"You're okay. You're alive." His breath was coming erratically. He still couldn't believe he'd found her. He had her back.

She stared up at everyone. Then slowly, comprehension filled her face.

"Oh God, you thought I was dead. Duke, I'm fine. I promise."

He started running his hands over her body. He needed to make sure for himself.

"Duke, really. I'm all right."

"Did he hurt you? If he hurt you, I'll fucking kill him."

"He didn't hurt me, I promise. He brought me here and then he left. I'm fine."

"We should get going in case he comes back," Reyes warned.

"He won't come back here," she said confidently, swinging her legs over the edge of the bed.

Duke placed his hand on her shoulder. "Don't move."

"Duke, really. He didn't hurt me. He locked me in here and told me you guys were coming for me. That's all."

"Why don't you think he'll be back?" Ink asked, moving around the room. "What the fuck is this place?"

Sunny's face grew red. "Ah, well, this is one of his safe houses. Apparently, he decorated it like this to make me feel more comfortable."

"He created this room so when he fucking kidnapped you and locked you up you were more comfortable?" Duke asked.

"Um. Yeah. He's a strange man. I think he might have some psychopathic tendencies. Or at least his brain doesn't work the same way other people's does. He has a warped sense of right and wrong. I think to him, kidnapping me and bringing me here was his way of keeping me safe. And all of you."

"All of us?" Reyes asked. "Why the fuck would he care about us?"

"He doesn't," she said softly. "He cares about me and he knows killing you guys would hurt me."

"What?" Duke barked. "Are you saying that he. . .that he. . ." He couldn't get the words out.

"That he wants you?" Jason asked. "Has feelings for you?"

"They're not normal feelings. I don't think he's attracted to me." She frowned slightly. "I don't know. He's difficult to understand. He went into disguise as Marv—"

"Wait," Duke barked. "The Fox is that old homeless guy?"

"Yes. And he was, uh, also one of your weekly clients."

She winced as he swore.

"This can all wait," Reyes barked. "Let's get out of here. I don't want to leave it up to chance that he won't be back."

Duke nodded. Much as he'd like to stay and wait for the Fox, Sunny was his priority. He reached down and picked her up.

"Wait." She wiggled out of his arms. He set her feet down, but kept hold of her.

She picked up a book from the nightstand. He gave her a curious look as he picked her back up. He held her cradled against his chest, bridal style. The book rested in her lap.

"It's a first edition *Alice in Wonderland*," she told him. "I can't leave it behind."

He growled. "How the fuck did he know that was your favorite story?" How had he known that she was a Little? That she used to keep her housekeys under plants on her porch?

"He bugged the shop," she told him as they moved out of the cabin. "And maybe our houses."

"That fucking bastard, I'm going to kill him."

"I know he shouldn't have done any of it," she told him. "But if he didn't care about not upsetting me, you guys would all be dead. He would have killed you. I don't like that he kidnapped me and held me, but he did rescue me from Horse and Rory." She shuddered. "And they were going to hurt me. They were pissed about not being let into the Iron Shadows. Horse. . .he had this knife. . ." she trailed off, looking pensive and scared.

"You don't have to worry about those assholes, he took care of them. They can't hurt you again."

She let out a shuddering breath and nodded. "As wrong as Fox was for the way he went about things, he did save me."

Duke still wanted to kill him. There were a lot of things that bastard could have done differently. But for now, he wouldn't argue with her. He reached Ink's bike and set her down. Fuck. He didn't have a helmet for her. Or more clothing. He pulled off his leather jacket and helped her put it on. She smiled up at him, looking tiny in his big jacket.

He pulled her close, aware of everyone starting their bikes and waiting for them. "Don't ever fucking do this to me again, understand? I was fucking terrified, chasing down each of that asshole's clues, wondering if you were all right. I'm not fucking letting you leave my sight again, understand?"

She just hugged him tighter. "I love you too."

25

Pleasure filled her.

She moaned as her clit was gently sucked. Her eyes fluttered as she floated in that place between consciousness and sleep.

A finger slid down her slit, pushing inside her and she sighed. Oh, yes. His tongue flicked at her clit as he added a second finger.

She groaned. "A girl could get used to waking up this way." She attempted to touch him, to run her fingers through his hair. She frowned. She couldn't move her arms, her hands were stuck above her head. Then she let out another groan as she realized why.

He'd tied her up.

Again.

To say Duke was having a few lingering issues from her being kidnapped was putting it mildly. Over a week had passed since he'd rescued her from the Fox's safe house and he was sticking to his vow of not letting her out of his sight.

It was kind of cute.

Except when she needed to go to the bathroom.

Eventually, she knew she'd need her own space. However, for

the moment she needed him nearby just as much as he had to be close.

But as well as sticking to her like glue, he'd ramped up his needs in the bedroom. The man was insatiable. And demanding. And she was loving every second of it.

After the guys had rescued her, they'd decided to all head to the compound, thinking it would be safer. She knew the Fox wouldn't hurt them, but she hadn't argued.

Turned out that Duke actually had a room there. He'd dragged her into it, stripped her bare and inspected every inch of her, only letting her get dressed once he was absolutely certain she was unharmed. He'd been pissed about the bruises, especially the one on her face. When she'd told him that had been Horse, his face had grown so dark she'd known that if the Fox hadn't taken care of those two then he would have.

Maybe she should have felt disturbed by that. That they were both dead at the Fox's hands, but they'd been going to hurt her, probably worse.

So yeah, they didn't deserve her sympathy.

Only then had they joined the others in Reyes' office so she could explain everything. Ink had met them there, and after she'd told them everything, he'd wasted no time dispatching guys to the check for listening devices. Bugs had been found in both of their houses, the tattoo parlor, the compound, and the bar. Nobody knew how long they'd been there or what he'd overheard.

He mustn't have been able to get into Reyes' office, as it had been all clear. Spike was cursing himself, thinking the Fox must have overheard him talking about his meeting with Frankie, the pimp at Duke's place. But she figured the Fox would have found out about the pimp anyway. And in the end, it had all turned out, right?

As she'd relayed everything that had happened, Duke had grown increasingly more and more upset. When she'd finished her story, down to finding a card from the Fox in the first edition of *Alice in Wonderland*, Duke had finally exploded. He'd punched a hole in the wall of Reyes' office and if Jason and Spike hadn't pinned him down, he might have done worse.

But as soon as she hugged him, he'd calmed.

The senator's murder was big news. What was even bigger news was the fact that he'd been buying underaged girls and raping them. Yep, somehow the Fox had completely blown the lid on that.

His bodyguards had been in on it. They'd buy a girl from Frankie, take her out to the cabin owned by one of the bodyguards, where the senator would have his sick fun. There had been a poor girl there the night the Fox murdered the three men. All she'd been able to tell the police was that one minute they were all there, then the next they were gone and she could hear sirens in the distance.

The senator and his bodyguards had been evil. They all deserved what they got.

Duke lapped at her clit. She tugged at the restraints, feeling another surge of desire hit her. She loved being restrained. Duke had worried she would have some hang-ups with it after her kidnapping, but she assured him that no one had tied her up.

But knife play was never going to happen.

He flicked her clit harder, faster. She clenched down around the three fingers he now had thrusting inside her. Then just as her orgasm came within reach, he pulled back.

"Please let me come," she begged. "Please."

"In a minute. I'm playing." He moved one damp finger down to her asshole and she groaned as he slid it partially inside.

So good.

He ran his tongue along her slit, careful not to touch her clit before driving his tongue deep into her passage.

She cried out, driving her hips up into his face as he

tongue-fucked her.

"Please! Please!"

He pulled away once more and she let out a cry of protest. "No!"

"Shh," he told her. "I need you." He settled his cock against her entrance then thrust deep inside her.

So full. So delicious.

"Yes, yes, take me."

He set a fast pace, dropping his mouth to her nipple to suck on it strongly. He found that spot inside her and ran his shaft over it. Again and again.

"Yes. Yes. More." She wasn't capable of speaking in sentences. Her clit was swollen, throbbing, desperate. He moved a finger between their bodies, flicking at her clit with sure, firm strokes.

She screamed, pushing herself up against him as he increased his pace, fucking her fast and furious. Her orgasm overwhelmed her, sent her mind spinning. He roared his own release, filling her. She buried her face into his neck, her lungs gasping for breath, her body trembling in reaction.

Duke rolled off her onto his side, cupping her breast in his hand.

"Duke? Untie me please."

"No." He latched onto her nipple, sucking. Hard. She groaned.

"Please. I want to hold you."

"No. I'm keeping you tied to my bed all day." He ran his tongue over her nipple. She shuddered. Felt so good.

"While that sounds nice, there's a few problems with that."

"I'll let you up to pee," he told her.

"So kind of you," she said dryly. "But remember we've got people coming over later?"

"They can all fuck off," he muttered. "I don't want people coming here."

"Duke, we can't hide here forever," she told him gently. "We have to get back to work. You need to go back to the club. Your friends miss you."

With a groan, he lay on his back and placed his arm over his eyes. "Fuck it. Fine. You get your way this time. But I'm spanking your ass later."

"What? Why?"

"In exchange for me letting you out of my bed. You have to be punished for that." He quickly undid the handcuffs he'd somehow managed to sneak around her wrists while she was sleeping.

Sneaky.

"All right then. I guess I'll submit to a spanking." She sighed exaggeratedly, knowing he wasn't being serious. Oh, he'd likely spank her tonight.

But it would be one they'd both enjoy.

~

SUNNY LAID the food out on the outside table, glancing over at Duke as he manned the grill. Most of the guys were here already, sitting on the porch and drinking beers. Duke laughed at something Ink said to him, looking more relaxed than she'd seen him in ages. Having his friends over had been a good idea.

Of course, the blow job she'd given him earlier might have helped. Or maybe it was the spanking he'd delivered to her ass. She had to bite back a smile. She might not be sitting comfortably this afternoon, but it was totally worth it.

She just wished that Jewel could have joined them for dinner. She'd said she had something going on, although her excuse felt kind of weak.

"Hey, Sunny," Razor called out, stepping onto the porch. He walked over and wrapped an arm around her waist, pulling her close to kiss her cheek, ignoring Duke's possessive growl.

"Hey, Razor. Want a beer?" She moved towards the beer fridge

Duke had installed out here, but Razor tightened his hold.

"Not yet, sweets. Hey, Duke. There's a guy next door at Sunny's place. Skinny, brown hair, wearing a suit," Razor's voice held disbelief. But then it was a Sunday and eighty-two degrees out.

She stiffened in his hold, having a fair idea of who that could be.

"That right?" Duke met her gaze questioningly.

"Sounds like Greg," she said to him.

"Your ex?" Ink asked, standing up.

Jason moved to take over the grill. Duke stepped towards her and held out his hand. She slipped her hand into his much larger one as he led her through the house. She gave him a surprised look. She'd half-expected him to tell her to wait there while he checked things out.

"So long as you've got back-up and don't get close to him, I'll let you take the lead," he told her, obviously spotting her disbelief.

She was aware of all the guys, except Jason, following them.

She'd decided to put her house on the market. There was no point in keeping two houses. She'd get the equity out and use it to help Duke pay his mortgage. Not that he knew that yet.

She'd save that argument for another day.

They all walked up her small driveway to find Greg pulling up her flower pots and setting them down, muttering to himself.

"Greg? What are you doing?"

She'd moved a lot of her pots over to Duke's place and he'd even dug her up a garden in the back for more flowers.

Greg stood and whirled, his eyes widening as he saw her. Then his mouth dropped open as he spotted Duke and the others.

"Sunny?" He ran his gaze over her. "What the hell are you wearing?"

She glanced down at her cut-off shorts and tight tank-top. She thought she looked cute and she knew that Duke definitely thought her outfit was sexy.

"Clothes," she replied dryly. "Now, mind telling me why you're here? And looking for the key to my house, I'm guessing?"

He looked disheveled. His suit was messy, almost dirty and his hair was sticking up as though he'd been running his fingers through it repeatedly.

She'd never seen him this way. He was always impeccably dressed and put together.

"You always keep a key out here. Where is it?"

"I don't keep a key out here anymore, Greg. Even if I did, you have no right to just waltz on inside. This is my house. What are you doing here?"

"I need more money," he said frantically. "From the house. You got it from me for a steal and I want more money."

She narrowed her gaze, placing her hand on Duke's arm as he stepped forward. "Let me."

Greg's gaze moved from her hand to Duke. "What the fuck is going on here? What are you doing with my wife?"

"I'm not your wife, Greg," she said firmly. "And Duke is none of your business."

"Duke? Seriously? You're fucking a gang member now?"

Anger filled her. "Leave Greg. Now. You're not getting more money from me. You were paid a fair price for your share of the house." Why did he want to get inside, anyway? It made her feel uneasy, wondering if he'd been going to wait and ambush her.

"I fucking paid the mortgage!"

"We both did and you know it," she snapped back. "I don't know why you were trying to get into the house, but you need to leave."

"I want to check that there's nothing in there that's mine."

She frowned. "Everything was settled in the divorce. Nothing in there is yours anymore."

"There might be! There's got to be something I can sell!"

"Greg, you need to leave. Before I call the police."

He sneered. "Maybe I'll call them now, tell them I'm being harassed by a gang."

Duke snorted. "We're not a gang, douchebag. And you're the one fucking trespassing."

"Screw it, I'm going to go call them now. Before our lunch gets cold." She turned away, to head back next door.

"Wait, no, Sunny, don't! I'm broke!"

She turned back. "What? How?"

He ran his fingers through his hair. "I don't know. It's all gone. Disappeared a week ago. The bank keeps saying that I did it, but I fucking didn't! Then I got a letter in the mail thanking me for my large donation to a charity for foxes in freaking England. Someone stole my money and donated it in my name to a fox charity. Who the fuck would do that?"

She heard a snort of laughter from behind her. She had to fight hard to hold back her grin.

The Fox strikes again.

"Go away, Greg. You're not getting anything from me. You still have a job, right?" A job he was well-paid for.

"Yes, but I've got an image to keep up. I've got a trip to the Bahamas I can't even pay for. I'll lose the deposit."

"Our heart bleeds for you man, now beat it," Duke rumbled.

Greg stared at them all. "I'll take you back, Sunny."

"What?" She gaped at him in disbelief.

"I'll take you back. Move back in. We can be together. You can ditch this loser."

She burst into laughter. She laughed until she was out of breath and had to lean against Duke to steady herself.

"You'll have me back? Have me back?"

"Well, yes. You'd have to get rid of those clothes and your hair needs work and we'd have to move to get away from these unsavory characters."

She linked her arm through Duke's and turned him away.

"Wait. . .so. . .is that no?"

"Greg, I wouldn't take you back if you were the last man on Earth. Duke is my dream man and I thank God every day that I met him. And that I no longer have to put up with you. Goodbye, you douche."

Duke grinned down at her.

They left him standing there as they made their way back home.

"Razor," Duke called out, loud enough for Greg to hear. "Call the cops if he's not gone in the next three minutes. Don't want him bringing down property prices since we're selling Sunny's place and she's moving in here."

Several hours later, she wandered into her playroom and pulled out first edition, *Alice in Wonderland* book. She opened it up and stared at the card inside. She thought about calling him to say thank you. But she figured she didn't need to. He'd know how she felt.

She carefully put the book back and left to go find Duke. He was in the kitchen, putting away the left-over food. When she walked in, he drew her close to him.

"I've changed my mind; I'm going to let the Fox live. So long as he doesn't make any unwanted appearances in your life."

"I'm pretty sure you're safe there."

He lifted her onto the counter before cupping her face with his hands. "I know I'm being painfully overprotective at the moment. I want to tell you that I'll ease up, but I don't know when that will happen."

"I understand. But just so you know, I'm going nowhere." She placed her hands over his. "I'm right where I want to be. For the rest of my long, awesome life."

"Fuck. Yes."

EPILOGUE

"Come on, Daddy, let's go for a ride!"

Sunny bounced around Duke as he wiped his rag over his motorcycle. They were in his small garage with the door open.

"Weather ain't looking good today, baby girl."

"But it's not raining right now," she wheedled. "And you promised." She widened her eyes pleadingly, clasping her hands together and bringing them up to her chest.

Classic cute begging face.

He crossed his arms over his chest. "You really think pulling that face is going to get you what you want?"

"Please, best Daddy in the whole wide world. You did promise."

He shook his head but his mouth was twitching. "All right."

She jumped up and down with a squeal. "Yes!"

"But only for a short time," he warned. "And don't think that face will get you whatever you want, little rebel."

"But Daddy, I'm irresistible." She pouted and batted her eyelashes.

"You're something, all right." He turned her around and landed a sharp slap on her bottom. "Go get some warmer clothes on then grab your gear."

"Yay, Daddy! You're the best." She raced off and put on some trackpants and a long-sleeved shirt. It wasn't that cold, but she knew Duke would insist on a sweatshirt. So she grabbed that as well and hurriedly put on her sneakers without bothering to tie up the shoe laces.

No time for that!

"I'm ready! I'm ready!" She raced into the garage, her feet tangling up as she stood on a loose shoe lace and she went flying.

Duke raced for her, catching her in his arms.

"Whoopsie." She looked up at him guiltily.

He gave her a stern look as he picked her up in his arms and carried her over to his workbench. Setting her down, he grabbed one foot and started to tie her shoe laces.

"What have I told you about shoe laces, little rebel?"

"That I need to ask for help and not try putting on any shoes with shoe laces myself. Sorry, Daddy."

"You could have really hurt yourself and then we wouldn't be able to go for a ride, would we?"

She shook her head. "No, Daddy." She brought her thumb to her mouth to comfort herself.

He finished tying off her other shoe then pulled her thumb free to lightly kiss her lips.

"Right. Let's get your protective gear."

She sighed. "I really don't think I need it."

"You want to go for a ride, then you need protection. That's nonnegotiable."

"Okie-dokie."

He helped her down from the bench and then they walked over to where her protective gear was stored. He picked up the bag that held it as Sunny grabbed her bike, kicking off the kickstand and pushing it outside.

It only took a few seconds to get to the park, which was devoid of people this early on a Sunday morning. Perfect time for her to practice.

"Right. Protective gear first." He knelt to put on her knee pads.

She pulled on her riding gloves. "Daddy, I've seen four-year-old's with less protective gear on than I have."

He stood and fastened on her elbow pads. Her helmet followed.

"Well, you're my baby and you'll wear what I tell you since it's my job to keep you safe. Now, do you want to stand here and argue or would you like to practice riding?"

"Ride! Ride! I wanna ride!"

Sunny bounced in excitement as Duke's phone buzzed. He texted something and put his phone away. "Ink's on his way here. That okay?"

"Yep!" she said cheerfully. "He can watch me ride on my own for the first time."

He looked skeptical. "We haven't practiced enough."

They'd practiced heaps. "Daddy. I got this. I promise."

"Yo!"

They both looked over at the greeting, and she smiled as she saw Ink walking towards them.

"Yo, Ink," she called back in a gruff voice. "How's it hanging, man?"

"Is that meant to be an impression of me?" Duke asked, raising an eyebrow.

She grinned up at him. "Totally nailed it, right?"

He just shook his head indulgently.

A wide smile crossed Ink's face as he grew closer. He looked from her to the bike. "Could that bike be any cuter?"

She glanced down at the bike fondly. It was bright pink with a white seat and a white basket with pink flowers and rhinestones along the front of it. Moody sat in the basket. She loved it.

"Nope."

"Do you think you put enough protective gear on her?" Ink asked Duke. "Maybe you should just wrap her up in bubble wrap."

"Don't give him ideas." She put her hands on her hips, tapping her foot. "This is our fourth time practicing, the first day he wouldn't even let me get on my bike!"

Ink burst into laughter.

"You could hurt yourself." Duke gave her a firm look.

"I'll be fine. I have to try doing it on my own sometime."

"Here. I'll stand down here. If she goes too far, I'll grab her, okay?" Ink asked, moving twenty feet down the path.

"Maybe you should try on the grass," Duke muttered. "Less chance of hurting yourself if you fall off."

She reached up and cupped his face with her hands. "I got this, Daddy. Trust me."

He blew out a breath. "Fine. But don't go past Ink."

She climbed on the bike. She was so ready for this. She put her feet on the pedals, her tongue sticking out in concentration. Duke pushed her off, running with her for a few feet before letting her go. She wobbled. Oh no, she couldn't do this!

She tried to regain her balance, but she slid off the path onto the grass and landed on her side with a thump.

Tears immediately filled her eyes, spilling down her cheeks. Not because of the pain but due to the shock of falling off. Also, she was kind of embarrassed she'd done that in front of Ink.

Duke had been right. She wasn't ready.

She sniffled.

"Baby girl, you okay? You hurt?" Duke raced over and knelt down behind her.

"Sunny-girl, did you hurt yourself?" Ink rushed over, picking up the bike and carefully moving it away from her.

"Where are you in pain?" Duke asked urgently, moving around to face her so he could run his hands all over her.

"Does she need to go to the hospital?" Ink asked. "I can run back and get my truck."

Duke nodded. "Do that."

"No! No, I'm fine!" They were totally overreacting. "I didn't hurt myself."

"Then why are you crying?" Duke demanded.

"'Cause I got a fright. And I thought I could do it and I couldn't." She hung her head. "You were right, I wasn't ready. I want to go home now."

She expected him to immediately agree. Even though he'd bought her the bike and told her he would teach her to ride, he had been extremely overprotective about the whole thing.

Over the past few months since the Fox kidnapped her, he'd eased up a bit on his protectiveness. A bit, but not totally. He still didn't like her out of his sight. And she was generally all right with that. Sometimes, she had to put her foot down. Like during shopping and spa days with Jewel.

Those were Duke-free days.

"Duke," Ink said in a low voice.

"I know," he said. "Give us a minute."

"I'll wait back down the path," Ink said. He reached out and tipped up her chin. "You were doing great, Sunny-girl. I know you can do this."

She turned to Duke as Ink left. "I can't do this, Daddy."

"Sure you can," he said tenderly as he wiped the tears from her cheeks with his thumbs. "My little rebel can do anything she puts her mind to. She's smart and brave and fierce. You got this."

She bit her lip. "I don't know."

He leaned down to kiss her, his forehead banging against the helmet and she giggled. He grinned at her. He tilted her head up and kissed both of her cheeks.

Then he stood and held out his hand. "Come on, little rebel."

She let out a deep breath and let him tug her up. She had this.

Nerves filled her as she climbed onto the bike. But Duke grasped hold of the seat and pressed his chest against her back.

"I know you can do this, baby girl. Now, let's go." He started to run and she peddled and then he let her go and she flew! She wobbled once but pushed through it, peddling towards Ink, giggling as she nearly ran him over, ignoring his yell and Duke's bellow to slow down.

Finally! This is what she'd been missing out on all these years. She came to a stop several yards away, and turned back to find Duke storming towards her.

Oops. She was in trouble.

Then his frown morphed into a smile and as he reached her, she climbed off the bike so he could pick her up and twirl her through the air. He set her down and undoing her helmet, kissed her.

"You did it, baby!"

"I did it! I did it, Daddy!"

She bounced up and down in excitement.

"I knew you could do it. You can do anything, Sunny." He tapped her nose. "But you're in trouble for not listening and going too far and too fast."

She just grinned. Totally worth it.

Who would have known that getting fired would have led to her finding more happiness than she ever thought possible? Sometimes she had to pinch herself.

Just to make sure it all wasn't a dream.

DADDY'S ANGEL

Montana Daddies #7

Coming June 10th

She's a Little in desperate need of a protective Daddy, but by the time he realizes he can trust her, it just might be too late...

On the surface Arianna has it all. Beauty. Talent. Wealth. But she's hiding a secret. Actually, more than one.

She's not perfect. She's not brave. And she's in a lot of trouble.

Luckily, help arrives. In the form of a huge, gruff, blunt man.

All Bain wants is a sweet, honest woman to be his Little. Arianna isn't that woman. Nope, definitely not. Despite how she tugs at all his Daddy instincts. He's just there to protect her.

Until he's no longer there

And his Little girl is left alone and vulnerable and in danger...

Printed in Great Britain
by Amazon

45019828R00169